FOREGONE CONFLICT

ACROSS HORIZONS - BOOK 2

STAN C. SMITH

A Skyra Publication

Copyright © 2020 by Stan C. Smith

All rights reserved.

No part of this book may be reproduced in any form or by any electronic or mechanical means, including information storage and retrieval systems, without written permission from the author, except for the use of brief quotations in a book review.

To those who can see what other people cannot.

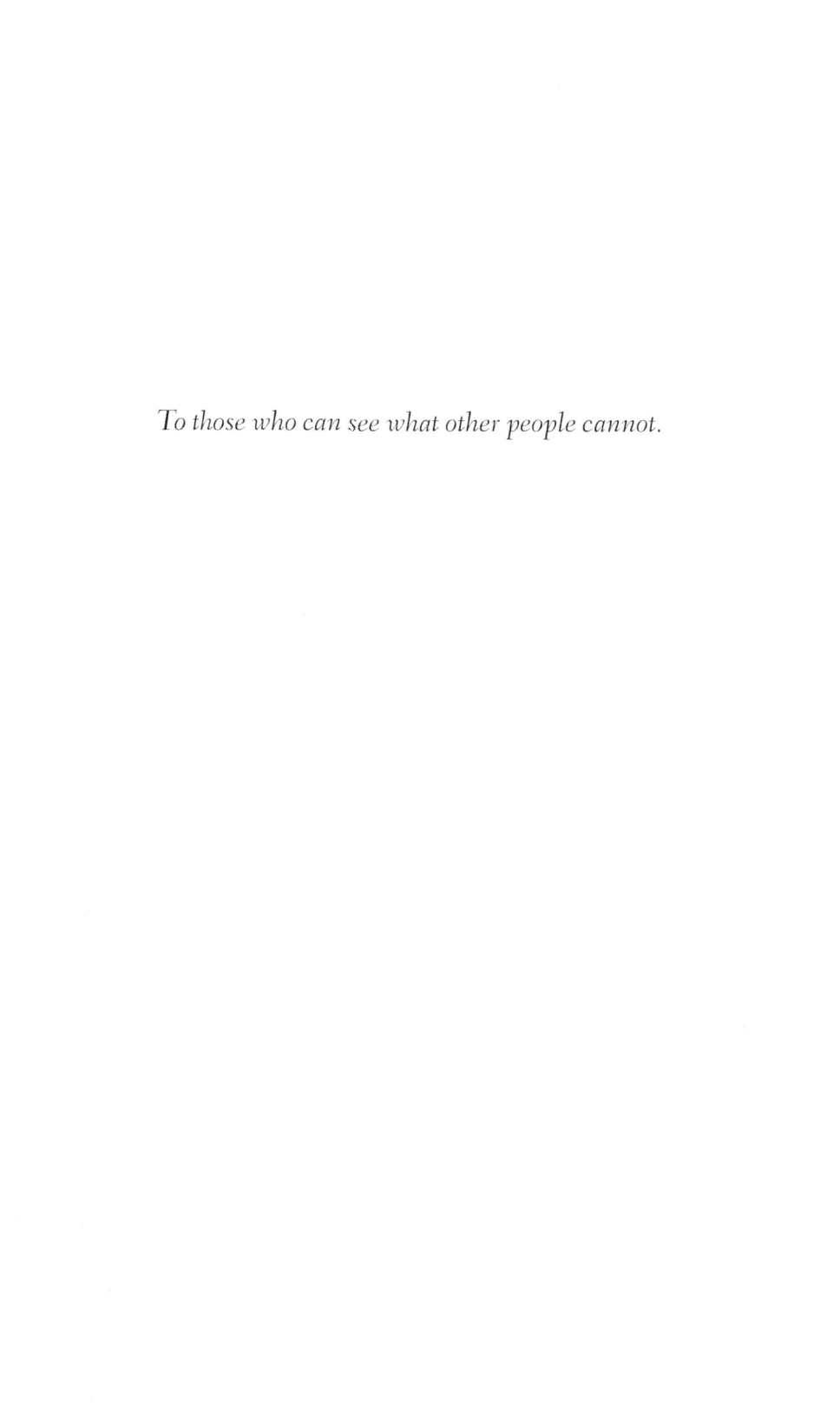

FOREGONE CONFLICT

May you have strength today, friend, to find your way home.

SKYRA-UNA-LOTO

1

AMBUSH

47,669 years ago - Zaragoza Province of Spain

Skyra-Una-Loto had lived through ten cold seasons. Now it was her time to kill. She gripped her spear with both hands to keep them from trembling. Skyra had waited many days for this opportunity, and she did not want to fail. Failure would result in a beating—not only for her, but also for her birthmate Veenah. If Skyra could make a kill, today would be a good day.

She sensed, however, that Veenah would rather be back at Una-Loto camp making capes and waist-skins or flint-knapping spear heads and khul blades.

"I killed an ibex on my first hunt in my tenth cold season," Skyra's birthmother said in the Una-Loto language. Skyra was listening intently, but Veenah was staring over the rock at the herd of ibexes feeding on the hillside. Their birthmother grabbed Veenah's scalp and turned her head. "I killed an ibex on my first hunt in my tenth cold season," she repeated. "Today you will each kill your own ibex. Show me where you will thrust your spear."

Skyra growled impatiently and pointed to her ribs near her armpit. Veenah did the same. They had practiced this more times than Skyra knew how to count, targeting an ibex pelt stretched over a bundle of dried grass. Her birthmother had good reason for being so persistent in her lessons for the two girls. Skyra and Veenah were different from the other nandups of the Una-Loto tribe. Because of this, their tribemates hated them. Some of the men even wanted to kill Skyra and Veenah, and if the two birthmates failed today, perhaps those men would finally convince the others to agree.

"Many of the males will run ahead of the females," their birthmother said. "You must be patient and wait for a female. Do you understand?"

"Rha-ofu," they both replied. *Yes.*

Skyra knew this. She had known for many days. Female ibexes didn't have horns and were easier to kill. They also provided better meat. Every Una-Loto hunter knew their first kill would be a female ibex. At least their first major kill while hunting with the adults—Skyra and Veenah had already killed pikas, rats, lizards, and vipers. Today, though, was different. Today they hunted with the tribe's best hunters.

Her birthmother grabbed Skyra's cape and pulled her to the other side of the gap between the rocks, leaving Veenah where she was. "One of you on each side. Do not show yourselves to the ibexes, even after you hear them running. Wait. Let the males run by, then look around the rock with only one eye. Choose your female before it gets close. Follow her with your eye. Thrust when you know it is time to thrust. Where will you thrust?"

Again the girls lifted their elbows and pointed to their ribs.

"Thrust hard, thrust true, then release. Do you understand?"

"Rha-ofu."

Skyra and Veenah had even practiced releasing their spears as their birthmother had run past them carrying the ibex pelt. Today, during the real hunt, if they released too early, their spears would not penetrate deep enough. If they released too late, the ibexes would tear the spears from their grip and break their wrists. A broken wrist would not heal quickly, which would give the men one more reason to want to kill them.

Their birthmother put a hand on Skyra's head, gazed into her eyes, and whispered, "Kami-fu-menga-ulmecko. Idi-bilaimo ati-de-lé-melu imbo-oh-nup-tekne-té." *Listen to me speak, woolly rhino and cave lion. My daughter submits to you in return for your strength.* She stepped past the gap, did the same with Veenah, then gave a hand signal to one of the other hunters.

It was time to kill.

Skyra peered over the rocks. Six hunters had already emerged onto the open meadow, spaced out evenly to convince the herd there was only one direction for retreat. Several of the creatures raised their heads and stared. They let out a few shrill whistles, sounding almost like birds, which prompted the other ibexes to raise their heads also. The approaching hunters made themselves appear wider by holding a weapon out to each side, in one hand a spear, and in the other a stone-bladed axe called a *khul*.

A wave of whistles passed through the herd. One of the males let out a huffing snort and took off running away from the driving hunters. The wave of whistles turned into an eruption of snorts as the other males broke away from the group to follow the first. Then the entire herd began pounding across the meadow toward Skyra, Veenah, and the other concealed hunters.

Skyra pressed her cheek against the rock, refusing to expose herself before it was time. A few breaths later, male ibexes charged through the gap, snorting and throwing up dust and bits of gravel with their hooves. Skyra gripped her spear as she watched them flying past, one set of curled horns after another.

There it was—the first ibex without horns. It was time. She leaned forward just enough to watch the remaining females coming toward her. Only a few were left. No time to be choosy. She eyed the very last female coming on her side of the gap, positioned her legs as she had practiced countless times, and pushed off against the dirt while thrusting.

Her spear hit the ibex's shoulder instead of its ribs. Skyra felt the solid impact before releasing her spear. The force of the thrust knocked the creature from its feet, but it immediately rolled over, throwing off the spear, and started getting up. With muscle memory due to endless practice, Skyra reached behind her head and pulled her khul from the sling on her back. She transferred the weapon's handle to her other hand as she scrambled toward the thrashing ibex.

On its feet now, the creature's back was as high as Skyra's chest. It was dazed enough to hesitate for a breath, which was more than enough time for Skyra to swing her khul downward to sever its spine behind its shoulders. The ibex went down again. It was still alive, but it wasn't going anywhere, so Skyra took this opportunity to check on her birthmate.

Veenah was on her knees, cradling her wrist against her

belly. She was hurt. Her spear was on the ground a short distance away, and her ibex had escaped.

Their birthmother was standing over Veenah with her khul drawn, ready to defend her daughter.

"Veenah has failed!" shouted Gelrut, one of the dominant men who hated the twins. Gelrut strode over, holding his spear up to make sure everyone could see the blood from his own kill.

Skyra scanned the ground near the gaps in the rocks where the other hunters had waited in ambush—three other ibexes had been taken in addition to her own.

Gelrut pointed his spear at Skyra's ibex, which was still gasping and trying to get up, although it could no longer use its hind legs. "Fusa," he ordered. *Kill.*

Skyra stepped over to the creature and drove her khul's stone blade into its skull, destroying its brain. She should have struck its neck, but she knew the brain was favored by the dominant men for its flavor, and Gelrut in particular was fond of challenging the other men for the right to eat it himself. Skyra glared at Gelrut in defiance as she pulled her blade from the split skull.

He shifted his gaze from the dead ibex and stared at Skyra for several long breaths, baring his teeth in an expression of hatred.

Gelrut had beaten Skyra so many times that she was no longer afraid of the man. He had seen twenty cold seasons and was twice Skyra's size, but he and the other men actually feared the twin sisters who had the strange ability to predict whatever the men were about to do. They didn't understand Skyra and Veenah, and some of them wanted to kill the girls to purify the tribe.

Gelrut turned to Veenah. "Sayleeh, you surely see now

that Veenah is worthless," he said to Skyra and Veenah's birthmother, who was still guarding her injured daughter. "The food and skins we have given that girl for ten cold seasons have been wasted. Now the worthless girl has a broken wrist. I propose we kill her now, as she will continue to be a burden on Una-Loto tribe." He turned to the other hunters. "We have been troubled by this worthless girl long enough! Today we must reach a consensus. Allow me to take Veenah's strength, as I should have done long ago."

Bolyu, one of the respected women, and a friend of Skyra's birthmother, spoke up. "Gelrut, you have no right to demand a vote where no vote is possible. Many of our tribemates are now at Una-Loto camp. You will not kill Sayleeh's daughter."

"Bolyu is correct," said Amlun, one of the dominant men. "There can be no vote here. Perhaps when we return to camp, Una-Loto tribe will vote to make you Veenah's caretaker. You can heal her wrist and then mentor her until she kills her first ibex."

The other hunters let out a chorus of laughter. *At-at-at-at-at.*

"My wrist is not broken!" Veenah said. "It hurts, but I can move it. Watch me move it!" She held it up and swiveled the hand. The others might not have noticed, but Skyra saw the pain concealed behind her twin's expression.

Gelrut glared at Veenah. He then stepped closer. "If I cannot kill this worthless girl now, I will give her a beating so that she will try harder next time." He shifted his spear in his hand to swing it as a club.

Skyra darted forward and stood at her birthmother's side. She held her khul ready, knowing that such a threat to a dominant tribemate was an offense punishable by death. The fact that she was defending her own sister, though, might convince the tribe to be lenient. She looked up into Gelrut's eyes. "Veenah will not get a beating today."

Gelrut bared his teeth and growled, but his eyes flicked to the side once, toward the other hunters. He was now in a bad situation. If he backed down, he would be ridiculed. If he stepped forward, he would have to fight both Skyra and Sayleeh to get to Veenah. This was obviously more effort than he had intended.

Skyra had never stood up to Gelrut before, and she truly felt the strength of the woolly rhino and cave lion flowing through her veins now. Their presence within her made her smile, which seemed to anger Gelrut even more.

Skyra saw it coming. Gelrut's face twitched slightly, and he tightened one shoulder. He intended to swing his spear. She raised her khul to block the blow, but she had failed to predict he was aiming at her birthmother. Sayleeh didn't have Skyra's ability to anticipate movements. The spear whisked over Skyra's head and hit something solid. Sayleeh's legs folded, and she hit the ground, moaning.

Skyra should have known Gelrut would attack her birthmother first. Sayleeh was a skilled fighter and would pose a serious threat, whereas Skyra and Veenah were only girls. Skyra wanted to look down at her birthmother, but she knew Gelrut's spear would strike her next if she averted her eyes.

The man prepared to swing again but then hesitated. He knew Skyra and Veenah could predict his movements, but he had no idea how skilled they were at it. They had tried to keep the ability hidden from their tribemates, only fully exploring it when playing and sparring with each other away from Una-Loto camp.

Gelrut feigned to one side like he was going to swing his

spear, but instead he leaned forward and struck Skyra's face with his fist.

She heard herself grunt, and she glimpsed the sky as her head popped backward.

Gelrut bared his teeth. "Today will be a good day. I will give you and your worthless sister a beating you will both remember." He thrust out the butt of his spear, which glanced off Skyra's chin and struck her throat.

She started choking but didn't drop her khul and didn't take her eyes off her attacker. She knew she was in for a severe beating, but this time she would fight back.

Veenah was now on her feet at Skyra's side. She pulled her own khul from her sling and shouted, "Gelrut, the great fighter and hunter, has hurt our birthmother! Today Veenah and Skyra are hunters, and we proclaim our right to defend ourselves as Sayleeh's daughters. Do we have that right?"

"You are now hunters and you have that right," replied Amlun. Several of the others grunted in agreement.

Gelrut sneered in anger, but again his eyes flitted to the side.

"No, do not fight," Sayleeh moaned. She was trying unsuccessfully to get to her knees.

Still struggling to catch her breath, Skyra swallowed. She studied Gelrut's face. The man had every intention of delivering the beating he had promised. In fact, he probably meant to kill, perhaps telling the tribe later he hadn't intended to hit so hard.

Skyra steadied herself and spread her feet apart. She extended one blocking hand in front of her and held her khul up beside her ear with the other hand, ready to strike. Beside her, Veenah took the same stance. Today, Gelrut would lose some of his own blood.

The man's face was now contorted with anger, and Skyra hoped his strange expressions wouldn't prevent her from sensing his intentions. She focused on his eyes, allowing her peripheral vision to catch all his other movements.

She didn't have long to wait. Gelrut twitched one of his cheeks and glanced at Skyra's khul as if he intended to knock the weapon from her hand, but then he turned one of his feet slightly. He was about to spin backwards and bring his spear around from the opposite side to strike Veenah instead. His intention was now as obvious to read as his anger. Veenah must have seen it too—she dropped low and dove for his feet.

Skyra knew Veenah's move would surprise him. Feeding off her twin's action, she tried to distract him by raising her khul.

It worked. Gelrut hesitated, and Veenah's stone blade struck his leg below the knee with a stiff *chuck*.

His eyes grew wide, but only for a breath. Gelrut was a skilled fighter and wouldn't allow the injury's pain to give Veenah time to strike again. He leapt back out of khul range and immediately swung his longer spear at Skyra.

She saw the move coming, but he swung too low for her to duck beneath the spear. The shaft struck her shoulder, and Gelrut immediately swung it again, this time directly from above at Veenah's head. Veenah was already gone, and the spear struck the dirt.

Chuck. Another blow to Gelrut's leg, this time above the knee, and Veenah darted back out of range.

Gelrut flew into a rage, swinging and jabbing with his spear again and again, clearly attempting to kill one or both of the girls. His spear shaft caught Skyra's shoulder again, but she quickly got into a rhythm of studying his face and predicting each move before it was carried out. She didn't want to kill the man—that would force her and Veenah to leave the tribe, and two nandup girls wouldn't live through one season on their own. She did want to hurt him, though. She wanted the Una-Loto men to know that beating Skyra and Veenah would no longer be easy.

Veenah seemed to have found her own rhythm, anticipating and avoiding every thrust and swing, dodging out of the way at every charge, and inflicting one nonlethal wound after another. Soon Gelrut was bleeding from wounds on every part of his body. The other hunters even began shouting at Gelrut to stop his onslaught before losing all of his blood to the sand beneath his feet.

A figure darted from behind Skyra, skillfully avoided Gelrut's swinging spear, and took the man to the ground. With one hand on Gelrut's throat, Sayleeh sprawled to the side and kicked the spear from his hand. "Do not be a fool, Gelrut," she snarled down at him. "You are a skilled hunter and fighter of bolups. You are important to Una-Loto tribe. We do not want you to die today. My daughters do not want to kill you. Someday you will give up your strength to a woolly rhino or a cave lion, or you will give up your strength to raiding bolups, but you are a fool if you give up your strength to two girls of your tribe simply because they anger you."

Gelrut stopped struggling, but his breaths were still coming in snorts.

Sayleeh said, "Skyra and Veenah are not like the rest of us, but they *are* Una-Loto. I am Una-Loto. Their birthfather is Una-Loto. Therefore, Skyra and Veenah are Una-Loto. Perhaps my daughters are better than the rest of us. Perhaps we could learn from them and become better ourselves."

Gelrut's breathing was returning to normal. "I will not give my strength to those girls today. Let me up."

Sayleeh gazed down at him for a few breaths. Then she turned to her daughters. "Go. Do not return to Una-Loto camp until the sun has slept four times. When you return, bring meat and hides with you. If you bring meat and hides, you will be welcomed back into Una-Loto. Go!"

Skyra exchanged a glance with Veenah then shoved her khul into its sling on her back and picked up her hunting spear. She waited while Veenah did the same. Together they walked away from the hunters, heading deeper into the foothills of the Kapolsek mountains.

They moved up the first slope, picking their way through the ridges of rocks that made the area ideal for ambushing ibexes. Without speaking, Skyra took Veenah's hand and was comforted by her birthmate's skin against hers. Skyra turned to look back just once. The hunters were gathered around Gelrut, and she could no longer make out her birthmother among them.

2

WAR

47,669 years later - Present time - Arizona, USA - Day 1

If Skyra hadn't already been on her knees, she would have collapsed. Her fingers and toes felt numb. A whooshing sound, like wind blowing over yano grass on the slopes of the Kapolsek foothills, filled her ears and seemed to steal away her self awareness. The scene before her couldn't possibly be real, yet she saw the dead bodies. She smelled burning flesh and heard growling beasts feeding on the bodies waiting to be heaped into piles and set on fire. There were so many bodies. She had never imagined so many people—alive or dead—could exist in the entire world.

"Skyra, are you okay?" Lincoln was speaking to her in his language. His voice seemed far away, even though he was right beside her. He grabbed her arm. "Skyra?"

Skyra had known violence and death since she had been a

young girl, but she had never seen anything like this. What was happening here, and how could she be in this unfamiliar place? It was completely different from her homeland, yet she hadn't walked to get here. She and Lincoln and Lincoln's tribemates had enclosed themselves within strange skin bags. Then the bags were gone. Skyra had opened her eyes to find she was in a new land. The place had been strange and beautiful at first. But now this—a vast field of countless bodies. The smells. The sounds.

Lincoln shook her arm. "Skyra, are you okay?"

She closed her eyes, trying to force away the confusion before she turned to him. "What is a *war*?" Lincoln had spoken this word only moments before as he stared out over the field of bodies.

"A war is a big fight between two groups of people. It can go on for years, and sometimes thousands of people are killed. There's definitely a war going on here, and from what I can tell, the war is between bolups and nandups."

She gazed out over the field again. Black smoke was billowing from mounds of charred bodies. Other bodies were still scattered on the ground, including dead creatures that were at least the size of aurochs. "This is the place you are from?"

"That's not as easy to answer as you might think. It's the place I'm from, but it's completely different now."

"I don't understand."

"Eventually I'll try to explain it all. Right now we—" He stopped speaking and turned to look down toward the base of the hill they were hiding on. "Here comes another cart."

A rumbling sound grew louder. Soon another four humpbacked creatures came around the curve of the hill, again pulling a flat, wooden object mounted on turning circles of wood. Walking beside the creatures and the wooden object were men and women, all of them short and broad, with large eyes and thick brows. They were nandups, like Skyra. Injured, bleeding men were tied down on top of the rolling wooden object. Like Lincoln's, their bodies were long and thin, and they had tiny eyes and flat faces. They were bolups —humans.

"I do not like the place you are from, Lincoln," she whispered.

"Yeah, I'm not surprised. I just hope we aren't stuck here. We need to get back to the T3."

"Khambap-bolmuna!"

Skyra turned to the voice. A nandup woman who had been walking beside the humpbacked creatures had stopped and was pointing up the hillside toward Skyra and Lincoln. She had spotted them even though they were on their knees in the brush.

Skyra's leg muscles began twitching, commanding her to move. She grabbed Lincoln's arm and held tight. It was time to run.

3

CHOICES

PRESENT TIME - DAY 1

LINCOLN WOODHOUSE STARED at the Neanderthal woman who had shouted. His gut tightened as he imagined being captured and strapped onto the wagon among the other prisoners. He couldn't even consider what might happen after that. The captured men on the wagon were humans—*Homo sapiens* rather than *Homo neanderthalensis*—and they appeared to be warriors or soldiers. All of them were bleeding, some were even missing limbs, but Lincoln doubted they were being taken to a hospital.

Skyra squeezed his arm hard enough to make him wince.

"I don't think she saw us," he whispered. "See, she's not pointing at us."

The woman was trying to draw her companions' attention to something at the top of the hill beyond Lincoln and Skyra's hiding spot. Lincoln resisted the temptation to turn and look—any movement might be detected. The temptation became even stronger when a faint moaning sound filtered down through the brush from higher up the slope.

"I want to leave this place," Skyra muttered. "I do not understand these nandups. What are they doing?"

"They're taking prisoners. This is a war, and they're hauling off their enemies—the ones they haven't killed."

"Nandups do not eat bolups! Why are they taking them?"

"I have no idea, and I really don't want to find out."

The Neanderthals stared at the hilltop for a few seconds as they exchanged incomprehensible words. Then the entire group resumed walking and caught up with the camel-drawn wagon. Soon the entire procession disappeared over a low rise, apparently following the previous wagon that had passed by a few minutes ago.

Lincoln turned to Skyra. Her huge nandup eyes were fixated on the battlefield. She was gripping her long, copper-colored hair with one hand, twisting the strands repeatedly around two fingers. Four days ago, when Lincoln had first met her, he had assumed this was a nervous habit, but now he knew it served a much darker purpose. She would often do this to keep her hand close to the stone blade of the khul hanging in the sling on her back. He had seen her wield the khul with deadly skill, and the resulting carnage was horrifying to witness. She now had two khuls in her sling, following a vicious fight with her tribemates, and Lincoln had hoped bringing Skyra with him on the jump back to his present time would mean she'd never have to use them again. However, this wasn't his world—it was a nightmare, possibly worse than Skyra's own brutal world 47,000 years in the past.

"Are you okay?" he asked for the third time.

Her eyes flicked toward his. "Why do you keep asking me that? I thought *okay* means I am good and happy. Right now my belly needs food and water, and my head does not understand where I am or how I got here. I did not walk to this place, but I am here." She gestured toward the smoking battlefield. "Sometimes when I sleep I have bad visions of hurting and killing and fear, but I do not have sleep visions as terrible as what I see here. I am not okay, Lincoln. Are you okay?"

"I'm sorry." Then he remembered Skyra didn't understand *sorry* either. "I mean, I realize it's a meaningless question. It's just something my people say when we're worried about someone." He got to his feet. "We should get back to the T3—make sure my team is safe and figure out what to do next."

"What to do next is to go away from this place."

He nodded. "I hope we can."

She stood and looked up toward the hill's summit. "We will walk around the hill, not over it."

"I agree," he said, assuming she was thinking of whatever the Neanderthals had pointed at higher up the slope. He followed her gaze up the hill but saw nothing but cacti and thick brush.

They made their way around the hillside, taking advantage of available cover to avoid detection. The low area on the backside of the hill was more open, but they needed to cross it to return the way they had come. Lincoln picked up the pace.

Jogging now, they skirted around a thick patch of ocotillo-like plants. Lincoln abruptly came to a stop, and Skyra ran into his shoulder. They were almost face-to-face with a creature the size of a grizzly bear. The beast let out a growling moan and reared back, obviously startled.

Lincoln immediately backpedaled, then he turned to run. Skyra grabbed his arm. "That is not a predator."

He hesitated, struggling to control his flight instinct. The creature was standing on its back legs, its head at least eight feet off the ground, with its clawed forefeet held out in defense.

"What is it?" he stammered. Maybe the thing wasn't a predator, but its claws were six inches long, and it looked like it could pick up a car if it wanted to.

"I do not know what it is. This is the place where you are from, Lincoln!"

"We didn't have anything like this when I was here."

The creature seemed to be frozen in place, like a grizzly about to attack a cowboy on his horse in one of those old western paintings. Its neck was much longer than a bear's, though, and it had a thick tail it was using for stability, like a third leg. Its hind legs were massive pedestals upon club-like feet. It let out another moan, causing its lips to quiver and drip saliva. The creature then began lowering itself back to all fours, moving slowly, inch by inch. Finally, it folded its curved claws upward toward its belly and rested its weight on its knuckles.

"I'll be damned," Lincoln said. "I think it's a giant sloth."

"It smells bad," Skyra said matter-of-factly.

She was right. The air already carried the stench from the battlefield, but the sloth's wretched odor was pungent despite that. This may have been why the creature hadn't already been killed for food to support the countless soldiers.

The sloth started backing away, clearly not in a hurry.

"We will get your tribemates and leave this place now," Skyra said. She resumed walking toward the T3.

Lincoln glanced at the massive creature once more then caught up. He studied Skyra's face for a moment as they started up the next hill. How could he possibly explain their situation without compounding her confusion?

"Here's the problem," he began. "The T3 is a device that takes us from one place to a different place." There was probably no point in trying to explain that the T3 also took them to a different *time*. "We got inside the body bags, then the T3 took us from your homeland to this place, but the body bags stayed behind in your homeland. That's how the T3 works—the body bags stay behind. Those bags are important. We can't use the T3 to travel to a new place without them. We have extra body bags—enough to travel two more times, but that's it. The bags will be gone, and we'll be stuck forever in the place the T3 last took us. If we make a mistake and go somewhere dangerous, we'll never be able to leave that place."

She seemed to consider this. "We will make new body bags."

"Those bags are impossible to make without specialized... well, we just can't make them."

"We will go back to my homeland and get the body bags that we left there. Then you will have more body bags."

Lincoln shot her a glance. She was catching on quickly, although this idea wouldn't work. "If we did that, we would have to leave body bags behind here in order to go there, then we'd have to leave bags there to come back here. We'd end up with the same number of bags. I suppose it's possible just one of us could go back for the bags, in which case the person could retrieve the five bags then leave behind only two bags in your homeland—one for the person and one for the T3." He shook his head at the thought. "There's just too many things that could go wrong. The T3 itself would have to go with that person, which might result in stranding everyone else here. Not only that, but I'm not even sure the T3 will work a third time, let alone a fourth."

They reached the hilltop, and Lincoln scanned the

surrounding area. The battlefield was now hidden from view. This was fine with him—it was a sight he hoped he'd never witness again. They continued hiking back toward the T3 in relative silence. Lincoln struggled to rationalize why he had allowed Skyra to make the jump with him and his team. Yes, she had insisted, but what right did he have to remove her from her native time and place? He had known all along it would be impossible to return to his own timeline. After all, he was the one who had formulated the Temporal Bridge Theorem, which proved that jumping back in time created a new timeline—a new universe. It was impossible to go back in time then return to the same present you left behind. So, why had he been willing to bring Skyra into a future he knew nothing about, a future as likely to be a treacherous wasteland as a peaceful utopia?

At the time, he had justified it as trying to protect Skyra, or as simply granting her request. Deep down, though, he knew he wanted her with him. During four days of shared traumatic experiences in her homeland, in which they'd both nearly been killed numerous times, and in which Skyra had lost her twin sister to an act of brutality, he had developed an undeniable attraction to this Neanderthal woman. He was fascinated by every aspect of her, and he simply liked being with her. Basically, he had done something unforgivably selfish.

"I have an idea," Lincoln finally said. "We can send you back to your homeland. You know how to survive there. It wasn't fair for me to bring you here."

She stopped walking and grabbed his arm. "What is *fair*?"

Lincoln knew she was asking about the literal meaning. "*Fair* is when you choose to do something that is the best thing for everyone involved. When I brought you to this place, it was definitely not the best thing for you. I thought it was at the time, but now I know it wasn't fair to you. We can send you back to your homeland."

She squeezed his arm with her powerful fingers. "I cannot go back to Una-Loto tribe. They will kill me like Gelrut killed Veenah. I cannot live in my homeland without a tribe. Bolups would take me or predators would kill me. Do you think it is *fair* to send me back to my homeland alone?"

"No, I didn't really mean that. I just... I don't know. I just feel bad for bringing you here, only to find that we're in the middle of a brutal war."

She finally released his arm. "I go where you go, Lincoln Woodhouse."

He smiled in spite of the circumstances. "Actually, I find that comforting."

They made their way back to the T3 without further incident. Lincoln was relieved to see Jazzlyn, Virgil, and Derek safely back from their own scouting excursion. Waiting dutifully beside the T3 was Ripple, the mysterious autonomous drone Lincoln himself had supposedly designed, coded, and built fourteen years in his future.

"We may have made a big-ass mistake jumping here," Derek said as Lincoln and Skyra approached. "We only went out a mile or so before we found about a dozen human bodies. Someone had piled them up and left them there to rot. Considering that, and the awful smell in the air, this place gives me the flippin' creeps."

Derek Dagger was Lincoln's all-around assistant, competent at just about any task Lincoln needed done.

"Please tell us you found at least something to give us hope," Jazzlyn added.

Lincoln had hired several paleontologists when he'd

started sending research drones into the past to gather data, but Jazzlyn Shields had proven herself not only brilliant but also unwavering in her commitment to the program. This was why Lincoln had asked her to come on this now disastrous mission.

"Well..." Lincoln said. He exchanged a glance with Skyra, but she didn't say anything. "We found a few more than a dozen bodies."

All three of them frowned.

"What do you mean?" Derek asked.

"I mean we've jumped into the middle of an all-out war of unimaginable brutality. From what we saw, I'm pretty sure it's a war between bolups and nandups."

He got three incredulous looks.

Virgil said, "Wait, Nandups? You're talking about Neanderthals? Here? Now?"

Virgil Brodigan was Lincoln's top physicist and had been immensely helpful in the rush to develop the T3 to meet the deadline. As with the other two, Lincoln now wished he hadn't asked Virgil to give up his life for an endeavor that would probably have no benefit to their own original civilization.

"They looked like Neanderthals to me," Lincoln replied. "Skyra agrees, and she would know."

"Neanderthals aren't extinct in this timeline?" Jazzlyn asked.

"Technically, we're in the same timeline we jumped forward from," Virgil said. "We're just not in the same timeline we originally jumped back in time from four days ago."

"Who gives a flying frazzle-monkey about technicalities!" Derek said in his booming voice. "We jumped into the middle of a freakin' war. Between hominid species, no less. We can't stay here."

"No, you should not stay here, and we should not have come here," Ripple said, stepping away from the T3 upon its four jointed legs. The drone's voice was neutral, neither male nor female. Apparently, at some point in the next fourteen years, Lincoln had decided his time-jumping drones would be less likely to alienate past humans if they sounded distinctly non-human. Ripple came to a stop beside Lincoln. "You must jump back 47,659 years, back to Skyra's time, to her original geographic region."

Lincoln sighed. "This isn't the time to promulgate your absurd scheme, Ripple. You need to forget about it." The damn drone was the reason Lincoln and his team had been forced to jump back in time in the first place, leaving their own world forever.

"My scheme happens to be the culmination of thousands of calculations and—"

"Not now!" Lincoln ordered.

This time the drone remained silent, but it flashed the circle of red lights that surrounded its vision lens, perhaps in frustration or in protest.

"We will leave this place," Skyra said.

Derek tilted his head toward Skyra. "I'm with her. We gotta go. I don't know where, but we gotta go."

"We all agree this place isn't ideal," Lincoln said, "but we have to be realistic. We have ten body bags left. We managed to jump here using only five bags, so it's possible we can make two more jumps. That's assuming the T3 can even continue functioning."

"Which is not a given," Virgil added. "We're already well into uncharted territory with its capabilities."

"Listen, you guys," Jazzlyn said. "We have three choices—stay where we are, jump into the past, or jump into the future. We already know we don't want to stay here, right?"

Derek nodded vigorously. "Damn right. We don't want to jump into the past either. We just left Skyra's time, and that place was a goddamn land of claws, teeth, and skull smashing. Any time before that was probably even worse. The thing is, in the 47,000 years following that, things obviously didn't get any better. Neanderthals didn't go extinct, and now they're at war with humans. For all we know, the two species have been at war the entire 47,000 years! I don't see any reason whatsoever why we would consider going back in time to any point at all in this wretched timeline."

"What is *extinct*?" Skyra asked.

Lincoln and the others eyed her silently. Lincoln still hadn't told Skyra that her species had gone extinct several thousand years after her lifetime. Of course, that had been in his own original timeline. In this new timeline, Neanderthals were apparently alive and well, possibly because of the actions of Lincoln and his team during the four days they had been in Skyra's time 47,000 years ago. Perhaps, because Lincoln had shown Skyra's tribe how to use a bow and arrow, that one simple act had given Neanderthals the competitive edge they needed, thus changing all of history. Or maybe it had simply been caused by a multitude of random events occurring in the new timeline created by the jump.

"You wanna tell her what we're talking about, Lincoln?" Jazzlyn asked.

Lincoln turned to Skyra. How could he tell her without first trying to explain about jumping through time? "Extinct means all of some kind of living thing have died. In the place where I'm really from, nandups no longer exist. They went extinct. Here in this place, though, nandups did *not* go extinct. Here they are still alive."

She gazed at him, her disarmingly large, penetrating eyes so intense that he found it difficult to look away. "Did you and the other bolups kill all the nandups in the place you are from?"

"No. It happened a long time ago. We don't really know why all the nandups died in that place."

"Why did you want to bring me to a place where nandups died?"

He resisted the urge to rub his forehead in frustration. "Because I thought it would be a safe place for all of us, including you. Now I know it's impossible for us to get there from here. I'm sorry. I mean... I wish things were different."

She continued staring, her ample lips working back and forth as if she were chewing on something.

Lincoln turned to his team. "Um... it's possible the war here is a result of something I did in Skyra's time. I kind of showed her tribemates how to use a bow and arrow. That one thing could have given Neanderthals enough of an edge to prevent their extinction."

"And with both species surviving, this war was inevitable... a foregone conflict," Jazzlyn said. Then she shook her head. "No, Lincoln. You need to forget that. Billions of other factors contributed to this. It's not rational to blame yourself for something happening on a global scale."

"Dude, not everything is about *you*," Derek added. He didn't smile, but his eyes twinkled enough to let Lincoln know he was just ribbing.

Lincoln half-smiled and nodded. "You may underestimate my ability to cause trouble." He took a deep breath and gazed at the T3 for a moment before turning back to his team. "Let's look at the practical aspects of this situation. Our goal is to jump to a time and place where we can live out the rest of our lives, preferably in peace. At most, we have only two jumps to accomplish this goal. We have a good idea about what this world was like at Skyra's time, based on what we experienced there. We also know a lot about what this world was like *before* Skyra's time, based on all the paleontology and climatology research done by humans of our timeline."

"Yep, that too. Now let's consider the period between Skyra's time and now—the last 47,000 years. All we know about it is what we've learned today. Neanderthals survived, and they are at war with *Homo sapiens*. Also, from what I could see, neither species appears to be very technologically advanced. Camel-drawn wagons, for example, as well as weapons that looked somewhat medieval."

Derek crossed his arms. "Like I said, the chances of finding anything pleasant in the gap between Skyra's time and now are basically zip. Zero. Zilch."

Lincoln nodded. "Do you all concur?"

More nods all around, except from Skyra, who was now staring toward the trees and hills to Lincoln's right.

"Does my opinion count?" Ripple asked.

"Not really," Lincoln replied. He let out a long breath. "So, we attempt to jump to the future. How far?"

Virgil raised a finger as if he intended to make a point. "There is one potential benefit of jumping forward. If we're lucky, and if we jump forward far enough, we may find a society sufficiently advanced to assist us in constructing additional body bags."

Jazzlyn gave Virgil's shoulder a light shove. "Good thinking, Virg. If they're that advanced, though, wouldn't we just choose to stay there?"

Virgil reddened slightly and adjusted his glasses. "Just a thought."

"Right." Lincoln said. "We need to consider all possibilities. Here's what I propose. It'll take considerable time for the T3 to calculate spatial placement for a jump to the future—up to thirty hours, depending. However, it has already run complete placement calculations for our first jump back to Skyra's time, as well as the calculations for the reverse jump back to this present. If we have the T3 use the same calculations, except carried forward the same amount of time into the future, then much of the hardcore number crunching can be avoided. I'm guessing it will be ready before we can even prepare the body bags and the rest of the gear. Twenty minutes, tops."

Virgil held up a finger again, but not without giving Jazzlyn a wary glance. "Uh, I might point out that if the current war escalates to the point of nuclear conflict, even if it takes a few thousand years for the beings here to develop the capability, then jumping 47,659 years into the future should give us plenty of time to skirt around the resulting nuclear winter as well as the long-term global climate devastation."

This was why Lincoln had hired Virgil in the first place—the guy had a knack for filling in the missing blanks in Lincoln's own reasoning.

"Okay then," Lincoln said. "Does anyone have an objection to jumping 47,659 years into the future?"

Jazzlyn, Virgil, and Derek shook their heads.

Lincoln turned to Skyra. There wasn't time to explain jumping through time, but she deserved to have some say in the decision. "Skyra, instead of going back to your homeland, we are thinking of going to a place that is very different. Do you agree?"

She was still staring into the distance, but she shot him a glance. "I go where you go, Lincoln Woodhouse."

Lincoln turned back to his team to face raised eyebrows and smirks. They obviously didn't know what to think of his newfound attachment to the Neanderthal. "It's unanimous," he said curtly.

"Technically, it is not unanimous," Ripple said.

"It's unanimous!" Lincoln repeated.

"I'll start prepping," Virgil said, heading for the duffel bag containing the last ten body bags.

Jazzlyn and Derek followed Virgil.

Lincoln eyed Skyra. She was again staring out into the trees and brush, but now she was frowning.

"Is something wrong?" he asked.

"Wolves. I hear them."

He spun around and scanned the area. "Here? How far?"

She pulled out her khuls and handed him one, keeping the other for herself. "They are coming. If we cannot scare them away, you will have to use that khul." She grabbed Lincoln's elbow and dragged him over to the T3. Then she gestured to Jazzlyn, Virgil, and Derek. "Bolups! Gather here with us. Together we will scare away the wolves."

"Wolves?" Derek said, spinning around to look.

"Do what she says," Lincoln ordered.

The three darted over, and Skyra pushed them each into position about a foot apart. She pulled her two stone knives from her wrist sheath and gave one to Derek and one to Virgil. "Jazzlyn, you must use your hand weapon," Skyra said, referring to Jazzlyn's prosthetic hand. The carbon fiber polymer appendage wasn't originally designed to be a weapon, but Skyra had seen how formidable it could be.

Ripple moved to Skyra's side. "Perhaps I can be of assistance."

Now Lincoln could hear them—soft, brief yips, which he had thought were just birds. The yips were getting louder.

"No way we can fight off a pack of wolves with knives!" Derek said.

Skyra stepped forward. "Stay behind me, and stay close."

Lincoln saw a flash of movement in the brush—something brown. Then the creatures were there, in plain sight, no more than fifty yards away. Six of them. They were huge, at least 200 pounds each. One of them obviously spotted Lincoln's group. It stopped and stared. Then it emitted several soft yips, and the entire pack stopped.

"Do not fight until I tell you to," Skyra said, her voice firm and confident. "If they come to attack, we will all charge them together, and we will all yell."

"God almighty," Virgil muttered, his voice shaky. "We can't possibly fight those monsters off. Look at them!"

The wolves exchanged several yips, then they charged.

4
FOUND

PRESENT TIME - DAY 1

SKYRA WASN'T TERRIBLY WORRIED. Wolves could usually be frightened away. She had faced wolves before in her homeland, although none as large as these.

The creatures slowed to a walk, but they kept coming. The nearest one let out a low growl.

"Now?" Derek asked.

"Wait," she said quietly. The closer the creatures came, the more likely the scare effort would work. If scared enough, the wolves would turn around and leave instead of backing off and circling. Skyra wished she had a flaming stick of firewood —throwing fire at wolves would usually scare them off for good.

The creatures started spreading out—it was time.

"Run together and yell!" she shouted.

They all rushed forward as a group, screaming and waving their weapons.

The wolves didn't flee. They didn't even flinch or take a step back. Instead, they held their ground, snarling.

"It's not working," Lincoln said.

"Stop!" Skyra ordered. Something wasn't right. The creatures were staring only at her, ignoring Lincoln and his tribemates.

The others fell silent. Skyra was nearly close enough to swing her khul at the nearest wolf's head, but still the creatures didn't run. She took a step back and to the side, moving behind Lincoln. The wolves followed her every movement with their eyes. When she hid her face behind his shoulder, they stopped snarling.

"Uh, what are we supposed to do now?" Jazzlyn asked.

Skyra stepped from behind Lincoln. The wolves rushed at her, snarling again.

Lincoln raised his khul. "Shit!"

Skyra stepped behind him again and the wolves stopped, their snouts almost touching Lincoln's belly. She peeked around his shoulder with one eye. The wolves weren't tearing into Lincoln's gut or lunging for his throat. Instead, they were quiet again, staring past his shoulder at Skyra.

Skyra spoke firmly. "Do not attack the wolves."

"They're not after us, Skyra," Jazzlyn said. "They just want you."

"These canines are displaying evidence of domestication," Ripple said. "Based upon their size and proportions, they are likely modern descendants of the dire wolf, *Canis dirus*."

"That's not helpful right now!" Derek said. "They're inches away, and all we have are stone tools that probably won't even slow them down."

Ripple continued talking. "I must agree with Skyra at this

moment. If you attempt to hurt the wolves now, the consequences would be *dire*, pardon the pun."

Lincoln and the other bolups gave Ripple a strange look Skyra didn't understand—Ripple's statement was meaningless to her. What she did understand was that Lincoln was now the only thing between her and six wolves that clearly considered her to be either food or a threat. She remained silent.

Jazzlyn pushed the sleeve of her strange blue garment up to her elbow and extended her hand weapon toward the creatures. She spoke softly. "Nice dogs. Are you domesticated?"

"Please don't do that, Jazzlyn," Virgil said.

One of the wolves stepped closer to sniff the hand weapon. It took another step and sniffed Jazzlyn's dark skin and the strange blue garment bunched up at her elbow.

Jazzlyn turned and bared her teeth in a bolup smile. "Ripple is right," she said. "They're tame."

A second wolf approached Jazzlyn, and the two creatures began licking her arm where it joined with her hand weapon.

Skyra heard new sounds rising in the distance. The wolves must have heard them too because they turned to look back the way they had come. The sounds were getting louder—movement, footsteps, creatures much larger than the wolves. "Lincoln, we must leave this place," she whispered into his shoulder.

"Yeah, I hear it too. Virgil, let's get those body bags ready right now."

Virgil took a step toward the T3 then paused. "Um, how am I supposed to do that when we're in a stand-off with killer wolves?"

"Just move slowly," Jazzlyn said. "Lincoln, you better stay between Skyra and the dogs. I have a suspicion they are trained to hunt Neanderthals."

Jazzlyn, Virgil, and Derek started moving away.

Before coming to this place, Skyra had watched the others prepare the T_3, and she knew it would take too long. The sounds of larger creatures—grunts and heavy footsteps—were getting closer with every breath. She moved away from Lincoln, intending to help prepare the bags.

The wolves growled and lunged again.

Lincoln darted in front of her, and the creatures stopped. "They recognize you as different," he said. "Please stay behind me. When we're ready, I'll keep them away while you get inside one of the body bags."

"I detect the voices of men, in addition to the movements of large creatures," said Ripple, still standing beside Skyra.

The wolves glanced at Ripple when they heard its voice then returned their attention to Skyra.

She gripped the handle of her khul and listened. A faint voice arose from the direction of the approaching creatures. The wolves must have heard it too—they all turned their heads to stare.

"I hear them!" Virgil said. He quickly grabbed one of the brown bags on the ground beside the T_3 as Jazzlyn and Derek joined him.

Skyra's instincts commanded her to run, but the wolves kept her hiding behind Lincoln.

Ripple said, "It would be prudent for us to conceal ourselves at this time, until we better understand the intentions of the approaching men."

"Okay, there's no time for the T_3," Lincoln said to his tribemates. "Gather around me. We'll make a human barrier around Skyra and move off together." He looked around as if trying to decide which direction.

"We will hide beyond that hill," Skyra said, pointing to the nearest rise.

The others gathered around. Lincoln put his arms back to keep Skyra behind him, and they all started backing away from the wolves.

The creatures watched for a few breaths then spread out and circled the group.

"Just keep going," Lincoln said.

Three of the wolves came together to block their path, growling and baring their teeth.

Ripple stepped away from the group and scuttled toward the creatures. "Away with you! We shall pass."

The wolves glanced at Ripple again but held their ground. Ripple rammed its body into the nearest creature. The wolf lunged forward, knocked Ripple over, and went back to baring its teeth at Skyra and the others.

Derek said, "Dammit, we don't have time for—"

The wolves raised their snouts toward the sky and began howling, cutting off Derek's words. Together, the six creatures created a chorus that could probably be heard as far away as the smoking battlefield.

"Kalufo dup!"

The wolves fell silent, and everyone turned toward the voice.

Another wave of confusion washed over Skyra, this time twisting her belly until it threatened to toss out any food that might still remain inside. She tried swallowing to get it under control. What she was seeing made no sense. There were men —bolups. Many of them. The men were sitting upon the backs of great creatures. She had seen such creatures dead and rotting upon the battlefield. The beasts were as large as aurochs but with high shoulders and enormous heads. Two short, curved horns protruded from the creatures' heads, one just above each ear.

What most confused Skyra, though, was that the men were riding upon the creatures' backs. She had never seen such a strange thing. How could these men get on top of these massive beasts without being killed? Why were the beasts so calm, as if they didn't notice or care that men were sitting upon their backs?

The men wore strange garments upon their bodies, similar to those worn by Lincoln and his tribemates, although these were dark brown instead of sky blue. The garments covered these men so only their hands and faces were visible. Their skin was slightly darker than Skyra's, lighter than Jazzlyn's but darker than Lincoln's. Each man had a long spear and a khul with a broad, shiny blade. Several men carried bows, like the one Lincoln had taken from bolups in Skyra's homeland.

After standing in place for several breaths, the great beasts began lumbering forward, carrying the men toward Skyra's group.

"Kalufo dup!" one of the men repeated.

The beasts came to a stop, and the men upon their backs stared at Lincoln and his tribemates. Skyra remained behind Lincoln, watching warily over his shoulder.

The men began talking in a language Skyra had never heard before. They pointed at the T_3 and the bags on the ground beside it. They pointed at Lincoln and his tribemates, perhaps confused by their strange faces and blue garments. During all of this the wolves stayed calm, as if they weren't frightened at all by the men on their massive beasts.

One man pointed directly at Skyra. He leaned to the side to get a better look around Lincoln's shoulder. "Amo bo diamo," he said.

Skyra squeezed her khul's handle then raised the weapon to show the man she was prepared to fight. She moved to the side, exposing her face.

The man's eyes narrowed. "Yu-te khakhul!" He whistled and swiped his hand from the side until his fingers pointed at Skyra.

The wolves charged toward her.

"No!" Lincoln said. He and his tribemates bunched up around her, stopping the wolves' advance.

"Call off your confounded dogs!" shouted Ripple, now back on its feet.

The men seemed to notice Ripple for the first time. They stared for a few breaths, obviously having never seen such a strange creature before. Unfazed, the first man again whistled and swiped his hand toward Skyra.

The wolves began snarling, pushing their snouts between Lincoln and his tribemates to get at her.

It was time to fight. Skyra didn't know why these wolves were ignoring Lincoln and his tribemates, but they obviously intended to kill her. Maybe if she hurt one of them, the others would run away.

She shoved Lincoln aside and immediately swung her khul into the face of the wolf trying to force its way past him. Her stone blade split the creature's forehead, and it collapsed at Lincoln's feet without a sound. Another wolf leapt over the body. She swung again, cracking the bones in its snout. It let out a yelp and ran off.

Something solid hit Skyra from behind. She went down along with her four protectors. Among squirming bodies and flailing limbs, she rolled to her back to see one of the massive beasts standing over her, its forelegs planted on either side of her belly. The man sitting on the creature leaned to one side and thrust his spear down at Skyra's face. She jerked to the side and the spear's tip hit the dirt by her ear. Dropping her khul, she grabbed the spear's shaft before the man could pull back for another thrust. She yanked the spear to the side with all her strength. The man tumbled from the creature's back and landed on top of Lincoln and Jazzlyn.

Amidst the screaming people, snarling wolves, and thrashing limbs, Skyra grabbed her khul, crawled from beneath the huge beast, and got to her feet. She leapt over the fallen wolf and ran. The remaining wolves would chase her, she was sure of that. Maybe the men on beasts would chase her too, then Lincoln and his tribemates could quickly prepare the T3 and leave this place.

Before Skyra even reached the nearest trees, she was cut off by one of the horned beasts and its rider. She switched directions but was cut off by a second rider, then a third. The wolves hung back behind the men, waiting for an opportunity to charge in for the kill.

Skyra had nowhere to run, so she turned and faced the nearest rider. Now she wished she had held on to the other rider's spear. Her khul was her only weapon—she would have to make good use of it. She got into her fighting stance, one hand positioned forward to block, the other holding her khul beside her ear.

"Lincoln, go now!" she shouted. She glanced toward the T3, hoping to see Lincoln and his tribemates preparing to leave.

Instead, they were running toward her. They darted past the riders and formed a barrier around her.

"Don't hurt her!" Lincoln shouted at the riders. He had dropped his khul and was holding his hands out with his palms toward the men and wolves. "She's with us. We didn't come here to fight with you. Please!"

The great beasts pawed the ground and paced restlessly back and forth as their riders glared at Lincoln.

Ripple moved from behind one of the riders then stood beside Lincoln, becoming part of the barrier around Skyra. "These men have spoken their language enough for my translator to begin preliminary analyses," Ripple said. The creature then spoke loudly. "Yu-te khakhul. Boon-belol yasul-un."

One of the men pointed his spear at Ripple. "Yasul-un yu-te khakhul."

Ripple replied with a long string of even more words Skyra couldn't understand.

The men looked at each other and exchanged words.

"What the hell's going on?" Derek said. "That drone's translator hasn't had anywhere near enough time to learn the language."

Skyra didn't know the word *translator*, but she understood the rest, and she did not agree. After all, Ripple had somehow learned the Una-Loto language of Skyra's tribe after visiting the tribe's camp on only one occasion.

"I do not yet know the language to the point of conversing fluently," Ripple said. "I hope, however, to intrigue these men enough to dispel their desire to slaughter all of you on the spot."

The man Skyra had thrown from his beast stepped forward, holding his recovered spear toward Skyra's group. He held the spear with its strangely-smooth, sharp tip almost touching Lincoln's face. The man then spoke a long string of words.

The other men slid from their beasts, their feet thumping

the ground. They advanced, holding their spears ready. The wolves advanced with them.

The first man spoke again. Ripple spoke back, repeating some of the man's same words. This went back and forth several times, which seemed to anger the men even more. They stepped closer, and the wolves started growling all over again.

"I fear I am not making progress," Ripple said in Lincoln's language. "The likelihood that all of you will survive is decreasing precipitously."

Jazzlyn said, "Lincoln, can't you get that damn drone to shut up?"

Skyra gazed over Lincoln's shoulder, studying the nearest man's face. His eyes flitted from Ripple to Lincoln, to Lincoln's tribemates, to Skyra, and to one of the other men beside him. He was angry but also frightened—a dangerous combination. Abruptly, he furrowed his brows and cocked his head.

The wolves became silent.

Then Skyra heard it too. She had been too caught up in the conflict to notice sooner. Something else was coming— voices of men and women, heavy animals, and the rumble of something large moving upon turning circles of wood.

5

NEGOTIATION

Present Time - Day 1

LINCOLN DASHED FORWARD and picked up the broad-bladed axe one of the men had dropped in a frenzied rush to get back onto his bison.

Four camels came into view, pulling a flat cart flanked by Neanderthals on foot. Seconds later, another camel-drawn cart appeared behind it. The bison-riding humans were still trying to get situated on their mounts, but their wolves had no such constraints. The four remaining creatures charged toward the newcomers.

Shouting and dashing about in apparent confusion, some of the nandups scurried back, while others rushed forward to meet the attacking wolves. Lincoln then realized the movements were far more coordinated than he'd thought. As he watched, the leading defenders instantly pulled short swords from their belts. Then they each raised one arm just as the wolves closed the last few yards of distance and launched themselves at the nandups. The creatures' teeth clamped onto the nandups' arms, which were covered in massively-padded sleeves. The defenders thrust their short swords into the wolves' chests while agilely stepping to the side to avoid being knocked off their feet.

All four of the wolves were now writhing on the ground and coughing up blood, unable to even yelp or howl. The second line of nandups stepped forward in unison and thrust metal-tipped spears into the creatures to finish them off.

The bison riders, all eight of them, let out enraged shouts and goaded their mounts into charging the Neanderthals. Hooves thundered against the ground as they picked up speed, apparently intending to plow directly into the more numerous nandups and their carts.

Skyra grabbed Lincoln's arm. "We must run."

"Go, go, go!" Derek growled as they made a run for the nearest brush-covered hill.

Lincoln turned to look back as he started up the hillside. A tree and several tall saguaros partially blocked his view, but what he did see, as well as the horrifying sounds he heard, indicated the confrontation had become a full-blown battle. Screams of fury and pain intermingled with clashing weapons and pounding hooves. A bison reared up on its hind feet then collapsed onto its back on top of its rider. An axe, like the one in Lincoln's hand, flew end-over-end and struck either a human or a Neanderthal, resulting in a pitiful cry as the victim fell. Clouds of dust were beginning to enshroud the entire scene.

"Hurry up, Lincoln!" Jazzlyn cried. She and the others, including Ripple, were almost to the top of the slope.

"Wait a second!" Lincoln said as he cleared the crest of

the hill. He stopped and took up a position where he could look back without being seen by the nandups or humans.

The others came back and crouched beside him.

Virgil said, "You're thinking of the T3, aren't you?"

Lincoln nodded. Whoever survived the battle would see the T3 and the duffel bags beside it. The T3, which was the size of an office desk, had been designed to look vaguely like a natural boulder, but it didn't match the color of the gravel and rocks here.

"If those bolups kill the nandups, they will come for us," Skyra said. "We must run far away."

Lincoln shook his head. "The T3 is our only way out of here. Let's at least see what happens. Maybe we'll have a chance to go back, get it ready, and jump to a new place."

They crouched in silence, watching as the shouts and clanging of weapons steadily diminished. Within a few minutes the area was silent. Lincoln could see figures walking back and forth beside the two carts, but the leafy branches of a tree made it hard to tell what they were doing. One of the figures swung an axe at something on the ground, producing a faint but sickening *chunk*.

Lincoln studied the weapon he'd collected. Its handle was polished wood, etched with some kind of design. He brought it closer to his face. The design was a spiderweb, encircling the entire handle all the way to the blade. The blade itself was metal, perhaps steel, or at least bronze. Its workmanship was far from perfect—numerous rough spots and blemishes gave it a rustic, almost primitive appearance. One side of the blade was fashioned into a chisel-like stabbing tool, while the other side was a broad axe with at least ten inches of sharpened edge.

He turned the weapon over and looked at the butt end of

the handle. Nailed into the wood was a surprisingly-intricate metal ornament. There could be no mistaking it—the ornament was in the shape of a spider.

"I have never seen a khul like this," Skyra said. She was crouched beside him, staring at the battle axe. She touched the blade then ran two fingers over the sharpened edge. "I do not like this khul. It is too sharp. If I put it in the sling on my back, it would cut me while I am sleeping."

Lincoln touched the blade edge. "I don't think you're supposed to sleep on it. I mean, you could.... well, you're right. It's too dangerous."

"Oh, no." Jazzlyn said. "Don't you even think about touching that."

Lincoln followed her gaze to the scene below. At least a dozen figures were now standing around the T3, obviously curious about it. Several of them kneeled beside the duffel bags and began pushing and pulling as if trying to get them open. It was only a matter of time before they figured out the zippers.

"That's it, man," Derek said. "We're gonna be stuck in this hellhole forever. Or in our case, until we die within the next few hours—or minutes."

Lincoln silently willed the figures to leave the duffel bags and go on about their business. The chances of that, though, were approximately zero. "Be patient," he said. "Maybe they'll be confused by the gear and just leave it alone."

One of the figures stepped over to the T3 and lifted the end of it off the ground. Faint voices drifted up the hillside as they exchanged words. Then the entire group gathered around the device, picked it up, and carried it to one of the carts.

Derek pounded his knee. "Oh, man. We're screwed!"

Ripple spoke up. "Those people are nandups—Neanderthals. Perhaps Skyra can approach them without provoking their ire. I can accompany her, with the objective of quickly processing enough of their language to initiate rudimentary negotiations. With any luck, we may convince them to return your property."

Lincoln glanced at the drone, trying to decide whether to laugh at the plan or give it serious consideration. Whatever he decided to do, it would have to be quick. The Neanderthals would haul away the T3 at any moment.

Skyra turned to Lincoln. "You do not want the nandups to take your T3."

He shook his head. "If they take it, we'll never be able to leave this place."

She rose to her full height, khul in hand. "I will stop them." She stepped away and started down the hillside.

"I will provide assistance," Ripple said, following her.

Lincoln moaned and rubbed his eyes. This wasn't likely to end well. These nandups were appallingly brutal. They would probably kill Skyra before Ripple even began to analyze their language.

"I don't know about this, Lincoln," Jazzlyn said. "Maybe we should stop her."

Lincoln stood up. "Skyra, wait. Let's think about this."

She paused and looked back.

Beyond her, the camel-drawn carts started moving.

"We're completely, utterly screwed!" Derek said. "Now they're leaving."

There was no time left. Something had to be done quickly.

"We're coming with you, Skyra," Lincoln said. "He shot a

glance at his team. We have to stay together, and we can't lose the T3. I've got an idea." He started jogging down the hill.

"Ripple, when we get down there I need you to do exactly what I tell you to," Lincoln said as he caught up. The nandups appeared to be turning the carts around to head back the way they had come. There would be time to reach them before they were gone.

"I understand," the drone replied.

Jazzlyn, Virgil, and Derek caught up and descended the hill with them.

"I don't know about this," Virgil said. "I really, really don't know."

"Hey!" Lincoln shouted as he hit level ground. "Hey, wait!"

The Neanderthals were still a hundred yards away, but one of them pointed and called out to the others. The carts stopped moving.

"Ripple, do you have enough power to levitate? Even for just a few seconds?"

The drone was now between Lincoln and Skyra, galloping on its four jointed legs. "I should be capable of levitating for up to one hundred and twenty seconds. Lincoln, as you know, I am not well equipped for combat. I have had to improvise at times, but I am not—"

"I know! I just need you to do what I say."

The nandups were now fifty yards away. Several of them were preparing to fight, brandishing spears or axes.

"Derek, Jazzlyn, Virgil, hang back behind me and Skyra. Be ready to follow my lead, okay?"

They all muttered brief words of confirmation.

It was too late to give up this insane attempt now, but

Lincoln was starting to second-guess himself. He had no right to lead his team to their deaths. What had he been thinking? One of the Neanderthals shouted, "Yu-te khakhul! Apofu layop nu-te!" The voice belonged to a woman, who was pointing at Skyra while wielding an axe with her other hand.

Lincoln brought his group to a stop ten yards from the nandups, now in a defensive line. The ground around them was littered with dead wolves and humans, and Lincoln glanced briefly at the carcasses of two bison the Neanderthals had somehow already loaded onto their carts.

"Apofu layop nu-te," Lincoln said with as much confidence as he could muster. He had no idea what the words meant but had heard them spoken by the bison-riding humans as well as these Neanderthals. He then parroted the other words he'd just heard the woman speak. "Yu-te khakhul!"

Other than exchanging a few glances, the nandup men and women didn't move.

Lincoln placed his stolen axe on the ground at his feet. He turned to his team and raised his eyebrows. Derek and Virgil understood and dropped their stone knives. Jazzlyn was not holding a weapon, but she concealed her prosthetic hand behind her back. "Skyra, would you please put your khul on the ground?" Lincoln said.

She glanced at him with furrowed brows. "I will not."

Arguing would make things worse, so Lincoln faced the nandups and proclaimed, "I am the great and powerful Oz." He pointed down at the drone standing beside him. "This is Ripple, robot ruler of Rohan." He then lowered his voice and said, "Ripple, without scaring the crap out of them, impress them with levitation, lights, and sound."

Without any discernible delay, Ripple emitted a low buzzing sound. The drone rose from the ground to the height of Lincoln's shoulders, withdrawing its legs into its shell. Its red circle of lights pulsed and rotated. Seconds later, mild, orchestral music began playing from Ripple's speakers. The music started with a few violins then swelled to include woodwinds and some subtle brass.

Lincoln studied the nandups' faces. They watched Ripple's performance with eyes as large and intense as Skyra's, but their expressions didn't change in any way that Lincoln could detect. Still, he hoped for the best. Perhaps it was a long shot, but with luck the Neanderthals would become interested enough to find out more. This would result in talking, which in turn would allow Ripple's translation software to learn enough to allow real communication. Lincoln's only goal now was simply to convince these people to return the T3 and body bags so he and his group could jump the hell out of this place.

Ripple began swaying, propelling itself several feet to the left then back to the right, as the music continued playing. The nandups followed its movements with their eyes, apparently fascinated, and Lincoln began to think his plan might actually work. As ruthless and barbaric as these beings were, they had obviously developed some degree of technology—at least enough metallurgy to produce rough metal weapons, as well as some ornaments and the hardware needed for the camel-drawn carts. They had to have some measure of curiosity. After all, they had collected the T3. Surely they would want to know more about what Ripple was and what made the drone work. Or at least about the music emanating from its speakers.

One of the nandup women spoke to her companions and took a few steps closer to Ripple. Several of the others replied without taking their eyes off the drone.

Lincoln saw the woman's intent before she acted. Her face tightened, as did her grip on the axe in her hand. He had no time to process this observation, though. The woman drew the axe back and threw it. The weapon hit Ripple's shell with a loud *crack* and ricocheted to the side, almost striking Lincoln's leg before bouncing to a stop on the ground.

Ripple's music stopped. The drone rolled to the side and nearly hit the ground before getting its levitation under control. A split-second later, it started emitting an ear-splitting siren.

Everything went to hell. Skyra raised her khul and rushed the woman but was immediately assailed by a half dozen nandups. The overwhelming force of bodies drove her to the ground. Lincoln froze for several seconds, struggling to comprehend what was happening, before he decided to dive for his discarded axe. Derek was there on the ground beside him, grabbing the nandup woman's thrown axe. His wide eyes met Lincoln's for a brief moment before they both started to get up.

Neither of them made it to their feet. Derek was struck from the side and swept out of Lincoln's view an instant before Lincoln felt a crushing weight upon his back. His chest and chin hit the dirt. Someone wrenched the axe from his grip. A knee mashed painfully into his lower back.

Ripple's siren fell silent.

As Lincoln fought to catch his breath, fingers probed his fleece shirt and pants. The nandups spoke rapidly to each other. They bent his right leg at the knee to lift his foot. The fingers then prodded his running shoe, resulting in more words exchanged.

Powerful hands rolled him onto his back, then a knee pressed into his gut. Nandup faces stared down at him. Again, fingers probed his clothing. One of the Neanderthals discovered the only object Lincoln had in his pocket. The man fumbled for several seconds to remove it, then he held it up to get a closer look. It was Maddy's cognitive module. Lincoln had removed it from Maddy's broken shell after the drone had thrown herself off a cliff to save Lincoln and his team.

"No!" Lincoln sputtered. "Please don't break that."

The man turned the module over a few times while studying it, then he passed it to one of his companions.

Lincoln twisted his neck to look for Skyra. She was getting the same treatment he was—a group of nandups holding her on the ground and prodding her. Based on the obvious effort they were putting into it, she hadn't yet been killed or seriously wounded. Jazzlyn, Virgil, and Derek were also still alive, all of them now subdued by beings who had just used nothing more than handheld weapons to kill four wolves, at least two bison, and a team of human warriors. The fact that Lincoln and his group were still alive was little comfort. That could change within seconds.

"Alep memo-tole tohn-lee-aful."

The words had been spoken in Ripple's oddly-neutral voice. Lincoln spotted the drone. It was now on its feet, walking freely among the groups of Neanderthals gathered around their captives.

One of the men examining Lincoln lifted his head and spoke to Ripple. Ripple replied, now using words Lincoln was pretty sure the Neanderthals hadn't yet spoken in his presence.

The man got up, leaving Lincoln to the three other nandups still holding him down. The man stepped to within a few feet of Ripple and spoke at length.

Ripple replied at length.

This went on for several minutes. The other nandups had, at least for now, lost interest in their captives and were watching and listening intently. Several of them joined in the conversation. All the while, Ripple spoke without pausing or repeating words, as if the language had already been coded into its memory.

Lincoln had never studied foreign languages—he had never been particularly interested. He had always focused his attention on mathematics and science. Now he needed to apply his cognitive skills to learning this language, and fast. He was already beginning to recognize patterns. Surprisingly, these nandups seemed to be speaking the same language as the human warriors they had killed. What events could possibly lead to two different species at war with each other speaking the same language? Regardless, if he had a few days to listen to these people talk, he could probably learn enough to converse with them.

"Lincoln," Jazzlyn called out from her prone position beneath three nandups, "since we're about to die and all... I just want to tell you I don't regret coming with you on this crazy-ass mission. Maybe it was doomed from the start, but still, it's been the honor of my life to be on your team."

"I have to say I agree," Virgil said, "although I'd rather not die if I have a choice."

Derek grunted from pain or from trying to move, then he said, "Shit, now I'm obligated to say something too. Well, sure, I'm—" He grunted again.

Lincoln strained his neck to look. Four nandups were now dragging Derek toward the nearest wagon.

Brawny hands gripped Lincoln's arms and yanked him to his feet.

"Wait, let me get my glasses," Virgil said, nodding his head toward a spot on the ground.

As Lincoln was being pulled toward the wagon, he glimpsed one of the nandups scooping up Virgil's glasses.

"Skyra, please stop struggling," Lincoln said as he was guided past her and her attackers. "Don't give them a reason to kill you."

"I do not... want to be taken!" she grunted, still fighting.

Several nandups hoisted Lincoln and slammed him down onto the wood surface of one of the carts, only a few feet from a dead bison. Within seconds, his arms and legs were restrained by leather straps with metal buckles that appeared to be built into the platform for this very purpose. Dozens of similar straps were situated in rows, and soon Derek, Jazzlyn, and Virgil were also restrained.

Skyra was literally tossed onto the cart. She rolled over and immediately started to get up, but one of the nandup women rammed the butt of her spear into the side of Skyra's head. Skyra went limp and hit the wood like a rag doll. Seconds later she pushed herself up to a sitting position. Her eyes didn't appear to be focused, though, and she just sat there with her arms on her knees, staring at her feet.

The cart began moving. Most of the nandups jumped off to walk alongside, but four of them stayed beside Skyra. For some reason, they didn't strap her to the platform. In fact, the woman who had struck Skyra sat down and gently parted Skyra's hair to examine the wound she had inflicted. She snapped her fingers in front of Skyra's face and spoke softly to her.

In spite of the creaking and jostling of the moving cart, Lincoln heard a familiar buzzing sound. He lifted his head to see Ripple fly to catch up to the cart, extend its legs, and gently alight between Skyra and the bison carcass.

"I'm feeling rather enthusiastic about the success of our efforts," the drone said.

Derek jerked against his restraints, knocking his elbows against the platform. "This is what you call success? I don't even want to *know* what failure would look like."

Ripple ignored this. "Not only have I succeeded in making some sense of the language, which I must point out is quite different from any language of your original timeline, but I have convinced these nandups that you and your devices are of great scientific importance."

Derek let his head thump back onto the wood. "Great. They're going to dissect us."

"Perhaps you could allow the drone to explain," said Virgil.

"What exactly did you learn from them?" Lincoln asked Ripple.

"I learned that these nandups are warriors. They are not very curious, and they have no interest in scientific pursuits, unless those pursuits involve better ways to kill their enemies. If you anger them, they may disembowel you, but they have no interest in dissecting you."

"So where are they taking us?" Jazzlyn asked.

"They are taking us to those of their kind who *are* interested in scientific pursuits. I do not know what might happen to us there. It is a bridge we must cross when we get there, as they say. For the time being, though, you are all alive. You're welcome."

Lincoln sighed and laid his head back on the platform. He stared at the sky, trying to ignore the gamey smell of the dead bison only a few feet away. He raised his head again to check on Skyra. She was now staring back at him, and her eyes seemed more focused than they were before.

"Are you okay?" he asked, knowing she considered that question to be ridiculous.

Her lips parted slightly in a hint of a nandup smile.

Lincoln exhaled in relief. As Ripple had said, cross one bridge at a time. He turned his attention to the Neanderthal woman beside Skyra. She was older, although how much older he couldn't even guess. Compared to Skyra, she was weathered and drawn, perhaps from a lifetime of battle and deprivation. However, Lincoln could still see the same penetrating and disarming look in her oversized eyes that he had noticed so many times in Skyra. This was apparently a universal Neanderthal trait.

Like the other nandups on and beside the cart, the woman wore dark-colored clothing made of woven cloth, simple but functional. Unlike the bolups who had almost killed Lincoln and his team earlier, the nandups here apparently didn't like clothing covering their arms and legs, except for the thick, padded sleeve some of them wore on one arm for protection from bolup-trained wolves. Like Skyra, these Neanderthal women and men had little to no facial or body hair. Lincoln focused on the wide leather belt around the woman's waist, which provided loops to hold her weapons—a short sword on her left, an axe on her right, and a sheathed dagger between the two.

A bronze-colored buckle was affixed to the belt beside the knife. At first, Lincoln had thought it was merely functional, but now he saw it was more of an adornment. He squinted. There was no mistaking it—the buckle, about three inches across, was fashioned into the likeness of a spider.

6
CARGO

PRESENT TIME - DAY 1

THE FOG gradually lifted from Skyra's mind. A nandup woman was sitting beside her. The woman was touching Skyra's head, speaking the same language Skyra had heard the beast-riding bolups speak. Lincoln was here, and his tribemates, all of them tied to the rolling wooden structure, while Skyra had been left untied for some reason. Ripple was here, also not tied to the platform.

Skyra looked down at her hands. Her khul was gone. Her two hand blades from her wrist sheath were gone. She had no weapons, although she doubted she could fight at this moment anyway. At least not until her head fully cleared.

What had happened to her? She had been thrown onto the wooden platform, and then... nothing. Pain. There had been pain. She pushed the nandup woman's hand away and felt her own scalp. It was tender and swollen. Something had hit her. She looked at her hand. No blood, which meant she hadn't been hit with a khul, especially not one of the shiny, sharp ones used by the bolups and nandups here.

She turned and watched Lincoln until he met her gaze.

"Are you okay?" he asked. He knew it was a question that didn't make sense to Skyra, especially under the circumstances. She grimaced at him, to let him know what she thought of the question.

At least Lincoln and his tribemates were still alive, though they probably wouldn't be for long. In Skyra's homeland, nandups did not eat bolups or other nandups. In this land, she was not so sure. In her homeland, nandups did not take bolup women to put children in their bellies. Perhaps the nandups here did take bolup women. Why, then, would they take Lincoln, Derek, and Virgil, unless they intended to eat them?

She turned and looked at the second wooden platform being pulled ahead of hers. On it was the T_3 and the second of the dead beasts Lincoln had called bison. Both platforms were being pulled by camels. Skyra had never imagined animals could be made to follow commands or to carry people on their backs. This was a strange land indeed, and the confusing things Skyra had seen made her want to close her eyes and wake up back in her own homeland. At least there she understood the dangers.

The camels continued walking, pulling the wooden structures along a well-worn path that wound back and forth through countless hills. On the hillsides grew trees, grasses, and bushes unlike any that grew in Skyra's homeland. Large birds that looked like vultures and eagles occasionally soared overhead, but not the types she could recognize.

Lincoln and his tribemates began speaking to each other about the things they had seen. Skyra still didn't understand some of their words, but she continued to learn more with each day she spent with these strange bolups. At this moment, they seemed as confused as Skyra about what was happening.

She kicked her heel against the wooden platform to get their attention. "These nandups will kill us. I can run away from them, but I do not want to be alone in this land. I will watch for a good time to take one of their weapons. Then I will kill. I will release all of you, and we can run away."

"Impossible," Derek said without lifting his head.

Lincoln said, "Please don't try anything like that. There are too many of them."

"They are going to kill us," Skyra said simply.

Ripple turned its vision orb toward Skyra. "I have been your companion for many days, Skyra, have I not?"

She gazed at the creature without answering.

Ripple continued. "I have tried only to help you and protect you from danger. As you have recently become aware, I have an important plan. My plan requires that you and Lincoln survive, to travel back to your homeland and live as partners there, producing children and therefore setting in motion a series of events that will make the world a far better place. All my actions are carried out with the hope of making that plan succeed. Please trust me when I say you should not try to escape from, or fight, these nandups at this time."

Skyra stared at the creature's transparent orb. Ripple had taken care to use words Skyra knew, which somehow made its words seem more important.

"Mafum genul-ulelo," the woman beside Skyra said. She was looking at Ripple.

Ripple spoke back to her, and the two went back and forth as if the woman were talking to one of her own kind.

"Ripple, what is she saying?" Jazzlyn asked.

"If it involves our deaths, I don't want to know," Virgil added.

Ripple waited for the woman to stop speaking and said, "This nandup woman simply wants to know what we are saying to each other. I am doing my best to explain we are concerned about our fate."

"Can I talk directly to her through you?" Lincoln asked.

"Yes, that is a function your future self has given me. Keep in mind that you will be getting direct translations based upon incomplete knowledge of the language. You will not have the benefit of my interpretations."

"I don't care," Lincoln said. "Please turn that function on."

Ripple's red lights glowed for a moment. "You may proceed."

Lincoln turned to the woman. "We are not your enemy. We ask that you release us and give us back our things."

Ripple spoke to the woman in her language.

The woman's face hardened. She glanced at the three other nandups sitting on the wooden platform. Then she turned to Lincoln and spoke directly to him.

When the woman was done speaking, Ripple said, "You humans-bolups. You enemy. But you not like other humans-bolups. We not release you. We take you village-city. Our scientists-learners-teachers decide what we do with you."

"I'll be damned," Lincoln said quietly. "Uh, don't translate that, Ripple."

"Tell her we *demand* to be released," Derek said.

"Can you ask her what she *thinks* their scientists will do with us?" Virgil asked.

Lincoln held up a hand. "Hold on. It'll be less confusing if only one of us talks to her. In fact, Ripple, from now on don't speak to these Neanderthals on your own, only as a direct translator. Understand?"

"I understand. I should point out, however, that my decisions are often based upon thousands of various parameters. You might be wise to reconsider."

"Duly noted, but for now just do what I say."

Skyra understood enough of the exchange to know what was happening—Ripple could speak the nandup language and help her and the others communicate. "Ripple, I will now talk to the nandup woman," she said.

Lincoln turned to her. "Um, I was just trying to explain why it might be best if just one of us—"

"I will talk to the nandup woman!"

He blew out a breath and laid his head back on the wood. "Alright."

Skyra faced the woman beside her. "I am a nandup from the Una-Loto tribe. You are also a nandup. We are the same kind of people. I honor you, and you honor me." She slapped the platform with her hand. "That is why you have not tied me to this wood. These bolups are my friends. You will not hurt them. If you do hurt them, I will challenge you to fight me. As a nandup, you must accept my challenge. I will then kill you. I will not kill you slowly. While your tribemates are watching, I will open your belly and pull out your intestines. I will wrap them around your neck, and you will die as you try to put them back into your belly. The strength of the woolly rhino and the cave lion is in my blood, and that is what I will do to you if you hurt my friends."

"Oh, shit," Lincoln said. "Maybe that's not—"

Ripple began speaking to the woman in her language. Ripple paused a few times as if thinking about what words to use then continued. The speaking went on and on.

As the woman listened, her face hardened even more. Now the other nandups on the platform were staring at Skyra, as were those walking beside the platform. This was what Skyra was hoping for. Now the woman would have to accept Skyra's challenge to fight, if it came to that.

When Ripple finally stopped speaking, Skyra eyed the woman again and said, "You will let us go now. We will leave this place, and I will not have to kill you."

Again, Ripple spoke the woman's language.

In response, the nandup woman moved her hand to the short blade on her leather waist strap. She used her free hand and her feet to scoot away from Skyra until she was sitting near the edge of the platform a body's length away. Then she just sat there, gripping her weapon and glaring at Skyra.

Skyra felt a growl escaping from her chest. "I challenge you to fight me!"

Ripple translated Skyra's words.

The woman's face softened, and she turned to one of the nandup men walking beside the platform and spoke. The man threw his head back and let out a laugh. "*At-at-at-at-at.*"

The other nandups joined in the laughter.

Skyra asked Ripple what the woman had said.

"The woman said, 'This little one brave. Or maybe I hit this little one too hard with my spear.'"

Skyra jumped to her feet and stepped toward the woman. "I challenge you to fight me!"

The woman and her companions stood up. Other nandups walking beside the structure leapt onto the platform. They attacked Skyra all at once. She had no weapons, and within a few breaths she was on her back on the platform. The nandups yanked her across the rough wood, wrapped some of the leather straps around her wrists and ankles, and cinched the straps tight.

Skyra fought against the restraints and spat at the woman. "I challenge you to fight me!" She then spat at one of the men. "I challenge *you* to fight me! You are nandups. You must accept. You are afraid I will kill you!"

Ripple spoke Skyra's words in the nandups' language. This resulted in another wave of laughter. Most of the nandups hopped off the platform and resumed walking. The woman Skyra had challenged sat back down and began staring out at the passing hills, no longer giving Skyra her attention.

"Skyra, are you hurt?" Lincoln asked.

She turned to look, but Lincoln's head was now hidden behind the dead bison. His tribemates were also behind the creature's body.

"I am not hurt, I am angry," she replied. "These nandups are not like my people. I do not understand them."

"Well, I'm glad you're not hurt. We'll just have to be patient and see what happens next."

Ripple stepped over to Skyra and stood over her. "Although reckless, your actions have helped us gather information. We now know these nandups do not wish to kill you, at least not before arriving at their destination. I do hope you take no further risks, as my plan requires that you and Lincoln survive this ordeal." Ripple pulled its legs up into its shell and settled its belly on the platform. "To keep your mind on more productive thoughts, I will now begin teaching you what I have learned about the language used by these nandups."

Skyra groaned and pulled at her straps. "No, I do not want to know."

Ripple's red lights brightened twice. "Perhaps you would

like me to tell you a story. I happen to be quite skilled at story-telling."

"Not now, Ripple!"

The creature fell silent but remained beside Skyra's head.

She pulled at her straps again, but the nandups had made them too tight to escape.

The wooden structure continued through the hills, creaking and rocking back and forth as it rolled over the bumps on the ground below. Skyra rested her head on the wood and stared out at the walking nandups and the scenery beyond. Other than their strange garments and different weapons, these people looked similar to the nandups of Skyra's tribe. However, many of them seemed to be much older. Some were even older than the oldest members of Una-Loto, members who had been forced to stop hunting and fighting many seasons ago. How could such ancient nandups fight the way Skyra had seen them fight? She let out a long breath. Everything about this new place was strange and confusing.

Voices came from ahead, and the platform stopped moving. Skyra twisted her neck to see. The camels had stopped walking, and two of them were pressing their noses together and licking the saliva from each other's drooping lips. The voices were coming from beyond the camels, but Skyra couldn't see the nandups who were talking. Her eyes were drawn to the horizon, and once again she was nearly overcome by a wave of confusion.

She had thought clouds were forming on the horizon, or perhaps that distant mountains were becoming visible. But now, as she focused on the dark layer that loomed ahead, it was obviously not clouds or mountains. Instead, it was a structure made of stones. The stones had impossibly-straight edges and square corners. Row after row, the stones had been neatly stacked, forming a solid wall even straighter than the sheerest cliff face or smoothest cave wall she had ever seen. She turned her head one way then the other. The wall went on seemingly forever, from one horizon to the other, disappearing into the distance in both directions. Along the top of the wall, spaced out evenly, were nandups, each of them holding a spear next to one shoulder and a long bow slung over the other shoulder.

Skyra had never even imagined such a structure before, but after staring at it for several breaths, she was sure these nandups had built it themselves. Somehow they had made these perfect stones and had placed them into the shape of a wall many times their own height. The thought of such an accomplishment made her thoughts swirl in her head.

Her scalp began to tingle as she made another connection. This wall had been built because of the war. Before today, Skyra had never conceived of a war and didn't know what one was. Seeing the battlefield had nearly overwhelmed her. But now, staring at this seemingly impossible wall, she started to truly understand. This war was not a raid of one tribe on the camp of another tribe, which would be over in only a small part of one day. This war was immense and ongoing, season after season, even generation after generation. She realized these people were born during the war, fought their entire lives, and died during the war, knowing their children and their children's children would have to do the same thing. Seeing this wall was almost more horrifying than seeing countless bodies burning and rotting on the battlefield.

Now, even more than before, Skyra wanted to leave this place. She would rather die than stay here.

The camels started walking again, and soon Skyra was staring up at the ceiling of a tunnel through the wall. As she came out the other side, she noticed three nandups staring down at her from atop the wall. The three, like those Skyra had already seen, were older, with scarred, leather-like skin the color of brown sand.

Shouts came from several directions. A great black slab with rows of square holes slid from one side until it slammed into place, blocking the tunnel.

Skyra turned and gazed out one direction then the other. Vast fields of waist-high grasses stretched into the distance. These fields were unlike any Skyra had seen—the grasses grew in rows, with bare soil between the rows. Scattered about in the fields were more nandups. Some of them appeared to be wearing no garments or footwraps, but they were so covered in dirt and mud it was hard to tell. Some were crouched low, engaged in unknown tasks. Others were carrying baskets balanced upon their heads. The baskets were like those Skyra's tribe used for collecting crayfish from the shallow rivers among the Kapolsek foothills, only many times larger.

The strange grassy fields went on and on, eventually replaced by fields of leafy green shrubs, many of them bearing red berries or brightly-colored fruits. Like the grasses, these plants grew in straight rows. More mud-covered nandups were working among them, some carrying empty baskets, some carrying baskets heavy with fruits, and some on their knees working, with no baskets at all. Many of the workers paused what they were doing to watch the camels and platforms pass by. After staring for only a few breaths, they went back to work.

After being silent for many breaths, Ripple spoke. "These are crop fields, Skyra. These nandups are growing food. The immense size of these crop fields, as well as the size of the defensive wall, suggests that we are headed toward a camp of many nandups. Perhaps it is even a *city*, which is a very large camp, perhaps with thousands of tribe members. If you are curious and want to ask questions of the nandups, I will translate your words. This is an opportunity to learn about their life in this land."

"I do not want to ask questions, I want to leave this place."

"I understand. Perhaps an opportunity might arise that will help us convince these nandups to release you. I will watch for such an opportunity."

The crop fields gave way to fields filled with animals. Camels grazed in large herds. Various deer-like creatures Skyra had never seen before lay together on the grass in groups, too many in each group to count. These animal groups were contained within their own vast enclosures. The enclosures had walls made with cords pulled tight between tall, black posts. One such enclosure contained waist-high creatures with snouts that wriggled back and forth like thick, fleshy fingers. The adults of these creatures were black, but the smaller young were tan with white spots. From the other side of the dead bison, Skyra heard Jazzlyn call these creatures *tapirs*. Within all these animal enclosures, nandups were pushing wheeled baskets filled with dried grasses, often dumping the contents, which were then quickly surrounded by hungry animals.

Eventually the fields of animals also came to an end, and the camels pulled the platform through a camp like nothing Skyra had ever seen. Rather than shelters made of skins stretched over pieces of wood, these nandups lived in shelters that appeared to be made of mud that had been smoothed into shape and allowed to dry. Unlike the massive wall Skyra had seen, these shelters were rounded, without straight sides. The shelters were embedded within frameworks of wooden poles.

Even the frameworks were not straight, and the poles stuck out in every direction. Many of the shelters were arranged above one another on these frameworks. Skyra saw some that were five shelters high. Instead of being stacked directly on top of each other, though, the dwellings were situated on the pole framework in random places, supported by the framework itself rather than the other shelters beneath them. Many of the poles extended outward and upward far beyond the mud shelters, and the overall appearance made Skyra think of the groups of mud swallow nests she had seen clinging to the branches of dofusofu trees in her homeland.

Countless nandups were climbing on the frameworks, gazing out of the round openings of the dried-mud dwellings, and walking in every direction on the ground. Many of them stopped what they were doing to watch the two wooden platforms passing by. Some of the nandups walking on the ground were carrying baskets balanced upon their heads or other objects tucked under their arms. Baskets were arranged in neat rows on the ground, and nandups were walking among them, talking to each other and pointing to whatever contents the baskets held. Entire animals, as well as severed heads, legs, and torsos, hung from wooden poles, perhaps drying in the sun. Young nandups, including many who had obviously seen fewer than six cold seasons, moved about in packs, often running and laughing, while the adults mostly ignored them. All the nandups were wearing dark-colored garments covering their shoulders, bellies, and groins but not their arms and legs. Their leather footwraps were similar to Skyra's.

Skyra laid her head back on the platform and closed her eyes. Her mind did not know what to do with all her thoughts. Never before had she imagined such a place—so many people, so many smells and sounds. How could it be that her Una-

Loto tribemates had never known of this place? Some of the hunters had traveled many days in search of mammoths in their attempts to earn recognition as the tribe's bravest hunters. Those hunters had never returned with reports of such a place as this. Lincoln's T3 must have taken Skyra much farther from her homeland than she had first thought.

Virgil's voice pulled Skyra from her thoughts. "God almighty, would you look at that?"

She opened her eyes and raised her head. The platform was nearing another wall, just as tall and impressive as the first, although this one curved more sharply as it receded into the distance, as if it enclosed a smaller area. Beyond this wall was a structure that made everything Skyra had seen so far seem insignificant. The structure rose unimaginably high, seemingly as tall as some of the foothills of the mountains of her homeland. The highest levels appeared faint through the smelly haze hanging in the air everywhere in this land.

Skyra realized she was pulling at her straps in her attempt to get a better look. Portions of the structure had been built with the same square stones used in the walls, but other portions were made of the rounded mud dwellings, with countless long, wooden poles protruding in all directions. Skyra's mind whirled. How could such a structure stand so high without collapsing, especially with the straight, flat walls randomly riddled with shapeless mud dwellings and odd arrangements of protruding poles?

The camels stopped at the wall's base. More nandup voices came from ahead. Soon the camels resumed their pace, passing through another tunnel to the other side of the wall. This time, although Skyra saw another great black slab with rows of square holes, the slab did not slide into place to seal the tunnel after the camels and platforms passed through. In fact, numerous nandups were walking through the tunnel in both directions, carrying baskets and other objects. Maybe this tunnel was sealed only when raiding bolups somehow got past the other, longer wall.

Their captors guided the camels and platforms directly to the base of the massive structure. Skyra no longer had to lift her head to gaze at the strange combination of straight stone walls and rounded dwellings—the structure loomed almost directly above her like a sheer cliff.

More voices came from ahead, this time speaking back and forth for many breaths.

"What's happening, Ripple?" Lincoln asked from around the edge of the dead bison.

Ripple pushed itself up by extending its legs from inside its shell. After apparently listening for several more breaths, it said, "It sounds like the nandups are trying to decide what to do with us, as well as with the T_3. The new voices here seem rather excited about the situation, which I believe is a most positive sign."

"Just do direct translation, like I told you before. We can do without your personal opinions."

"Very well, I will translate from the beginning of the conversation." Ripple waited a few more breaths then began speaking. "We have bolups-humans. These bolups-humans unlike other bolups-humans. Strange clothing. Strange tools. We bring to village-city. Scientists-learners-teachers will be pleased." Ripple made its voice slightly deeper, saying, "What is this?" Then its voice switched back, saying, "We do not knowledge what is this. This and this and this we find near strange bolups-humans. Strange bolups-humans know what is this and this and this. Strange bolups-humans know what is purpose of this and this and this. Scientists-learners-teachers will force-speak strange bolups-humans."

"Okay, I get the idea," Lincoln said. "Now please translate as I talk to the nandup woman sitting near Skyra."

"Very well."

Lincoln said, "What will happen to us now?"

Ripple spoke in the nandup's language.

The woman spoke back, and Ripple said, "We take you in public chamber-auditorium. Then scientists-learners-teachers take you in sanctuary-fortress."

"What will happen to us then?" Lincoln asked.

Ripple spoke to the woman then gave her reply. "We do not knowledge what happen to you there. Bolups-humans go in sanctuary-fortress. Bolups-humans not come out sanctuary-fortress."

7
WEBS

Present Time - Day 1

Lincoln told himself there was no point in fighting or resisting. He and his team were now deeply contained behind two massive walls within a city of thousands of Neanderthals. Ruthless warriors, armed to the teeth, were all around them. In spite of his previous resolve, when four nandups removed his restraints and pulled him off the cart, his fear took over. He instinctively dug his heels in as they started dragging him toward a metal cage.

The cage was actually a smaller cart, no more than five feet wide and eight feet long, covered by a dome of black metal latticework. Like Skyra, these Neanderthals were solid and surprisingly strong, and they easily overpowered his pitiful resistance. They shoved him through an opening at the back of the cage and slammed the door shut.

Lincoln got to his knees and watched as the nandups returned to the larger cart and dragged Derek to the cage.

Derek didn't physically resist, but he did use his booming voice to cuss at his captors, including a detailed statement about how ugly and stupid they were.

"Ripple, please don't translate any of that," Virgil said.

"Understood," the drone replied.

For some reason, the Neanderthals hadn't restrained Ripple in any way. In fact, the drone would have been left behind at the jump site if it hadn't voluntarily flown onto the cart.

The nandups shoved Derek into the cage with Lincoln, and within minutes they had added Jazzlyn and Virgil. Skyra and Ripple remained on the larger flatbed cart, watching silently, ignored for now by the nandups.

Another cage on wheels was brought out through the open doorway of the massive structure the woman had called the *public chamber-auditorium*. Nandups went to the second flatbed cart, retrieved the two duffel bags—one containing the rolled-up body bags, the other containing the remaining survival gear—and loaded these into the second cage. Then they hefted the T3 from the cart, carried it to the second cage, and pushed it through the cage's door, scraping its sides in the process.

The woman Skyra had challenged held her dagger to Skyra's throat as one of the men unbuckled her straps. Both of the nandups leapt from the cart and waved for Skyra and Ripple to do the same. Skyra dropped to the ground easily, but Ripple had to levitate for a moment before alighting on all four legs beside her. This drew some attention from the nandups who had gathered around to watch, although not nearly as much as Lincoln would have assumed. Either these people were accustomed to seeing levitating robot drones, or the sight was so foreign it hardly even registered as noteworthy. The former seemed unlikely. The latter seemed plausible, as Lincoln had observed this exact same indifference in the humans and Neanderthals of Skyra's time.

The nandups that had captured Lincoln's group promptly turned their camels around and hauled off the flatbed carts, which now only held two bison carcasses.

The staring crowd parted as Skyra was forced to walk through the entrance to the public chamber-auditorium. Nandups positioned themselves at each corner of the wheeled cages and commenced pushing them through the entrance behind Skyra.

With his face pressed to an opening in the metal cage, Lincoln saw a massive door on hinges that had been swung open to the inside of the building. Affixed to the door's surface, on the side that would face outward when the door was shut, was a metal spider at least six feet wide and eight feet tall. Portions of the spider's spindly legs and bulbous abdomen had been worn to a reflective sheen, presumably a result of being rubbed by countless hands. These Neanderthals—and possibly the humans of this timeline, if the battle axe Lincoln had stolen from the bison rider was any indication—seemed to be inordinately fixated on spiders.

"Okay, I've seen some really weird stuff in the last few days," said Jazzlyn, "but this takes the proverbial cake." She was sitting beside Lincoln, staring out through the latticework of bars toward the interior of the building.

He turned and positioned his face in front of another opening. The chamber's interior was massive, with a roughly-domed ceiling at least eighty feet high and a hundred fifty feet in diameter. The walls and ceiling had no particular pattern. The supporting structure obviously consisted of cut stones or bricks of the same type used to construct the impressive defensive walls outside. However, these stone walls were randomly disrupted by blob-shaped dwellings with posts sticking out of them in weird directions. As with the similar dwellings Lincoln had seen outside, the mud or clay used to make these dwellings extended a foot or more out on each of the posts protruding from them, giving each dwelling the odd appearance of a wet, sticky blob sagging from its supports. For whatever reason, or perhaps no reason at all, many of the posts stuck out beyond the dwellings into the open air as far as twenty feet.

Most of the dwellings had round or oval holes, providing the occupants with a view of the vast chamber. Others had no holes, looking very much like giant, solid spit wads stuck to the stone walls. No large doorways were visible, only the smaller window holes, so Lincoln could only assume the dwellings were accessible from the other side of the stone walls in which they were embedded.

The ceiling and some of the higher portions of the walls were equally as impressive and puzzling. Huge sections consisted entirely of what could only be described as stained-glass windows. Thousands of small pieces of glass, most of them clear but others blue and gray, were arranged in a metal frame in the shape of an intricate spider web spanning the entire chamber. These glass fragments allowed enough sunlight through to make the huge room almost as bright as outside.

"Not up there, Lincoln," Jazzlyn said. "Over there."

He followed her gaze. Dominating the center of the chamber was a fenced-in courtyard containing a dozen or so trees twenty to thirty feet high. A treed courtyard wouldn't have seemed so strange. However, these trees were almost entirely covered in one massive network of webs. It looked as if a fifty-foot-wide sheet of gray silk had been spread out above the trees and allowed to settle down upon them, conforming to the shapes of the branches as gravity dragged the silk downward.

The nandups stopped the cage beside this courtyard. Lincoln then realized the courtyard actually contained two areas of webbing. The second portion contained no trees, and the web there was stretched over the ground, elevated here and there by rocks no more than a foot or two high. The ground web was lighter in color than the tree web—almost white—and it was nearly opaque, as if the threads were more densely woven together.

One of the men shouted something loud enough for everyone in the chamber to hear, resulting in dozens of people gathering around. The man stepped to the cage, pointed at Virgil, then gestured for Virgil to come closer to the latticework of bars.

"What?" Virgil said. "What do you want with me?"

The man growled and slammed his palm against the bars. He extended his hand through one of the holes, making it obvious he wanted Virgil to move closer and take his hand.

"Don't do it, Virg," Jazzlyn said.

Virgil turned to Lincoln and shook his head, obviously terrified.

Lincoln looked out the front of the cage. Skyra was trying to look back, but she and Ripple were still being led away, and now they were too far away to ask Ripple what the hell was going on. "I have no idea what he wants," he said to Virgil.

A nandup woman on the other side of the cage inserted a metal-tipped spear through one of the holes and pressed the point into Virgil's back, forcing him toward the waiting man. Virgil finally took the nandup's hand.

The man yanked back, causing Virgil's face and chest to slam into the bars. He then pushed Virgil's sleeve up to the elbow and pulled his dagger from his belt. He bared his teeth in a fierce smile and began slicing the flesh on Virgil's forearm.

Virgil let out a pained cry and fought to pull his arm back.

Before Lincoln could get to Virgil's side, the Neanderthal had cut off a chunk of flesh the size of a silver dollar. The chunk dropped to the stone floor, and the man released Virgil's arm.

Virgil fell back, hitting his head on the opposite latticework bars. "What the hell, man?" he cried, staring at the wound, which was just starting to ooze blood.

Jazzlyn moved to his side and grabbed his arm. "It's okay, Virg. Really, it's not that deep."

Lincoln threw himself against the bars and cursed at the nandup.

The man ignored him and picked up the chunk of flesh from the floor. He strode to the chest-high fence surrounding the courtyard, holding the flesh above his head for the crowd to see, then he threw it over the fence. It bounced once on a slanted portion of the web about twelve feet off the ground and stopped, as if it had stuck to the strands.

A wave of nandup words and laughter rolled through the audience.

Almost immediately, dots on the web's surface began moving toward the disturbed spot. At this distance Lincoln couldn't tell for sure, but he assumed the dots were spiders. Most of them were pouring out from funnel-like holes in the vast web. Hundreds of spiders converged on the chunk of Virgil's flesh.

"This is seriously, severely screwed up," Derek said. He

was now at Lincoln's side, watching through the bars. "They're going to feed us to those spiders piece by piece."

The nandups resumed pushing the cart of prisoners away from the courtyard, and Lincoln felt a surge of relief. Maybe Derek was right, but at least they weren't going to be sliced to pieces at this very moment.

The crowd that had been following the carts now hung back, apparently more interested in watching the spiders feed. The nandups brought the cages to a stop before yet another door embellished with a huge metal spider. Unlike the first door, this one was closed. Skyra and Ripple were now beside this door, surrounded by Neanderthals, with the T3 cart between them and Lincoln's cart. The nandups who had been pushing Lincoln's cart exchanged a few words, then they stood silently beside the cage as if waiting for someone to open the door.

Lincoln moved to Virgil's side to inspect his injured arm. The divot in his flesh was about a quarter-inch deep and two inches in diameter. Blood was trickling but not flowing.

"We need to get a clean compress on that at least," Jazzlyn said, sitting cross-legged on the cage's floor beside Virgil. "It won't be easy to stitch up a wound this wide."

Virgil grimaced while staring at his arm. "I'd be surprised if any of these people have the inclination to help with this, and I doubt they're familiar with the concept of *clean*."

Lincoln sighed and leaned against the bars. "Well, we'll have to convince them to give us access to our gear. We have plenty of first aid supplies left."

The spider-adorned door still hadn't opened. At least six nandups were gathered around Skyra and Ripple, apparently talking to them. Lincoln couldn't hear them, so he took a moment to look out over the chamber again. The crowd of nandups watching the spider feeding frenzy was starting to disperse. Apparently the show was over.

Lincoln stared at the massive webs. The only spider webs he'd ever seen were no more than a few feet across. This web was at least fifty feet from one end to the other, with portions of it attached to the ground and other portions extending more than twenty feet into the trees.

He reached over and tapped Jazzlyn's elbow. "Any idea what kind of spider could make a web this massive?"

She shifted her body without releasing Virgil's arm. "No single spider could that I know of. Hundreds could, or thousands. In our timeline there are certain species of spiders that live together in colonies. They're called social spiders. They combine their efforts to make huge webs, allowing them to catch more prey than they could individually. It's one of those *combined-whole-is-greater-than-the-sum-of-its-parts* kind of things." She pointed toward the ground web on the far side of the courtyard. "Looks to me like they might have a second species of social spider over there."

Lincoln stared out through the bars. "Any idea why these people are so fixated on spiders? It's a major deal with them."

"No kidding," she said. "Even their houses and buildings are designed to look like this web."

Lincoln blinked. He hadn't made this connection, but Jazzlyn was right. The wood frameworks, with their long, protruding poles, had indeed been positioned to resemble webs. The clay dwellings had been shaped upon the pole frameworks to resemble spider egg sacs, or perhaps the funnel holes in which the spiders hid until an unsuspecting insect— or a chunk of human flesh—hit the web.

Derek smacked his palm against the latticework of bars.

"Like I said, this is seriously screwed up. They're going to feed us to their damn pet spiders."

Lincoln gritted his teeth and glared at Derek. "Hey, we need you to be Derek Danger right now, not the guy who screams, '*we're all gonna die!*'"

"Sorry, man." Derek pursed his lips and looked down at the cage floor. "You're right. I'm a little freaked out right now. Three times in the last hour I've felt an episode coming on. I'm trying to keep those at bay while dealing with all this crazy shit." His eyes met Lincoln's. "I'm Derek freakin' Danger."

Lincoln felt a pang of regret for his admonishment. Derek had—quite literally—his own demons to deal with. He was the only person Lincoln had ever known with a rare disorder called clinical lycanthropy. The episodes he had referred to involved an overwhelming belief that he was transforming into a nonhuman creature. These episodes usually happened after Derek saw an animal, particularly if the animal had frightened him or was strange or remarkable in some way. This disorder was one of the reasons Lincoln had hired Derek, similar to the reasons he had hired Jazzlyn with her prosthetic hand and Virgil with his deep psychological scars resulting from an unthinkable childhood trauma. Lincoln believed people compensated for their disabilities by developing certain strengths, including cognitive strengths that he found to be valuable.

"That's right," Lincoln said to his assistant. "You're Derek freakin' Danger, certified badass. Whatever these Neanderthals are planning to do to us, together we'll figure out a way to get through it and get access to the T_3. Then we'll jump 47,000 years forward."

Derek stroked his long, gray beard and nodded. "It's gotta be better than this place."

A clank echoed across the chamber, and the massive door ahead began to swing inward. Lincoln crawled forward and pressed his face to the bars. Six people stood waiting beyond the door. In contrast to everyone else, these people were dressed in orange. They each wore a single garment, which hung loosely like a long sack with a hood at the top and holes cut for the arms. Encircling each of their waists was a broad leather belt with a buckle in the shape of a spider, like all the others but without loops for weapons.

The orange-clad people stepped out through the doorway, and even with their hoods, Lincoln could now see three were men and three were women. They were nandups, without a doubt, with large eyes and well-defined features. Several things were different about them, however. Their skin was comparatively paler, and their arms were slightly thinner than those of the other nandups here. These had to be the ones Ripple's translator had referred to as *scientists-learners-teachers*. If so, these were the people who would decide the fate of Lincoln and his companions. It would be best not to offend them.

"Skyra!" Lincoln shouted.

She turned to look back.

"Please do not threaten or attack these people. They can—"

A spear slammed against the bars in front of Lincoln's face. The nandup beside the cage then shoved the weapon's tip between the bars, forcing Lincoln to back away.

Several minutes passed as the orange-clad nandups exchanged words with the guards and apparently with Skyra and Ripple also.

Finally, these new nandups stepped forward, grabbed the corners of the first cage, and wheeled it through the door.

Then they came back out and did the same with the cage containing Lincoln and his team.

The door slammed shut, and one of the pale nandups threw a massive bolt to lock it in place.

"I guess we're now in the place bolups never leave," Virgil said.

Lincoln put his face to the bars and scanned the area. They were in another tall chamber, although not nearly as wide as the outer one. More stained-glass windows in the ceiling and upper walls provided light. Like the others, these windows resembled spiderwebs. Assorted ladders and walkways were attached to the walls, providing access to the entry doors of dried-clay dwellings. These were the backsides—or perhaps the frontsides—of the dwellings Lincoln had seen embedded in the walls out in the larger chamber. A few orange-clad nandups stared down from the walkways above.

The nandups wheeled the two cages across the stone floor, through an open doorway, and into a smaller chamber, this one illuminated by sunlight streaming through an entire wall of stained-glass windows. The nandups closed and latched the door.

In the center of the room was a massive, oval-shaped wooden table. Just the table—no chairs or other furniture.

Skyra stepped away from the other Neanderthals and approached Lincoln's cage. She pressed her face to one of the openings. "These nandups ask many questions. They know I am from a different tribe, in my homeland. They have my khul and my hand blades. If I can get my weapons back, I will kill them. But I do not think we can run away from this place."

"No, please don't try to hurt them," Lincoln said. "That would get us all killed. We don't have to run away from this place—we just have to convince them to give us the T3 and the body bags. Do you think we can do that?"

Skyra seemed to consider this for a moment. "It will be easier if I kill them."

Lincoln exchanged a glance with Derek, who shook his head ambiguously. "Let's talk to them first then see what happens," he said to Skyra.

All six of the Neanderthals, as well as Ripple, gathered beside Skyra and faced the cage. One of the men spoke, pronouncing his words carefully, as if he knew Ripple needed to hear them clearly.

Ripple translated. "Speak us what land you from."

"I'll talk to him," Lincoln muttered to the others. Then he looked through the bars. "We are from a land far away, called Arizona. We came here in peace, and we are not happy your people put us in a cage. Please let us out."

Ripple spoke in the nandup language.

The man stared at Lincoln as he listened to the translation. He continued staring even after Ripple fell silent. Then he gestured with one hand to the others. One of the women walked around the wooden table, unlatched a small door on the far side of the chamber, and disappeared.

Seconds later she came back through the door, followed by two nandups wearing the more typical dark garments with short swords, axes, and daggers hanging from their belts. They came around the table, and the woman returned to her position among the orange-clad nandups while the two newcomers stayed back a few yards. Lincoln thought one of the two was probably a woman, but they were both weathered and scarred to the point that it was hard to tell. These two were obviously here to protect the thin, pale nandups, and every aspect of their appearance suggested they were formidable fighters.

The man who had first spoken to the group casually stepped to the end of the cage, pressed an odd-looking flat key into the locking mechanism, then pulled open the door. He stepped back, apparently waiting for them to get out.

"Go ahead," Lincoln said to his team.

Virgil crawled out first, still cupping his palm over the wound on his arm. Seconds later, they were all standing beside the cage, anxiously waiting for whatever might come next.

One of the women gestured for them to step over to the table. The orange-clad nandups circled the table to the opposite side and stood shoulder to shoulder. Lincoln, Skyra, Jazzlyn, Virgil, and Derek lined up at the table, while the two guards stood menacingly behind them.

It seemed odd to have such a large table without any chairs, but Lincoln wasn't about to complain.

All heads turned as Ripple emitted a low buzz and lifted off the stone floor. The levitating drone propelled itself forward and alighted softly in the center of the table. Its gender-neutral voice said, "As the official translator, I will assume a convenient position." Ripple then spoke in the nandup language, presumably saying something similar.

The orange-clad nandups stared at Ripple for a moment then turned their eyes toward Lincoln and his team, as if the humans were more interesting than an autonomous flying drone with sophisticated AI.

One of the nandup men looked at Skyra and spoke, then Ripple translated. "We do not knowledge what kingdom-district you from. We do not knowledge Arizona. You not like other citizens-nandups. You not like other humans-bolups.

You have strange tools-technology. Tell us please kingdom-district Arizona knowledge."

Skyra turned to Lincoln. "You talk to them. I will watch for a chance to kill."

"Don't translate that," Lincoln quickly said to Ripple. Then to Skyra he said, "We can't possibly get away now. We have to convince them to give us the T3 and body bags. Please don't attack anyone." He glanced at his team.

"This is all you, Lincoln," Jazzlyn said.

He turned to the nandup man across the table. "Start translating now, Ripple. We are from a kingdom far away from here. We traveled many days to get here. We are tired and hungry and thirsty. We have come here in peace. We have much knowledge we can share with you, but your people have treated us badly." He pointed to Virgil, who was still clamping one hand over his bleeding arm. "Your people have hurt my friend. We would like to be treated with kindness and respect."

The man appeared to be watching Skyra as Ripple translated the words. When the drone fell silent, the man spoke to Skyra. Ripple translated. "You citizen-nandup. You in citizen-nandup village-city. Why does human-bolup speak for you?"

Lincoln was preparing to coach Skyra on what to say, but she spoke firmly to the man, "This bolup is my friend. I want him to speak to you. I want you to listen to him."

Ripple translated.

The Neanderthals exchanged looks. Several of them used rapid hand gestures, as if they understood Ripple might translate their words if they spoke aloud. Finally, the man looked directly at Lincoln, put both his hands on his own chest, and spoke.

Ripple translated. "You friend of citizen-nandup. We

listen to you. We happy-proud you come to our village-city. We happy-proud you share your knowledge. Now we give you food. We give you liquid-drink. We give you sleep-bed. We not hurt your friend. Warrior-guard hurt your friend. Warrior-guards are much stupid-cruel. Now we death-punish warrior-guard who hurt your friend. We much happy-proud you come to our village-city."

Lincoln shook his head slightly, momentarily confused. "Ripple, was that an accurate translation?"

"As accurate as I could manage. And if you'll allow me a brief anecdotal note, I am quite pleased."

"Hot damn," Derek boomed. "This is a freakin' unexpected turn of events."

8
SANCTUARY-FORTRESS

Present Time - Day 1

Skyra inspected the interior of the tiny cave-like chamber. It had smooth walls made of stacked stones, with flat pieces of clear stone placed near the top of one wall to let in sunlight. Half of the chamber's floor was made of the same smooth stones as the walls, but the other half was covered in ankle-deep flowing water. It seemed like the entire structure had been built on top of a small river.

This chamber was where the strange nandups had told her she could relieve herself. Skyra had always relieved herself beside one of the rivers in her homeland, then she would wash herself in the cold, clear water. Here it appeared she was supposed to urinate and defecate directly into the river then wash herself in the same water. This flowing water would carry her waste away, but it was not cold, and it was definitely not clear. In fact, it stunk.

She pulled up her waist-skin, squatted beside the flowing

water, and did the job as quickly as possible. Then, instead of sitting in the river as she normally would, she used her hand to splash the smelly water onto her body to clean herself. When she finally stood up, she frowned at her wet hand. Hanging upon a stick protruding from one wall was a garment of some kind, apparently made of the same soft-looking material worn by most of the nandups here. The garment had several wet spots and smudges on it, so Skyra assumed its purpose was to wipe off excess water. She found a relatively unstained portion and used it to dry her hand. She took one last disapproving look at the tiny chamber before stepping out.

Jazzlyn had already used the chamber and was waiting outside for Skyra. Jazzlyn said, "I don't know how you're used to doin' it, girl, but that is *not* my idea of a bathroom. Although it *is* a step up from what I've had to do the last four days." She held up her hand weapon and flexed the strange, black fingers. "This thing came in handy this time."

Skyra wasn't sure what Jazzlyn's words meant, so she said, "A river is flowing through the floor."

Jazzlyn bared her teeth in a bolup smile. Her dark skin made her teeth seem very white. "Yeah, I guess we should give them credit for that—indoor plumbing of sorts. I wonder, though, what kinds of parasites are in that water."

Skyra didn't understand this either, so she remained silent.

Jazzlyn made a strange face that Skyra couldn't read. "I'm sorry. I'm starting to think of you as a regular friend—one of the team, you know? Sometimes I almost forget you've had a completely different life, and English isn't your language. I wish you and I had more time to talk. You know, girl to girl."

"Why?" Skyra asked.

Jazzlyn's strange look became even stranger. "Why?

Because I like you. I know Lincoln *really* likes you. You seem to like him too. That's probably strange for both of you. Maybe if you and I could talk more, I could help you with... you know, how to figure out what love is all about to a bolup."

"What is *love is all about?*"

More baring of white teeth. "Love. Just the one word—love. Love is when someone likes someone else so much they want to be together with that person all the time. I think Lincoln might be falling in love with you."

Skyra stared at her, confused. Sometimes in the Una-Loto tribe, some of the older nandups would defy the tribe's traditions and share a shelter together until they died. The other tribemates would allow this because the paired nandups were too old to participate in *ilmekho*, which was how the dominant men would put children into the bellies of women who had seen twenty cold seasons. Skyra had now seen twenty cold seasons—it was time for her ilmekho, but Lincoln and his tribemates had come along, which had changed everything in Skyra's life.

"You have no idea what I'm talking about, do you?" Jazzlyn asked.

"I am too young to be together with another person all the time."

Jazzlyn narrowed her eyes. "How old are you anyway?"

"I have seen twenty cold seasons."

"Twenty years old is *not* too young to be in love with someone."

Skyra shook her head. She liked learning about Lincoln and his strange bolup tribemates, but these ideas were too confusing to think about now. She was tired, hungry, and thirsty, and her head was still filled with sadness following the violent death of her birthmate Veenah, not to mention visions of all the fighting and killing of the last few days. She turned and walked away from Jazzlyn. "Now we will put food and water in our bellies."

As Skyra reentered the larger chamber, she paused to stare. Jazzlyn came up from behind and stopped beside her.

The wooden platform Ripple had called a *table* was now covered with strange foods and containers of liquid. Ripple was standing on the table amidst the food and drink, translating English to the nandups' language and the nandups' language to English. Virgil now had a brown garment bound around his arm to cover his wound, and he was actually smiling at something that had been said.

Skyra's thoughts were still jumbled, and now this new apparent friendliness of the pale nandups wasn't helping. Skyra couldn't imagine why Lincoln and his tribemates were behaving like they trusted these people. Skyra did not trust them at all, and she was still watching for an opportunity to kill as many of them as she could.

Jazzlyn grabbed Skyra's elbow and pulled her toward the table. "We better get some before the guys eat it all."

The whole situation made Skyra nervous, so she was glad when Lincoln moved to the side and motioned for her to stand beside him at the table.

"Wish I could offer you a chair," he said.

Skyra didn't know what a chair was, and Lincoln didn't explain. Instead, he picked up a transparent bowl filled with brown liquid. He looked at her like he wanted to make sure she was watching, then he put the bowl to his lips and drank.

"I know how to drink from a bowl," she said.

"Actually, this is a glass." He pointed to another bowl, this one made of wood and containing a pile of red fruits. "That's a bowl. In case you want to know the difference."

She picked up a glass in front of her and smelled the brown liquid.

"I should warn you," Lincoln said. "It's fermented."

Skyra had not heard that word before, but she understood what he meant. The liquid smelled similar to monlopi, a drink members of the Mano-Loto tribe would make from the sap they brought back from certain trees that grew far from the Kapolsek foothills. Skyra's Una-Loto tribe would carry loads of woolly rhino meat to the Mano-Loto camp at the end of each cold season, to celebrate the upcoming greening of the foothills. Nandups of the two tribes would tell many stories, challenge each other in fighting contests, eat the rhino meat, and drink the monlopi. The drink would make the nandups laugh and talk long after the sun had hidden itself beyond the hills. Skyra and Veenah had enjoyed these celebrations because on these nights the Una-Loto men would not beat them or even call them names. Skyra didn't like the next mornings, though—her head would hurt, and sometimes she would lose the rhino meat she had eaten.

She took a careful drink from the glass. The fermented liquid was good. She was thirsty, so she drank the rest of it. She spotted more full glasses on the table and pulled one of them over in front of her to claim it.

She needed food in her belly before drinking a second glass. Among the foods on the table she spotted what appeared to be the haunch of a reindeer-sized animal. It wasn't within her reach from where she was standing, so she crawled onto the table, dragged it back beside her drink, and dropped back to the floor. The meat had been well cooked and was tender, so she pulled off a piece the size of her forearm and started eating.

Lincoln held out a red fruit in one hand and a green seed pod in the other. "Do you eat many vegetables or fruits?"

"Not when there is meat," she replied around the food in her mouth.

Then he offered her a fist-sized chunk of brown food that looked like it might have been pulled from a dried mound of mammoth excrement. "This is bread. You should try it."

She took the chunk and sniffed it. It didn't smell like meat, but it also didn't smell like mammoth excrement. She bit off half of it and chewed. A few breaths later she shot him a glance. "I like bread."

He nodded and fell silent, pushing food into his mouth one piece after another.

Skyra was beginning to relax. Other than when sleeping, she hadn't felt this calm in many days. It was still possible the nandups would kill her and her friends. The two armed nandup fighters were still standing behind her, obviously ready to attack, but at this moment she could almost forget the danger. She just wanted food. And drink. And sleep.

One of the pale nandup women spoke, and Skyra listened intently. She was already starting to learn some of their words, which had become much easier since Ripple had begun translating. The woman was now saying something about the language Skyra's group had been speaking.

Ripple translated the woman's words. "You speak different language. We think you from much far away kingdom-district. All the citizens-nandups and all the humans-bolups we know speak the words we speak. You speak different words. Tell us please, where is Arizona."

Everyone turned to Lincoln.

Lincoln swallowed the food in his mouth then spoke. "You have no knowledge of Arizona because Arizona is very far away. We speak this different language in Arizona. We have much knowledge to offer you. Thank you for feeding us and treating us with respect."

Ripple translated.

The woman spoke again, and Ripple said, "We happy to learn your knowledge. We think you have much-great knowledge. We think Arizona must have much-great war between your citizens-nandups and your humans-bolups. Our war in Kyran-yufost not much-great. Some citizens-nandups and some humans-bolups no want to fight war. Now we learn your knowledge to make our war much-great like your war."

Skyra stared, trying to decide what the woman meant. It sounded like these nandups wanted their war to be bigger than it already was. That couldn't be right.

Lincoln said, "Ripple, are you sure your translations are accurate?"

"I am quite confident of it," Ripple replied. "This woman has stated she would like you to help her people increase the magnitude of their ongoing conflict with *Homo sapiens*. Perhaps what she means is she would like you to help her people *win* their war."

"Translate this, then." Lincoln turned to the nandups. "We are peaceful people. There is no war in Arizona. We cannot teach you how to win your war. However, we might be able to teach you how to live peacefully. Why are your people at war with the humans?"

Skyra watched the nandups' faces as Ripple translated. Their eyes grew wide with surprise. Then their expressions showed more than surprise. These people did not believe Lincoln's words, and they were starting to become angry and suspicious.

The nandups turned to each other and began talking

rapidly. Yes, they were definitely angry. Skyra could see it—in the tightness around their eyes, in the jerky movements of their heads when speaking. She had seen these little details countless times in her tribemates, right before they would come to deliver a beating. Lincoln and his tribemates were not nandups and would not recognize these details. They would not see the danger.

"Ripple, do not translate this," Skyra said. "Lincoln, these nandups are thinking of killing us. I am going to talk. You will agree with me and do what I do."

He began to say something, but she held up a hand to stop him. She said, "Ripple, now translate." She looked directly at the nandup woman and let out a loud, joyful nandup laugh. "*Aheeee... at-at-at-at-at... at-at-at-at.*"

The nandups quit speaking to each other and turned to stare.

Skyra let out one more loud laugh, trying to make it sound real. "*At-at-at-at-at.* The bolup's story confused you. It did, I can see that it confused you. *At-at-at-at.* This is our custom in Arizona! When we see people we do not know, we tell a story to see if we can confuse them. If they are confused, it is very funny. *At-at-at-at.* The truth is, in our Arizona homeland, we have a great war."

Skyra stopped to allow Ripple to translate. Her eyes met Lincoln's. He was frowning, but he nodded.

"Yes, we were telling a funny story!" Lincoln said after Ripple's translation. "We sure fooled you, didn't we?" He smiled, baring his white teeth. "Our war is very great. We have much knowledge to teach you, and someday your war will be as great as our Arizona war!" He fell silent and gave Skyra a strange look and a shrug of his shoulders.

The nandups listened to Ripple's translation. Their faces

relaxed. They did not smile or laugh, but they no longer wore the faces of nandups determined to give a beating.

"You are not laughing at our story!" Skyra said. "We told our story to make you laugh."

After Ripple translated Skyra's words, the nandups smiled. They looked at each other, then they began laughing. "*At-at-at-at-at.*"

Skyra grabbed her second glass and poured the brown, fermented drink into her mouth until the glass was empty. Then she smiled and shoved more food into her mouth.

This made the nandups laugh even harder.

That was all it took. It seemed the danger had passed, at least for now. Skyra was pleased with the way she had handled the problem. A warm, tingling sensation was working its way through her limbs to her fingers and toes, making the strange sights and experiences of the day now seem less overwhelming.

One of the nandup men spoke, and Ripple translated. "We happy to give you food and drink and rest. Tomorrow, we show you our sanctuary-fortress. We show you our spiders, and you tell us about your spiders. You will teach us how to make our war much-great. We will learn, and we will make our war much-great. We will make our war never end."

Skyra considered the man's words as she pulled another chunk of meat from the haunch. Tomorrow, he had said. Maybe tomorrow things would make sense. Right now she wanted to eat. She hadn't put much food in her belly in many days.

The man spoke again, this time looking directly at Skyra. Ripple hesitated before speaking the translation. "Skyra, I must warn you, this man's words are troubling."

She pointed her chunk of meat toward Ripple. "Tell me what he said."

Ripple's red circle of lights grew bright for a moment. "I am Mu-kailon. I have chosen human-bolup man to lie with you. This man is Amo-dho. Amo-dho makes good babies. Amo-dho has made two babies with citizen-nandup woman before. We happy you here to lie with Amo-dho."

"Say what?" Derek asked.

Skyra turned to Lincoln, who was now frowning.

"This is indeed troubling," Ripple said. "We cannot allow this. Skyra, you must only make babies with Lincoln. However, we must not anger these nandups. We are in a quandary."

Skyra growled and turned to size up the two fighters behind her. They were both large nandups, one a man and one a woman, and they had at least three weapons each. She might be able to kill one, but probably not both.

"Skyra, please don't do anything dangerous," Lincoln said. "Let me do the talking. I have an idea." He turned to the nandup named Mu-kailon and said, "We do not mean to be disrespectful, but we have different customs in Arizona." He gestured with his hand. "This is Skyra, and I am Lincoln. Skyra and I are married. We will stay together for the rest of our lives and will only lie with each other. We would like you to respect our custom, even though it may seem strange to you."

"Excellent," Ripple said, then began translating.

Again, Skyra watched the nandups' faces as they listened. Again, their eyes grew wide in surprise, and they began speaking rapidly to each other.

Before Ripple could explain what they were saying, Mu-kailon turned back to Lincoln and spoke. Ripple then translated. "Your custom not strange to us. Many citizens-nandups in Kyran-yufost are married. Tell us please, are all of you married?"

"You gotta be kidding me," Jazzlyn said. "Tell them Derek, Virgil, and I are all married to each other. Maybe they'll keep us together then. There's no way in hell I want to be alone in this place."

Lincoln nodded and spoke again to the nandup man.

Lincoln had told Skyra about the custom of being married. It was indeed a strange custom. Her people did not form long-lasting pairs or groups until they were too old to hunt. Once a woman saw twenty cold seasons, reaching her ilmekho, the dominant men would challenge each other to be the first to try to put a child in her belly. Then others would challenge to be the second, then the third, and so on. Skyra did not know which man was her birthfather. This was the way of her people, and she had never thought it could be any different.

Now Lincoln was saying he and Skyra were married, a custom of his people. Until this moment, Skyra did not know she and Lincoln were married. When had it happened? Apparently, being married did not involve any kind of ritual. Lincoln hadn't even told her. Skyra felt a growl growing in her throat as she gazed at Lincoln. What if she didn't want to be married?

The growl was drowned out by a burst of laughter from the nandups. A breath later, Lincoln and his tribemates started laughing.

Lincoln leaned toward Skyra. "I don't know what's so funny, but I thought we should laugh along with them. My goal at this point is just to keep them happy. We need to make sure they continue to believe we have come here from another land to share our knowledge. This story is probably the only thing keeping us alive."

Still laughing, one of the nandup women leaned across the table and pushed more food and more glasses of brown drink toward Skyra and her companions. The woman spoke between short bursts of laughter. Ripple translated. "We happy you come here. Eat and drink. Then you rest. Maybe you make babies when you rest. Tomorrow we learn your knowledge, and you learn our knowledge."

"I can't believe they actually did it," Lincoln said. He was standing beside Skyra, gazing at the T3.

Skyra stared at the T3 and the two large bags beside it, but the objects kept drifting in and out of focus. She grabbed Lincoln's arm to steady herself.

Lincoln had asked the nandups to give him back his belongings, and they had brought everything, including both of Skyra's stone-bladed khuls and her two hand blades. Skyra and Lincoln had been shown to a smaller chamber with smooth stone walls and strange sheets of garment material hanging in each corner. In the center of the chamber was a soft, flat object Lincoln had called a bed. It was for sleeping on. An opening in one wall led to another of the smaller chambers with a river flowing in the floor. This chamber, though, contained a waist-high container filled with clean water that did not smell bad like the flowing river water. Lincoln had said this clean water was for bathing.

"Damn," Lincoln said. "We should have asked them to let Jazzlyn, Virgil, and Derek come with us to this chamber. Then we'd all be here with the T3. Damn, damn, damn."

"You do not want to leave your tribemates behind, do you?" Skyra asked.

He shook his head. "I couldn't live with myself if I did that."

She felt her mouth forming a smile. "I do not know what that means. How could you not live with yourself?"

He turned to her. "I think you're a little tipsy."

Something about the way he was looking at her made her smile grow even wider. "I do not know what that means."

"It means you drank quite a bit of—"

"Lincoln, you did not tell me we are married!"

His tiny bolup eyes grew wide.

She took a step toward him then realized she was too close and took a half step back. "I was angry when you told the nandups we are married."

He shook his head slightly. "I was just trying... well, that was an idea I had to make sure they didn't make you sleep with someone else!"

"I was angry before because you did not tell me. I thought I might have to kill you then, but now I am not angry. I will not kill you. Now I am happy Skyra and Lincoln are married."

His expression became so funny that she had to hold back a laugh. He said, "Seriously, I was just... well, damn. Do you even know what being married means?"

"El-de-né! You told me about being married, remember? You told me when the sun was hiding behind the hills last night, and we slept together to stay warm."

He twisted his face into a bolup frown. "That was only last night? God, it seems like ages ago."

"And you told the nandups today. Being married is when two people live together for all their lives. They lie together, but they do not lie with others. You did not tell me Skyra and Lincoln are married. I was angry, but now I am not angry."

He blew out a long breath. "Okay, well... I'm glad you're not angry. Um, I should probably tell you—"

A rattling sound came from the chamber's wooden slab that Lincoln had called a door. The door swung open, and Ripple walked into the chamber, followed by one of the armed fighters who had stood behind Skyra while the group was eating. The man was carrying a black container with steam rising from within it. He carried it to the bathroom and dumped its contents into the bathing water.

With the empty container dangling from one hand, the man came back to face Skyra and Lincoln. He stared at them for a few breaths. The man was old, but Skyra could see he was still a fierce fighter and hunter. His hair was pulled back into a braid, like the way Lincoln had worn his hair when Skyra had first seen him. The man's face bore numerous scars, including one from the side of his forehead to his chin. This particular scar went through one of his eye sockets, and the eyeball on that side was missing, leaving a dark, empty hole. He stared at Skyra with his remaining eye, perhaps studying her in the same way she was studying him. After several breaths, the man spoke. Ripple said, "Hot water. You wash. What else you need? I get for you."

"Thank you," Lincoln said. "We do not need anything else at this time."

As Ripple translated, the man looked from Lincoln to Skyra and back to Lincoln. Skyra could see something in his expression—the man was confused. Maybe he didn't understand why a nandup and a bolup would be married. The man started to turn away.

"What name do your people call you?" Skyra asked.

Ripple translated.

"Belol-yan," he replied.

"Why do you and your tribemates fight with the bolups?"

Ripple translated.

Belol-yan spoke, and Ripple said, "Humans-bolups are filthy ground spiders. Humans-bolups must be killed." He shot a glance at Lincoln then looked down at the floor.

Skyra grabbed Lincoln's arm and pulled him closer. "My friend is a bolup. We are married. Do you believe my friend must be killed?"

The man continued looking at the floor. "What I believe is not important. I am only a guard in the sanctuary-fortress."

Something about this man fascinated Skyra. He was obviously a strong fighter. The orange-clothed nandups were skinny and weak, yet they seemed to be the dominant tribe members. This did not make sense. "Look at me," she said to Belol-yan. "I am a nandup. You are a nandup. We are the same kind of people. I honor you, and you honor me. I will tell you something important, and you will tell me something important."

After the translation, his single eye met hers, and Skyra could see he was cautious but willing.

"Now, what do you want me to tell you?" she asked.

"I do not believe you can help us make our war much-great. Your questions tell me you do not even understand our war. Why did you come here?"

"Skyra, be careful," Lincoln said quietly.

Skyra ignored him and spoke to Belol-yan. "We did not want to come here. Your people attacked us and brought us here. We want to leave this place."

After listening to Ripple's translation, Belol-yan's face did not show surprise. He seemed to think about this for a few breaths. Finally, he spoke. "What do you want me to tell you?"

Skyra did not hesitate. "You are correct. We do not understand your war. Your war is terrible. Tell me, do all of your tribemates want to make your war much-great?"

Belol-yan looked down at the floor again. "Our scientists-learners-teachers know what is best for Kyran-yufost kingdom-district. Our scientists-learners-teachers say we must make our war much-great."

Lincoln stepped forward. "Can you bring our other friends here to this room? We'd like to talk to them."

"Ripple, do not translate that," Skyra said.

"Why not?" Lincoln asked.

Ripple said, "Skyra, this could be your opportunity to jump back to your homeland."

"I do not want to go away from this place now," she said, although she wasn't entirely sure why.

Belol-yan started backing up toward the chamber's entrance. He spoke, and Ripple translated. "I go now. You wash. You make baby. You rest. If you need something, send your talking beast to get me. Your talking beast know where I am. I will get what you need." The man was gone from the chamber before Ripple had finished the translation.

"Perhaps I should resent being called a beast," Ripple said, "but I have been called worse."

"Do you want to tell me what's going on?" Lincoln asked, eyeing Skyra. "That guard may have actually brought Jazzlyn, Derek, and Virgil here. We could use the T_3 and leave this place."

Skyra didn't know what to say, so she went to the washing container in the bathroom. After feeling the warm water with one hand, she removed her cape, her waist-skin, and her footwraps. She crawled over the side and stood in the waist-deep water. It felt clean and soothing, so she dropped to her knees, which brought the water up to her neck. Water poured over the top and ran across the floor into the flowing river, but Skyra didn't care. Never had she bathed in water as warm as this. She submerged her head and ran her hands over every part of her body, washing away the dirt and dried blood.

She reluctantly climbed from the container, squeezed the water from her hair, and picked up her garments. She returned to the larger chamber, where Lincoln was now talking to Ripple. She said, "Lincoln, you did not tell me we are married, but now I know. We will lie together each night for all of our lives. I am ready to lie with you now."

His strange bolup expression helped her push aside all her troubled thoughts. Maybe she would never completely understand bolups, but she was becoming familiar with many of Lincoln's facial expressions. His surprised expression now made her giggle.

Lincoln didn't speak for several breaths.

Ripple broke the silence. "This is astoundingly positive news."

Lincoln stared at Ripple for a breath then stared at Skyra. He was obviously considering saying something, but he hesitated. He nodded. "Okay, I'm not sure how this happened, but I find I have little desire to change it." He headed to the bathroom, and soon Skyra could hear him getting into the water.

"Congratulations, Skyra," said Ripple.

"I don't know what that means." She placed her skins on the floor beside the bed and kneeled cautiously on the bed's soft surface.

"It means I am pleased you and Lincoln consider yourselves to be married. Skyra, I am assuming you have not slept on a bed before." The creature stepped to the side of the bed, held out one leg, and pulled back a wide garment that covered the entire platform. "This is a blanket. You put it on top of your body. It will keep you warm."

She slid in between the blanket and the bed. This bed was even softer than the pile of skins she had slept on with Veenah when she was a child. She stared up at the clear rocks near the chamber's ceiling. The sky was now gray, and Skyra realized the entire chamber had grown steadily darker.

"I wonder how far we are from my tribemates and Una-Loto camp," she said.

Ripple's circle of red lights briefly illuminated the side of the bed. "We are much farther than you realize. Would you like me to begin explaining how the T_3 works? It will take some time."

"No. I do not want you to do that now. Maybe another day."

"Would you like me to tell you a story?"

"No. I just want Lincoln to lie with me."

After a few breaths of silence, Ripple said, "Very well."

Lincoln came into the chamber wearing his blue garments and carrying his footwraps. He dropped the footwraps next to Skyra's and slid into the bed beside her. He stared up toward the clear rocks and fading sky.

Skyra could smell his wet hair and clean skin. There was something about this strange bolup—he made her belly tingle. She had never felt such a thing before, and her birthmother and tribemates had never talked about it. It made her want to move closer to Lincoln. So she did.

"Belol-yan said we will make a baby, then we will rest," she said, her mouth almost touching his ear.

Lincoln's body tensed up, which nearly made her laugh.

"Skyra, I know this year is your ilmekho, but do you even know *how* two people make a baby?"

"When a woman is in her ilmekho, the dominant man takes her to his shelter to put a baby in her belly."

He turned his head to look at her. "And? Do you know what happens in his shelter?"

"I have told you before, I left Una-Loto camp before my ilmekho celebration. Do *you* know what happens?"

"Well, I've never really made time to have a relationship, so I haven't really... but in an academic sense, I kind of know what happens."

"I do not know what that means."

Although the chamber was very dark now, Skyra sensed he was smiling. "I don't really know what it means either," he said.

She put a hand on his skinny neck. "You make me feel strange."

"Is that a good thing?"

"I think so. You make me not want to kill you."

"Yeah, that's definitely good." He gently pushed her hand aside and sat up. He pulled off his garments one at a time and dropped them on the floor.

Ripple's red lights glowed briefly. "I highly encourage such amorous behavior, as it meshes well with my plan."

"Ripple," Lincoln said, "go into sleep mode. Set a timer to wake up thirty minutes after sunrise."

"Very well. Initiating sleep mode. Carry on."

9

SPIDERS

Present Time - Day 2

LINCOLN DIDN'T WANT to open his eyes. He could tell the sun had risen, but opening his eyes would mean the hopelessness of their situation would become real again. It was easier to simply remain comfortable and go through every detail of last night in his mind—for the fourth time. This was the second night he had slept beside Skyra, but this night had been nothing like the first. If Lincoln somehow lived beyond today, this night would be forever burned into his memory.

Skyra's head was on his shoulder, and one of her legs was draped across his belly. Her hair smelled unlike any hair he had ever smelled before, perhaps because she was of a different species. Or perhaps because her hair had always been washed with natural river water. Never once had it been touched by shampoo or soap. Whatever the reason, he found the scent to be powerfully erotic.

Her rhythmic sleeping breaths stopped, and she inhaled

deeply. She ran her hand over his shoulder and onto his chest then spoke quietly. "I like that Skyra and Lincoln are married."

It was too late now to explain they were not actually married, and he had made that up to convince the nandups not to separate them. Actually, at this point he didn't even want to tell her. In fact, who was he to say they weren't really married? He would never see his own timeline again, therefore he would never again be subjected to any of the ridiculous rules of that world.

"I like that we're married, too," he whispered.

A mechanical whirring came from across the room, followed by a few clicks and taps. Dammit, he wasn't ready for their night alone to be over.

Ripple's gender-neutral voice said, "It is precisely thirty minutes after sunrise. Lincoln and Skyra, are you aware you are not alone in this room?"

Lincoln opened his eyes, and Skyra lifted her head from his chest. Belol-yan, the battle-worn, one-eyed guard, was silently standing a few feet from the foot of the bed. He was staring intently at Lincoln and Skyra, his arms crossed above the collection of weapons on his belt.

Lincoln blinked a few times and sat up, disentangling himself from Skyra's limbs. "Belol-yan, we didn't hear you come in."

Ripple translated.

The warrior's expression didn't change. He spoke, and Ripple said, "Your blood has not spilled in the night. May your blood not spill in the new day."

"Um, thanks." Was that a customary greeting—a way of saying good morning—or simply an observation?

Skyra sat up without bothering to pull up the blanket to

hide her breasts. "Melu tekne-té rha-ofu nokho muman lotup-mel-endü," she said in her own Uno-Loto language.

Ripple translated the words to Belol-yan's language. Then the drone said, "For your benefit, Lincoln, I'll point out that this is a greeting I have heard Skyra use before. Loosely translated, it means, 'May you have strength today, friend, to find your way home.'"

Skyra swung her legs out of the bed and got to her feet. In no apparent hurry, she pulled on her waist-skin and cape, then padded barefoot to the bathroom.

Belol-yan spoke while gazing after her with his one good eye, then Ripple translated. "That is a robust-handsome nandup woman. Strange that she would lie with such a skinny-frail human-bolup."

Lincoln eyed Ripple. "Is that an accurate translation?"

Ripple pulsed its red lights twice. "I did embellish it slightly, but only for the sake of levity. Good morning, Lincoln. I do hope your night was fruitful."

Lincoln reached for his clothes. "My night was just fine, until three minutes ago." He struggled into his pants while still trying to stay under the blanket, then he got off the bed and pulled on his fleece shirt. He turned to Belol-yan. "Do you know what is going to happen to us today?"

Ripple translated.

The man let out a brief grunt then spoke. Ripple said, "Our scientists-learners-teachers will want to learn your knowledge. I know you do not understand our war with the humans-bolups. I know you cannot help us make our war much-great. When our scientists-learners-teachers learn you cannot help us make our war much-great, your blood may spill."

"You think they will kill us?"

"They will kill you, or they will confine you with the others. I do not know what they will do to your nandup friend."

Skyra came back from the bathroom and pulled on her leather footwraps. "I heard you speaking. We must make the nandups believe we can help them."

Lincoln considered this. Skyra was right. Somehow they had to convince the orange-clad nandups that Lincoln and his team were useful. Or, the other option would be to jump out of here. He spoke to Belol-yan. "Can you bring our three friends here? We want to talk to them."

"Ripple, do not translate that," Skyra said.

Lincoln turned to her, recalling she had done the same thing last night. "If they allow us all to be alone with the T_3, we can leave this place."

"I do not want to leave this place. Not yet."

"Why?"

She moved her lips like she was chewing on something. "I do not know why. I do not have the right words to speak to you. I see things here that do not make sense to me. I want to change them so they make sense."

Lincoln blinked at her, genuinely surprised. She wanted to *fix* things? Like what, the war? The notion was insane and incredibly naive, but the simple honesty of her declaration, as well as the determination in her enormous nandup eyes, nearly took his breath away.

Before he could come up with a reply, she turned to Belol-yan. "We are nandups. I honor you, and you honor me. I will tell you something important, and you will tell me something important."

Ripple translated.

Belol-yan gazed at her without moving, his arms still

crossed above his weapons. Lincoln hadn't yet mastered nandup expressions, but he could see the man was intrigued, as he had been last night.

"I will choose what I tell you," Skyra said. "Nandups and bolups live in my homeland. Bolups sometimes raid nandup camps. They kill men and take women. Nandups sometimes attack bolups. We attack bolups so the bolups will not raid again. Nandups do not kill all the bolups. If my people killed them all, there would be no bolups to drive game into our hunting lands. If my people wanted to kill them all, we would have to hunt bolups every day from when the sun shows itself in the morning until the sun hides at the end of the day. There are too many bolups to kill. We would not have time to do anything else, and many of our own people would be killed. We cannot help you make your war much-great, but we can help you understand there are better ways to live than to always fight bolups."

Ripple hesitated for a few seconds as if processing the extensive speech before translating.

Belol-yan listened without moving a muscle. When Ripple finally fell silent, the nandup slowly dropped his arms to his sides. He stepped to the chamber's door and pushed it closed. Then he returned to his position facing Skyra and spoke. Ripple said, "I do not know of your homeland. Arizona must be far away indeed. You do not understand our land Kyran-yufost. This is strange, as Kyran-yufost is a great and wide kingdom-district. Everyone understands Kyran-yufost. Everyone except you."

Lincoln decided to join the discussion. "As we have said, Arizona is very far away."

The Neanderthal looked back at the door as if worried that someone else might come in. With Ripple translating, he continued the conversation. "Very far indeed. If there is such a place as Arizona, I would like to go there. I am weary of fighting humans-bolups. This is why I became a guard in the sanctuary-fortress. Many citizens-nandups of Kyran-yufost are weary of fighting the humans-bolups."

"If your people are weary, why do you continue to fight?" Skyra asked.

"There is much you do not understand about our land. When I was a warrior, fighting bolups, there was much that I, too, did not understand about Kyran-yufost. Now, as a guard in the sanctuary-fortress, I have learned things I wish I did not know."

"What things have you learned?" Skyra asked.

"Today, if your blood does not spill, you will learn more about Kyran-yufost. If our scientists-learners-teachers discover you cannot help make our war much-great, then your blood will spill. If you want to live, you must make our scientists-learners-teachers believe you can help make our war much-great. If your blood does not spill, I will tell you more, and you will tell me more. Now I must take you and your speaking beast to our scientists-learners-teachers."

Lincoln studied Skyra's face as she processed the man's words. What was going through her mind? He was now reasonably sure Skyra could talk the guard into bringing Jazzlyn, Derek, and Virgil to this chamber, at least for the ten minutes or so needed to prepare the T3 and jump to the future. Did she really want to stay here and try to change things? This was a side of her he hadn't seen before.

He touched her arm. "We might be able to jump away from here if we can—"

She snapped her head around to face him. "We cannot go away now!"

"Why not?"

"I told you before. I do not understand this place. The nandups here are doing things I do not understand. I do not want them to do these things."

He stared at her and sighed. "Skyra, these people have been at war for a long, long time. We can't possibly do anything to change what's happening here. In fact, they even want us to help them *escalate* their war—make it bigger than it already is."

Her enormous nandup eyes bore into him, expunging his will to disagree. She had lived a life of violence and was a ferocious fighter, but there was also a deep-rooted innocence about her. At this moment, her eyes indicated she wasn't willing to even consider her suggestion was impossible. Beyond impossible. It seemed to Lincoln it would be easier to stop the Earth's rotation than to make these people change traditions that were most likely tens of thousands of years old.

Belol-yan was waiting for them at the door.

"I do not recommend making the nandups wait for you," Ripple said.

Belol-yan took Lincoln and Skyra to the chamber with the large table. Lincoln half-expected the table to be covered with food again, but it was bare. Just as well—he had eaten too much the night before.

The same six orange-clad Neanderthals were there, waiting beside the table, along with the female warrior who had stood guard beside Belol-yan during the meal. Jazzlyn, Derek, and Virgil weren't there.

One of the orange-clad women spoke up immediately

upon seeing Lincoln and Skyra enter the chamber. Ripple translated. "We will do much speaking with you today. We know you are Lincoln and Skyra, but you do not know what names to call us." The woman introduced herself as Gedun-dal. Then, bypassing the need for translation, she quickly grabbed the arm of each of the others in turn and gave their names. The other two women were Lekhul-aup and Mahuon-afu. The three men: Khebum-khai, Mu-kailon, and Fayl-fudom.

Lincoln was aware of his own cognitive prowess. He could remember these names, but only by repeating them silently several times while looking at each nandup's face. He took the time to do this while Gedun-dal continued speaking. He completed the memorization process just in time to hear Ripple's translation.

"We have much to show you, but first we want to know, Skyra, what spiders do you align with? Lincoln, what spiders do you align with?"

Lincoln exchanged a glance with Skyra, but she looked as confused as he felt. He turned back to the woman Gedun-dal. "Can you explain? We do not know what you mean."

After Ripple's translation, the nandups spoke rapidly to each other. Lincoln was already learning some of the nuances of their tones and expressions. They were obviously confused by his need for explanation. They also showed signs of agitation.

"You must be cautious, Lincoln," Ripple said quietly. "These Neanderthals are again becoming suspicious."

Gedun-dal turned back to Lincoln and spoke. Ripple said, "If you do not align with spiders, how do you control your citizens-nandups?"

Again, Skyra offered no help, apparently choosing to simply observe.

Lincoln thought furiously, aware that his words were holding him and his companions over a knife's thin edge. "We have our own ways of controlling our citizens-nandups. Our ways work very well, and our citizens-nandups do everything we want them to. That is why our kingdom of Arizona is so great. That is why we have great technology."

He paused, then he tapped his watch to activate the tiny screen, which he held up for them to see. To connect his words to the gestures, he waited for Ripple to translate what he had already said before continuing. "We are curious about your spiders. First we will learn about your spiders, then we will explain how we control our people."

Again, the nandups exchanged words, and again Lincoln detected agitation, although less than before.

This time the man named Khebum-khai spoke. Ripple translated. "Yes, we are happy-proud to show you our spiders. You come with us."

Lincoln realized the nandups intended to lead them out of the chamber now. "Where are our friends?" he asked. "We thought we would be back together with Derek and Jazzlyn and Virgil today."

Gedun-dal said, "Your friends are learning today, as you are learning."

"But we thought we would all be learning together."

She listened to the translation without expression then repeated, "Your friends are learning."

Lincoln felt his anxiety rising. Should he demand to be reunited with his team, or would that be pushing his luck?

Without further discussion, the nandups led him, Skyra, and Ripple through a doorway and down a dim corridor with no windows. They stopped at a solid-looking door on the left. This door sported a miniature version of the eight-foot metal spiders seen on the larger doors out in the public portion of the compound.

Gedun-dal raised one leg and used her foot to pound on the door—three solid kicks, followed by a half dozen or so lighter bumps in an obvious pattern of timing. Lincoln thought it would be easier to do this with her fist, but perhaps these people had an aversion to knocking on doors with their hands.

A mechanical latch clicked a few times, then the door swung inward. Another orange-clad nandup, this one seemingly younger than the others, waited for them to enter then closed and latched the door.

They were now in a long chamber with light pouring in from an impressive array of stained-glass windows near the top of one wall. Situated in rows the entire length of the chamber were shoulder-high rectangular containers with walls of glass. Lincoln could already see networks of webs within some of the containers, and when the nandups started leading him and Skyra between two of the rows, it became obvious that every container housed spiders. Some containers held high webs stretched over sticks seemingly provided for that purpose, some contained ground webs, and others contained both high webs and ground webs.

Lincoln stopped beside a high-web cage where dozens of orange-colored spiders were out of their funnel-like holes, feeding on a chunk of meat with brown hair or fur on one edge. Was that human hair? It was hard to tell.

Skyra stopped beside him to look. "These spiders are orange. The nandups wear orange garments."

"Huh, you're right." Lincoln hadn't yet made the connection. "Why are these people so fascinated with spiders, of all things?"

Ripple said, "It is not unusual for pre-industrial populations to idolize specific objects or creatures. In your own timeline, Lincoln, indigenous Americans would—"

"Thanks, but I've got it," Lincoln said.

The nandups had paused to wait for them, so Lincoln urged Skyra and Ripple to move on. They passed cage after cage, each cage housing two species of spiders, the tree-web makers and the ground-web makers. The tree spiders were orange, the ground spiders were drab brown. Why not more diversity? If this was a spider zoo, people would get bored after looking at the first few cages.

The orange-clad nandups stopped at yet another spider-festooned door.

Khebum-khai spoke, and Ripple said, "This room-place is where we observe-study tree spiders and ground spiders. We have learned much in this room-place. We have made important changes to tree spiders and ground spiders in this room-place. If we do not make changes to spiders, we cannot make our war much-great. We much-proud of our changes. Now we show you room-place where we observe-study our changes. Some changes good. Other changes no good. Now we show you where we see if changes good or if changes no good."

The Neanderthals waited patiently for Ripple to finish translating, then Gedun-dal pushed open the door, this time without needing to kick it first. They all walked through.

Lincoln gazed around at a smaller version of the huge chamber-auditorium he'd seen at the outer reaches of the compound—the public area. Although only a fraction of the size, this auditorium was just as impressive. Stained-glass windows arranged to resemble a spider web made up most of the ceiling. Symmetrical stones, interspersed with seemingly random bulbous rooms constructed of dried clay, made up the tall walls. In the center of the space was another courtyard, this one without a fence to keep people out. Half of the courtyard featured several web-covered trees, the other half a nearly-white ground web.

The nandups moved directly to the courtyard and stopped where the tree web transitioned into ground web. Khebum-khai pointed to where the webs joined. He spoke, and Ripple translated. "Tree-web spiders we call nu-pa. Ground-web spiders we call kho-su. Citizens-nandups are tree-web spiders. Nu-pa. Humans-bolups are ground-web spiders. Kho-su."

Lincoln waited for more explanation, but Khebum-khai didn't elaborate.

"How can nandups be spiders?" Skyra asked.

Before Ripple could translate that, Lincoln stopped the drone and spoke to Skyra. "I think they're saying that the tree spiders *represent* nandups. They're using the spiders as a symbol. The nandups aren't really spiders."

Skyra kneeled to look closely at the floor where the two types of web met. "I understand now. The spiders have a war."

Lincoln kneeled beside her. The floor in this area was littered with dead spiders, some of them orange, some brown. Some were old and dried up, others were fresh. Some were partially eaten or missing legs, but most were intact.

Lincoln felt a chill penetrating his skin as the entire scenario started to make sense for the first time. Without getting up, he turned to Khebum-khai. "This is very interesting. We have not thought of this in Arizona. Can you please explain more?"

Ripple translated.

Khebum-khai delivered a long explanation, then Ripple said, "Citizens-nandups are tree spiders. Citizens-nandups much happy-proud to be tree spiders. We show citizens-nandups how to be tree spiders. We show how to make houses-structures like tree spiders. We show how to eat large animals like tree spiders. We show how to have much-great war like tree spiders. Citizens-nandups happy-proud to be tree spiders. We show citizens-nandups ground spiders kill tree spiders. Ground spiders destroy tree webs and make ground webs where tree webs used to be. Ground spiders do not eat like tree spiders. Ground spiders do not live like tree spiders. Citizens-nandups want to kill ground spiders. Citizens-nandups much happy-proud to go to war to kill ground spiders. War is what ground spiders and tree spiders always do. This is how we make our war always much-great."

After Ripple's translation, Lincoln got to his feet. The scenario was becoming clearer, except for one thing. Why did these scientists-learners-teachers have the desire to perpetuate the war? The resources needed, the cost in lives, the horrendous psychological toll—all of these things must be staggering. Why continue?

Asking them directly might be dangerous though. After all, these nandups believed Lincoln's group was here to help them escalate the war.

Skyra got to her feet beside Lincoln. "I understand now. I understand what these nandups are doing!"

"Ripple, don't translate that," Lincoln said. He spoke to Skyra. "Yeah, I'm starting to get it, too. But we have to be careful what we say."

"But Lincoln, I understand now! These nandups teach their tribemates they have the spiders' strength within their blood. They teach their tribemates to have the spiders' anger in their heads. My Una-Loto tribemates do this. We ask the cave lion and woolly rhino for their strength, for their anger. But we ask for their strength and anger only when we need it. These nandups teach their tribemates to have the spiders' strength and anger always, even when they do not need it!"

Lincoln paused. Skyra *did* understand, and she had just explained the situation better than he could have done himself.

Skyra's face hardened. "I understand what they are doing. They should not do these things! Their tribemates do not need the strength and anger of their tree spiders all the time. We must stop this!"

"Ripple, definitely don't translate that," Lincoln said.

"Understood," Ripple replied. "Good call, as you become fond of saying in your future years."

"Lincoln, we must change these things!" Skyra said.

"We can't change anything if they kill us, so we have to be careful what we say. They think we're here to help them."

"We *are* going to help them! Their tribemates cannot always have the spiders' strength and anger. We saw what the spiders' strength and anger does to their tribemates. They fight. They fight every day. They do not ever stop fighting!"

Lincoln glanced at the Neanderthals. They were watching the conversation, waiting. He gently grabbed Skyra's shoulders. "I agree with you—what these people are doing is terrible, but we have to be careful. Let's find out more about them. The more we learn, the better we can decide what we should do."

Actually, Lincoln knew exactly what they should do— jump the hell away from this place at the first opportunity.

10

ALINGA-UL

Present Time - Day 2

Skyra didn't understand what she was feeling. A fight was happening inside her head. She and Veenah, ever since they were young girls, had always found ways to avoid beatings from the men of Una-Loto tribe. Eventually, Skyra and Veenah had themselves become formidable fighters and hunters. This was the only way to stay safe, not only from their tribemates but also from raiding bolup men. Skyra's life had been about protecting herself and her birthmate—fighting and killing when necessary, but otherwise hiding, escaping, and outsmarting.

Her muscles and gut were now telling her to escape from these nandups right away. Her head, though, was telling her something different, something she had never considered before. She wanted to stay here and make things right. This place did not make sense to her. Skyra had been confused many times before by things she had experienced. She had seen a cave bear harmlessly step around one of her tribemates, a woman named Jezgo, only to charge and kill another woman, Khevni. She had also learned of a nandup man from the Alvi-Loto tribe who had killed all the children in his tribe after he had become sick from eating spoiled reindeer meat. As the dominant man in the tribe, he was probably the father of many of those children. Those events did not make sense to Skyra, but she had never felt the need to change what had been done.

Only a few days ago, however, she had finally found the woolly rhino that had killed her birthmother. She—as well as Lincoln—had almost been killed by the old bull rhino, but now it was dead, which helped to dull the pain she felt in her chest when thinking of her birthmother.

Then Skyra's tribemate Gelrut had killed her birthmate. Skyra ached for her sister's companionship, but she felt better knowing Gelrut would not be able to harm anyone again after what she and Lincoln had done to him.

Skyra was now starting to believe she could change the things that hurt or confused her, especially with Lincoln as her companion.

Here, in this place of strange nandups, her head was telling her she should do something to correct the source of her confusion. Her thoughts were pulling on her, trying to force her to ignore her lifelong habit of escaping from danger. She wanted to escape. She wanted to go away with Lincoln and find the real place he was from, the place where she would not have to worry about fighting or being killed by predators. She wanted that more than anything she had ever wanted, but still her head was telling her to first fix what was happening in this land—this place of deception and war.

The man named Khebum-khai began speaking, pulling

Skyra's thoughts away from the struggle in her head. Ripple translated. "Tree spiders are different from ground spiders. We show citizens-nandups how to live like tree spiders. Tree spiders work together to kill and eat large creatures. We show citizens-nandups how to eat large creatures. Ground spiders work together to make webs to catch many small creatures. Human-bolup scientists-learners-teachers show humans-bolups how to eat many small creatures. We make spider colonies in public chamber-auditorium. Spider colonies show citizens-nandups how spiders live. Spider colonies show citizens-nandups how spiders fight and kill. This is how we make our war much-great."

Skyra stared at the vast spider webs as she considered the man's words. These webs were much smaller than those in the great chamber for all the nandups to see, but they were larger than any she had seen in her homeland. The spiders she knew did not live in tribes like this.

Lincoln spoke to Khebum-khai. "You said the human scientists teach their people how to live like ground spiders. If you are at war with humans, how do you know this?"

Ripple translated.

Again, the nandups seemed confused about the question.

Khebum-khai answered, and Ripple said, "This is how we make our war much-great. Human-bolup scientists-learners-teachers show humans-bolups how to live like ground spiders. We show citizens-nandups how to live like tree spiders."

"Do you communicate with the human scientists-learners-teachers? If so, isn't that dangerous? I mean, you are at war with them, right?"

"Yes, we communicate. That is how we make our war much-great."

"Well, that's...." Lincoln said softly, not finishing his words.

Although she was still confused, Skyra was starting to understand what these nandups were doing. What she didn't understand was why. "Ripple, do not speak this," she said, then she turned to Lincoln. "Why do these nandups want this war? I want to ask them why."

He furrowed his skinny brows. "If you ask them, they're going to wonder why you're asking. We're supposed to help them escalate the fighting." He blew out a breath. "We do need to know, though."

Khebum-khai spoke again, and Ripple translated. "Teach us about Arizona. Tell us, how do you make your war much-great?"

Skyra's eyes met Lincoln's. She did not know how to answer this question. Now the nandups would understand she and Lincoln could not help them. She turned and looked at the two guards, wondering again if she could somehow kill them both. Belol-yan was watching her face. He probably knew what she was thinking, which would make it even harder to surprise him.

Belol-yan's face twitched. The movement was slight—a tightening in the skin below one eye and a slight nod of his head. Skyra read his expression—a skill that had saved her at times but had made her life miserable at other times. Belol-yan was hoping she and Lincoln would not anger the orange-clothed nandups. The guard wanted Skyra and Lincoln to live. But why? Skyra studied his face for another breath, although he did not reveal any more than he already had.

Lincoln began speaking to Khebum-khai. "We are now going to tell you the truth, and we hope you will not be angry. In Arizona, we are not fighting a war. In Arizona, nandups and bolups have learned to live in peace. I know this isn't what you—"

Skyra inhaled sharply. "No, do not translate those words, Ripple."

Lincoln turned to her with a bolup frown.

Belol-yan's expression had convinced Skyra of the danger of angering these nandups. "Now we must tell them what they want to hear," she said. "Maybe later we will tell them words that are true."

"Are you sure?"

She wasn't sure, but the risk was definitely real. "Ripple, translate my words." She took a step toward the orange-clothed nandups and looked at Khebum-khai's eyes. "Our homeland is Arizona. We have much knowledge in Arizona. We will teach you our knowledge. In our homeland, nandups fight bolups and bolups fight nandups. It is a great war. We do not show our tribemates how to live like tree spiders and ground spiders. I am a nandup. I make our war great by telling my nandup tribemates that bolups want to raid our camps and take our women and eat the bodies of our men. Lincoln is a bolup. Lincoln makes our war great by telling his bolup tribemates that nandups want to raid their camps and kill them all, their men and women and children. Our tribemates have much fear. Our tribemates want to fight and kill. They always want to fight and kill, because we tell them these things."

Ripple began translating.

This was the story Skyra's head had told her to tell, but she felt strange speaking such a lie. Her Una-Loto tribemates told untrue stories around campfires, but those stories were meant to be untrue. Those stories were fun and made her and her tribemates laugh. The punishment for telling a lie at any other time was a beating, and holding the liar's face over a campfire until the air smelled of burning hair and skin. Skyra had seen this punishment only once, but she had never forgotten the sight and smell. She glanced at Lincoln, feeling shame.

"Let's hope for the best," he said.

Skyra wasn't sure what that meant, but she gave him a twitch of one side of her mouth.

Ripple finished the translation and fell silent.

Before the nandups could reply, Skyra decided to keep their thoughts busy by speaking again. "We want our nandups and bolups to fight and kill because there are too many nandups and bolups in Arizona. Arizona does not have enough animals to kill and eat for so many people. That is why we make our war great. Tell me please, is that why you make your nandups and bolups fight and kill?"

Instead of translating, Ripple said, "Skyra, are you sure you wish to reveal that you do not know why they make their people continue fighting?"

"I want to know," she replied firmly.

"Very well." Ripple began translating.

Another of the nandups spoke for the first time, this one a woman named Lekhul-aup. Ripple translated. "Our citizens-nandups in Kyran-yufost grow many animals and plants for food. We have much food for all citizens-nandups. Humans-bolups have much food. We have different reasons for war. We do not want citizens-nandups to make babies with humans-bolups."

"Seriously?" Lincoln said. "Just last night they were *encouraging* us to make babies together—a nandup and a bolup."

The nandups watched Ripple, waiting. When Ripple did not translate Lincoln's words, Lekhul-aup spoke again. Ripple translated. "Surely in Arizona you do not allow your citizens-nandups to make babies with your humans-bolups. If you did, you would have too many scientists-learners-teachers. Is this not one of the reasons you make your citizens-nandups fight and kill?"

"What the hell?" Lincoln said in a whisper. "Are these guys hybrids?" When Skyra gave him a confused look, he said, "Hybrids. A hybrid is a baby from parents who are different species. Nandups and bolups are very similar—you and I are similar—but still, we are two different species."

"I do not believe these nandups are hybrids," Ripple said. "They have slightly less musculature and are slightly paler than the general population, but these characteristics appear to be caused by a more sedentary and sheltered life. Their height, build, and facial structure are well within the expected range for Neanderthals and well outside the expected range for *Homo sapiens*."

Skyra growled in frustration at Ripple's shift to speaking words only Lincoln would know. What she understood from Lekhul-aup's words was Lekhul-aup did not want nandups to make babies with bolups because those hybrid babies would become scientists-learners-teachers. She was confused again. Lekhul-aup herself was a scientist-learner-teacher, but Ripple just said Lekhul-aup was not a hybrid baby. Skyra growled yet again. How could she make things right in this place if she couldn't even understand what was happening?

The nandups were staring at her, probably wondering why she was growling. "Ripple, translate this," she said as she turned to Lekhul-aup. "Yes, that is one of the reasons we make our nandups fight and kill. Lincoln and Skyra lie together, but we do not want other nandups to lie with other bolups. We are happy you agree with us." She wasn't sure this was what they wanted to hear, but it was what her head had told her to say.

Ripple translated her words.

The nandups all bared their teeth in broad smiles. Lekhul-aup let out a brief laugh. Skyra exhaled. Apparently her answer had satisfied them for now.

Lekhul-aup spoke, and Ripple translated. "Tell us please, how many dali-tamons do you have in Arizona? How many alinga-uls do you have? Skyra and Lincoln, I am having difficulty translating these two words. The best I can do for dali-tamon is *second-level scientist*. The best I can do for alinga-ul is *first-level scientist*. If you are interested in my recommendation, I do not think you should let these nandups know you have no idea what these words mean."

The nandups were waiting for an answer.

"Ripple is probably right," Lincoln said.

Skyra spoke to Lekhul-aup. "We do not know how many dali-tamons and alinga-uls we have in Arizona. We have too many to count."

Ripple translated, and the nandups let out cries of happiness and respect. Skyra studied their faces and realized they were no longer showing signs of anger or suspicion.

"We really need to figure out what's going on," Lincoln said. "What the heck is a first-level or second-level scientist?"

"Perhaps the meaning will become clear without the need to ask," Ripple said.

The nandups' excitement continued for several more breaths. Then the man Khebum-khai stepped forward and spoke. Ripple translated. "We are much happy you have come here. We will learn from you. We do not have many dali-tamon, and we now have only one alinga-ul. We are much happy you have come here to help us make more alinga-uls.

Skyra, you must be an important citizen-nandup in Arizona. We are honored you have come here to make alinga-uls. Lincoln, you must be very happy to make alinga-ul with Skyra. Yes, we are all happy today. We will show you more of our sanctuary-fortress. We will consume more food and drink."

When Ripple finally fell silent, Khebum-khai reached within his orange garment and pulled out a thin, black object Skyra recognized. It was a piece of Maddy's body Lincoln had called a cognitive module. Khebum-khai held up the object and spoke to Lincoln. Ripple translated. "This was taken from you by our warrior-soldiers. We do not know what it is. We do not know the cloth-weave you use to make your garments. We do not know what kind of creature is your speaking beast. We do not know what is the black ornament you wear on your wrist. We have much to learn from you."

Lincoln stared at the object for a moment then held out his hand. "Could I please have that back? It is very important to me. We used to have a second talking beast named Maddy, and that object was part of Maddy. I hope to make another Maddy someday, and I will need that object to do so. I will tell you about these things, but telling you properly will take much time. Do you think we can continue this discussion later? Skyra and I are weary from talking and would like to rest."

After Ripple's translation, Khebum-khai smiled and handed the object to Lincoln. All of the nandups were now smiling, except for Belol-yan and the other guard. Skyra still had not seen either of them smile.

Lincoln nodded and pushed the black object into a pouch on the side of his waist garment. "Thank you. Um, do you think now we could see our friends, Jazzlyn, Virgil, and Derek? I'd like to talk to them again."

Ripple translated, Gedun-dal spoke, and Ripple translated again. "Your companions are learning from us and teaching us today, just as you are learning from us and teaching us."

Skyra watched Lincoln's face. He was not happy about this.

"I guess we know why I'm still alive," Lincoln said when they were finally alone again in their resting chamber. "For some reason, they want nandups to mate with bolups. Although the main reason they trick their people into fighting a war with bolups is to *prevent* nandups from mating with bolups! How does that make any sense?"

Skyra went straight to the bed and threw herself onto her belly. The soft platform felt so good, and it still smelled of Lincoln's body. Her head was tired of trying to understand all the strange things she had seen and heard. The nandups had shown them countless cages of spiders, each with an explanation she didn't even care to understand. They had asked many questions. She and Lincoln had answered with lies, but those lies seemed to please the nandups. She was tired of telling lies.

Skyra's belly was full again—the bolups had taken her and Lincoln to another table of food, this one in a chamber where the walls were covered with strange objects, most in the shape of spiders. She was glad the nandups hadn't offered more of the fermented drink—her head was still hurting slightly from the previous night. Finally, she and Lincoln had again told the nandups they were tired and wanted to rest.

She wanted Lincoln to lie beside her, but he was pacing back and forth, his footwraps squeaking against the stone floor each time he turned.

"It *does* make sense," she said. "The scientist nandups do not want the other nandups to mate with other bolups. They only want scientist nandups to mate with scientist bolups. They believe I am a scientist nandup and you are a scientist bolup."

He paused for a breath then resumed pacing. "Yeah, but why? And why won't they let us see Jazzlyn, Virgil, and Derek?"

Skyra pressed her face into the bed and breathed in the smell.

Ripple had been silent since returning to the chamber, but now the creature spoke. "I see the two of you are frustrated with today's events. I will, therefore, report two fortunate consequences."

"Use words I know," Skyra said.

"Very well. I will explain two outcomes from today that are good. First, I now know the language of these nandups quite well. I'm sure you have noticed improvement in my translations."

Skyra didn't reply, and neither did Lincoln.

"Second, my power level is now full. Skyra, forgive the words you do not know, but Lincoln may be interested to know my ambient-sound-harvesting charging unit, which utilizes the piezoelectric effect, was able to take advantage of the copious verbiage spewed forth by you and the nandups. You essentially talked me to a maximum charge."

Skyra growled into the soft bed.

"That's good to know, Ripple," Lincoln said.

Skyra felt the bed sink as Lincoln sat beside her. He put a hand on her back, and she lifted her head.

"I really think we need to leave this place," he said. "I know you want to do something about the terrible situation here, but it's only a matter of time before we say the wrong thing and these nandups realize we've been lying. I think we should ask Belol-yan to bring the others to this chamber. The T3 and all our other stuff is here. We can jump away, hopefully to a place where we can live in peace, a place more like the place I am from."

She pushed herself up and sat with her legs crossed. "You do not believe we can change what these nandups and bolups are doing here."

He shook his head. "It just seems impossible to me."

"My head tells me it *is* possible."

His mouth turned up at the edges just a little. He reached out and took one of her hands in both of his. No one had ever held her hand like this before, and she wasn't sure what it meant. She considered pulling back, but she decided she liked feeling his skinny fingers squeezing her hand.

"I can't tell you how amazing you are just for believing that," he said. "It means you are a very good person. I want us both to live, though. I want Jazzlyn, Virgil, and Derek to live." He rubbed her hand with his fingers. "I want to be with you and learn more about you. Sometimes there are wars in the place I am from—not this place, but the real place I am from. Many people want to stop those wars. They want to stop the killing and destruction, but stopping something so large is not easy. Wars are complex and hard to understand. They are usually the result of hatred that has built up for generations in thousands and thousands of people. You can't change all of that overnight. You may never be able to change it. Sometimes wars end just because one side is forced to give up, but the hatred may still be there for many years afterwards."

Skyra studied his face. He was speaking words he believed were true. "What is *one side is forced to give up*."

"Well, sometimes one side may be stronger, more powerful, with better weapons or more warriors. Sometimes one side may run out of resources, like food, water, or weapons. Sometimes the people on one side may decide they no longer want to support the war, so they force their leaders to stop it."

She flexed her folded legs, bouncing her body up and down on the bed. "That is what we will do, Lincoln! We will make these nandups decide they no longer want to support the war!"

He didn't look very excited about this. "I don't know."

She frowned. "Yes, you do know! It will be easy. I do not know why, but these orange-clothed nandups are the leaders here. They are skinny and weak, like you."

He made a face. "Okay, thanks."

She laughed. "The other nandups are not skinny. The other nandups are fighters and hunters. They will force the leaders to stop the war. See, Lincoln? It will be easy!"

He still didn't look excited.

Ripple spoke up. "I'm sure there are factors I have not considered, but I estimate a very slim chance of accomplishing such a thing here. The logistics of—"

"I am talking to Lincoln, Ripple!"

The creature fell silent.

Lincoln stared at Skyra with an expression she couldn't read. He let out a breath. "I have an idea, and I'd like you to agree to it. I will agree to look for opportunities to convince the other nandups here to force the orange-clad leaders to stop the war. In return, I'd like you to agree to something."

She bounced again, waiting for him to go on.

"I think we should also watch for opportunities to get Jazzlyn, Virgil, and Derek into this room so we can use the T3 to go away from here. We will try to accomplish *both* plans. Whichever plan works out first, that's what we'll do. Can we agree?"

She chewed on her lip for a few breaths. "Yes. You drive a hard bargain, Lincoln Woodhouse."

He bared his teeth. "Who taught you those words?"

"Guilty," Ripple said.

Skyra pulled her hand from Lincoln's grip, then pulled her cape off and dropped it to the floor. She sprawled face first onto the bed, enjoying the softness of it against her bare belly and breasts. She turned her head to the side and looked up at Lincoln through strands of her long hair. "Now I want you to tell me things."

"What do you want to know?"

"How can the T3 help us leave this land?"

"Oh, you would have to start with a really tough one."

She eased closer to him, squirming from side to side like a salamander from the shallow rivers of her homeland. "I do not understand how we can leave this place when so many nandups are here to stop us. We cannot run away, so how can the T3 help us?"

"Alright, where to begin." He pulled his legs up onto the bed and crossed them. "Remember yesterday how we connected body bags to the T3 then got inside those bags? Well, the T3 has a special way of sending whatever is inside those bags to a different place." He reached into the pouch on his waist garment, dug around with his fingers, then pulled his hand out. In his palm were several bits of rock and dirt that must have gotten into the pouch when he was lying on the ground. He picked out one of the rocks and tossed the rest away. "Imagine this pebble is you, and my hand is one of the body bags."

She frowned. "That does not make sense."

"Just... try to imagine it, okay? You are the rock. My hand is the body bag. Here is what the T_3 does to whatever is in the body bag." He struck the bottom of his hand with his other hand, sending the rock flying somewhere off the bed. "Do you see what happened? Now the rock is not in the bag. It is over there somewhere." He pointed. "The rock didn't have to walk there. The T_3 sent it there, and it happened very quickly."

Skyra rolled to her side and looked up. The chamber's ceiling was made of smooth stones and clear rocks Lincoln had called *glass*. "I do not understand how the T_3 can throw us all the way out of this land. We would hit the ceiling."

"Well, that's the interesting thing," he said. "The T_3 is very special. It sends us to a new place without throwing us." He tapped the black strap around his wrist. "I use this watch to tell the T_3 where to send us, and it sends us there. When it does, we will be gone from this place, then we will appear in the new place, but we do not travel through the space in between." He made a fist. "It's like this. The rock is inside the body bag, the T_3 sends the rock over to that corner, then the rock just appears in that corner. I do not throw it, I do not roll it, I do not carry it over there—it just appears there. Does that make sense?"

"It makes sense, but I do not understand how it is possible. It is what happened to us yesterday. We were in my land, then we were here. We did not walk here."

He nodded. "That's right. Now, do you want me to tell you more? There's an even stranger part of this I have not explained yet."

She pushed herself up and once again sat cross-legged. "Yes, tell me the stranger part. I will understand."

He twisted his mouth to the side. "You may wish I hadn't told you, but I'll do my best. The T3 can not only move us from one place to another place, it can also move us from one *time* to another time. It can move us from today to tomorrow, or to next year."

She let out a burst of laughter. "*At-at-at.* Are you trying to be funny?"

He bared his teeth and shook his head at the same time, which was confusing. "I'm not. The T3 can do that. It can also send us from today to yesterday, or to a year ago, or to ten years ago. As many years ago as you want. Or as many years after tomorrow as you want."

Skyra felt her smile fading. Lincoln believed what he was saying to be true.

He put his hands on her knees. "Listen carefully, okay? I'm going to tell you something that is hard to understand, but it is something I've been wanting to explain. It's something you should know. I'll do my best to explain, then you can ask questions if you want to. Is that okay with you?"

"Your question does not make sense."

He smiled. "Okay, then I'll just start. Fourteen years from this time, I will use the T3 to send Ripple back in time. Many, many years back in time. Ripple found you, or you found Ripple, and you became friends. Something happened when you were with Ripple, and you died." He paused and gazed at her.

Skyra was starting to think Lincoln was telling her a story, the kind of story her Una-Loto tribemates would tell around a campfire, the kind of story that could not be true. His expression, though, made her not so sure.

He went on. "Many, many years later, I found your remains—your bones. Ripple was still beside you. When I found your remains and Ripple's shell, I asked Jazzlyn, Virgil, and Derek to help me. We used the T_3 to jump many, many years back in time. We found you just before you would die. That's when you saw us for the first time. We saved you from dying, Skyra." Again he paused and watched her.

She did not know what to say. Lincoln was not laughing. He was not showing one of his bolup grins. He still believed what he was saying to be true. Now she understood why Ripple had told her Lincoln and his tribemates had saved her life that day.

"When we escaped from Gelrut and your other tribemates," Lincoln said, "we used the T_3 to jump forward to my time. The T_3 sent us many, many years to the future, and very far away to my land. You came with us, and that is why we are here."

"But this is not the place you are from," she said, surprising herself that she had even thought of a response.

He nodded. "Yeah, that's kind of the problem, isn't it? If we jump back in time then jump forward, we cannot end up in the same land we were in the first time we jumped. You can jump back then forward as many times as you want, but every time you jump forward, you will be in a different land—different from all the others."

She had understood most of what he had said until this last part.

He must have seen it in her face because he said, "Okay, let me put it this way. Let's imagine we take the T_3 now and use it to jump many, many years back to your time, back to your homeland. Then, instead of staying there, we use the T_3 again to jump right back to this time and place. If we do that, this time and place will be very different from the way it is right now."

"Why?"

"Because events don't happen the same way every time. Maybe one of your tribemates trips and falls while hunting and is trampled by a rhino. The rhino lives and your tribemate dies. Your tribemate then never has the chance to make babies, and those babies never make babies, and their babies never make babies. After a long time the whole world ends up being a different place because of that one incident when your tribemate tripped and fell. And, the thing is, there are many incidents like that happening every day. More than anyone could ever count. They could be little things, like the water in a stream rolling a rock over and crushing a crayfish. Or, they could be big things, like lightning starting a fire that burns an entire forest. All of these countless events result in a different tomorrow, and a different next year, and a very different land many, many years later."

He pushed his lips together and took a deep breath through his nose. "So, when you and I and Jazzlyn and Virgil and Derek jumped from your time to my time, we did not find the place where I am from. Well, it's the same *place*, but it's different now. Even if we would try to do it over and over again, we would never find the exact same place I am from. It is not possible. I knew that before asking you to come with us, but I still asked you to come. Because I wanted you to be with me. I'm very sorry about that."

She stared at him. He stared back. Skyra was sure of it now—he believed everything he was saying to be true. She had already decided she trusted Lincoln. If Lincoln believed it was true, she would try to believe it was true. "It does not make sense when you say *I'm sorry*. Stop saying it please."

He huffed out some air, a sound that may have been a short laugh. "Maybe you should just try to understand why people say it."

She tried huffing some air out the way he had, but it didn't feel like a laugh. She thought about the strange things he had said. "Why did you go many, many years to my land and save me from dying?"

"You can thank Ripple for that. Ripple left a message asking me to do it. Remember, Ripple had this crazy plan for me to jump back in time all those years so you and I could meet. Ripple thought we would fall in love, make babies, then our babies would grow up and have their own babies, and this would make the world a better place."

"Jazzlyn said you were falling in love with me."

Lincoln blinked at her. Twice. "Jazzlyn said that?"

Suddenly, a new thought jumped into Skyra's head. "You went many, many years to my land to save me from dying!"

He blinked again.

"Lincoln, you said I died, but you went many, many years to save me from dying. Gelrut killed Veenah—we will use your T3 to go many, many years to save Veenah from dying!"

He furrowed his brows in a bolup frown. "Um... I don't know. There are some serious issues with reprogramming and spatial placement."

"What does that mean?"

"Um... it's really complicated. The hardest part about jumping back in time is telling the T3 exactly where to put us. It takes a really long time to do that. The T3 already has the instructions to jump back to the exact time and place we jumped to when we went there to save you from dying, but I'm pretty sure we cannot jump to that exact time and place. We would get there at the same instant our other selves from my original world get there, and that would be a disaster. I would have to tell the T3 to jump to another time and place. That takes a lot of time, more than a whole day, and I'm not even sure it's possible without access to extensive 3D mapping of the area around the original destination site. Even if I had 3D mapping available here, I don't have a computer to view and analyze it."

Skyra leaned forward and put her hand over his mouth. "Your words do not make sense." She pulled her hand away. "Can we use your T3 to go many, many years to save Veenah from dying?"

He seemed to think about it. "I will be honest. It may be *possible*, but I don't think it's very *likely*. It would take a day or two—at least—for the T3 to get ready to jump us to a different destination than what the T3 has already learned. Then, of course, we'd have the problem of finding Veenah. If that takes more than just a few minutes, she probably won't be where she was last time because we will have created a new timeline the moment we arrived. Furthermore, we only have body bags for two more jumps. Not only that, but we'd have to convince the nandups here to let me work on the T3 for an extended—"

Skyra slapped her hand over his mouth again. "Too many words, Lincoln!"

She removed her hand, and he shook his head. "I don't think it can be done."

She studied his expression. He was speaking words he believed were true. If Lincoln believed it could not be done, she would try to believe it too.

"I'll try," he said, surprising her. "I'll start thinking about the placement issues. If I can come up with an idea, I'll tell the T3 to start processing the calculations."

Skyra wasn't sure what some of this meant, but she understood enough. Lincoln was willing to try to help her. She grabbed his hand the way he had grabbed hers before and held it tight.

Ripple spoke. "I have listened silently, assuming you would ask for my input at some point. Because you have not, I will offer it. Lincoln, perhaps I can be of assistance. After all, this endeavor is consistent with my plan. I happen to have spatial data for the area near your insertion point where you first found Skyra. The data is somewhat limited, but it should be enough to allow your T_3 device to calculate a new insertion point."

"Damn, you're right," Lincoln said. "I should have asked for your input. I'm skeptical that we could interface your system with the T_3, though."

"Once again you are underestimating the capabilities you will give your drones fourteen years in your future. I do not think interfacing will be a problem, although your T_3 may still take up to thirty hours to complete the placement calculations."

Lincoln said, "Well, in spite of the fact that I know you're just wanting to carry out your crazy plan, I appreciate knowing you may be able to help." He turned to Skyra and started to speak, but the door clicked and swung open.

Belol-yan entered the chamber, closed the door, and approached the bed. With his one good eye, he looked at Skyra, then at Lincoln, then back at Skyra. His eye flicked down to Skyra's chest. Finally, he spoke while looking at her face.

Although Skyra had already learned some of the words of these nandups' language, she still needed Ripple's translations to get a full understanding. Ripple said, "I am happy your blood has not spilled today. I honor you, and you honor me.

You will tell me something important, and I will tell you something important." His eye flicked to her chest again.

Lincoln leaned to the side and grabbed Skyra's cape from the floor. He handed it to her. "Maybe you should put this on. I think you're distracting him."

Skyra wasn't sure what that meant, but she pulled her cape on over her head. She spoke to Belol-yan. "I honor you, and you honor me. What do you want me to tell you?"

The warrior glanced back at the closed door. Then he spoke, and Ripple said, "I have listened to your words. You do not understand our war. I do not believe you when you say you want to make your war in Arizona much-great. I do not believe you want to help us make our war in Kyran-yufost much-great. Tell me, what do you want? Why are you here?"

"Be careful," Lincoln said softly.

Skyra did not want to be careful. Her head was telling her this old fighter had something important to say, and something about the man made her want to trust him. She said, "I do not want to leave this place because I do not understand why your tribemates fight and fight and fight with the bolups. I do not understand, so I want to make it stop."

Ripple said, "Skyra, are you sure you—"

"Yes! Translate my words."

Ripple translated. Belol-yan listened without taking his eye off of Skyra's face. When Ripple fell silent, he spoke again. Ripple translated. "Do you know I will be killed if our scientists-learners-teachers know we are speaking of these things?"

"I honor you, and you honor me," she replied. "I will fight beside you so you will not be killed."

Ripple translated, then the old guard stared down at the floor. He was frowning when he looked back up at her. He spoke for many breaths. Finally, Ripple translated. "We have always fought the humans-bolups. The humans-bolups have always fought us. Sometimes we want to fight, but sometimes many of us grow weary of fighting. We have grown weary of fighting three times during my lifetime. We are now growing weary again. Each time we grow weary of fighting, our scientists-learners-teachers renew our will to fight, and we begin fighting more fiercely than ever before. I have never seen people like you. I have never spoken to people like you. You have come here at a time when we are growing weary. I do not know why you are here, but your presence gives me hope. Therefore, I will speak to you now, although I may be killed for doing so."

Skyra's skin was beginning to prickle, a sensation she had always felt during a hunt just before the ambush, just as the reindeer or ibex or woolly rhino was almost near enough to attack. "What do you want to tell us, Belol-yan?" she asked.

Speaking through Ripple, the fighter said, "I have spoken to Di-woto. Di-woto is an alinga-ul—a first-level scientist-learner-teacher. She is the only alinga-ul we have in all of Kyran-yufost kingdom-district. I am only a guard in the sanctuary-fortress, but Di-woto has become my friend. She likes to hear me speak of my battles. She was very interested to hear me speak of you. Never have I seen Di-woto so interested. Di-woto would like to see you and speak to you. You must understand, Di-woto is an alinga-ul, so she is very important to all the scientists-learners-teachers. You must also understand that our citizens-nandups do not know Di-woto exists. They do not know we have an alinga-ul. They do not know we have dali-tamons—second-level scientists-learners-teachers. If our citizens-nandups were to find out, the result would be chaos. Do you understand? If you do not understand, I will have to kill you now."

Skyra realized Belol-yan was gripping the broad-bladed khul at his waist.

"Yes, we understand," Lincoln said.

"We understand," Skyra added. "When will we speak to Di-woto?"

Ripple translated.

Without speaking, Belol-yan stepped to the door and pulled it open. He turned his one eye back to Skyra and Lincoln and gestured for them to follow.

11

DI-WOTO

Present Time - Day 2

Belol-yan silently led Lincoln, Skyra, and Ripple through several unoccupied corridors, apparently taking them deeper into the compound's interior. Lincoln's curiosity was piqued, but his apprehension was higher. He and Skyra were lucky to have made it through the morning of intensive exchanges without getting themselves killed. Now they were being taken to one of the most important leaders of this Neanderthal society. What if this was a ploy designed to get them to reveal what the orange-clad nandups might be starting to suspect—that Lincoln and Skyra weren't actually here to help?

Perhaps even more frightening, Belol-yan had implied this visit with the woman Di-woto was somehow related to Skyra's determination to change what was happening to the nandup citizens of this kingdom—or district, or whatever it was. If so, what were they getting themselves into now?

Belol-yan led them past several open doors, each with two guards in drab clothing stationed in the corridor, probably to prevent unauthorized people from entering the chambers. Belol-yan exchanged a brief greeting with every guard they passed. Perhaps this formality was required, or maybe all the guards in this place knew each other and were a close-knit group. Lincoln wasn't able to see much through the first three open doorways, but through the fourth he briefly caught a glimpse of a wooden table with several orange-clad nandups standing around it.

The chambers were moderately to brightly lit—apparently the entire compound was designed so most of the rooms were exposed to the outside and were strategically walled or ceilinged with glass.

Belol-yan turned left and entered a room where at least fifteen other guards were engaged in what appeared to be hand-to-hand fighting drills. The group included about as many women as men. Just like Skyra's Una-Loto tribe, these Neanderthals apparently recognized little difference between males and females when it came to fighting. Some of the guards were paired up, but there were also several groups of three. Some were grappling on the floor, others were on their feet, jabbing and swinging bladed weapons without actually hitting each other.

Belol-yan shouted something, making the guards stop drilling and turn to look. Those on the ground got to their feet and stared. Belol-yan rattled off a quick string of words, pointing at the far end of the chamber. Several of the other guards replied, and they exchanged more words.

"There seems to be a negotiation taking place," Ripple said, its voice quieter than usual, probably to avoid attracting attention. "Belol-yan is explaining why he is taking us to a place he calls the atulan. Based on context clues, the atulan is heavily guarded, and only certain people are allowed to enter. I get the impression Belol-yan can be quite persuasive when he wants to be."

The discussion stopped, and Belol-yan gestured for Lincoln, Skyra, and Ripple to follow. They walked directly through the cluster of guards, who exuded an animal-like odor of sweat. A few of them stared at Lincoln or Skyra, but most of them watched Ripple. The drone's hard feet clacked on the stone floor as it walked just ahead of Lincoln.

Belol-yan led them to another door festooned with a metal spider. He raised one leg, gave the door three solid kicks, then followed with a distinct pattern of lighter kicks. Seconds later, the door clicked and swung inward. An orange-clad nandup Lincoln recognized as Khebum-khai stood there staring at them with an obvious nandup frown. Belol-yan spoke a few words, then Khebum-khai stepped aside, still frowning.

They passed through the doorway and started down yet another corridor. This corridor had several open doorways, but these had no guards stationed in front of them.

Lincoln glanced into one of the chambers as he was passing by. He abruptly stopped and stared. Standing around a table covered with unrecognizable items were several orange-clad nandups. Among the nandups were two women wearing the same sack-like garments, but these garments were brown instead of orange. The brown-clad women turned and stared through the doorway at Lincoln. They both had bronze skin, small eyes, and flat foreheads. They were bolups—*Homo sapiens*.

"Lincoln!" Skyra hissed. She was ahead of him, looking back.

Belol-yan was ahead of her, still walking, unaware that Lincoln had paused.

Lincoln jogged a few steps to catch up. "There are bolups here," he whispered.

Skyra shot him a glance. "I saw them too."

Belol-yan reached the end of the corridor and stopped. He gestured to a series of wooden poles protruding from the stone wall, obviously intended to be a stairway of sorts. They led up the wall about twenty feet to the doorway of one of the blob-shaped dwellings. About half of the dwelling was embedded in the top of the wall, the other half in the ceiling.

Belol-yan lifted one foot and rested it on the first of the protruding poles. He turned back to Lincoln and Skyra and spoke. Ripple translated. "You must remember Di-woto is an alinga-ul. She is the only alinga-ul we have. If you attempt to harm her, I will kill you and feed your body to the spiders. Do you understand?"

"I understand," Skyra said.

"We won't try to harm her," Lincoln said.

The guard listened to the translations then spoke again. Ripple said, "Many of our scientists-learners-teachers do not understand Di-woto. She does not speak like other scientists-learners-teachers, but her knowledge and skills are much-great. I, Belol-yan, know how to speak to Di-woto. I listen to her and I speak to her. That is why I have become a friend to Di-woto. That is why she chooses me to be her guard. That is why she ordered me to be your guard when she heard the news of your arrival. Now Di-woto wants to speak to you. Even with your talking beast to help you, maybe you will not know how to speak to Di-woto. Few people know how to speak to her."

Lincoln was tempted to ask what was so different about

this woman, but he decided Belol-yan might consider it offensive.

"What is wrong with Di-woto?" Skyra asked. "Did someone bash her in the head?"

Lincoln's chest immediately tightened. "Um, I don't think—"

"Do not worry," Ripple said. "I will temper the question with a dose of sensitivity." The drone then spoke to Belol-yan.

Lincoln held his breath. Belol-yan watched Skyra with his one eye as he listened to the translation. Then he bared his teeth. This was the first time Lincoln had seen him smile.

The guard spoke, then Ripple said, "You have asked me to explain a person who cannot be explained. Come. We will talk to Di-woto now." Belol-yan started climbing the pole stairway.

"This ascent may present logistical difficulties for me," Ripple said. "I cannot levitate higher than two hundred centimeters above the floor."

"What does that mean?" Skyra asked.

"I am not sure I can climb up there."

She held out a hand. "Give me your foot."

Ripple lifted one of its front legs. "I do not see how—"

Skyra snatched the leg, hoisted the drone off the floor, and slung it over her shoulder.

Ripple dangled against her back by one leg. "I was hoping for a more dignified solution."

"I carried you this way before," Skyra said. "You do not remember because you were sleeping." She started up the pole ladder after Belol-yan, apparently having no trouble with the extra weight.

Lincoln brought up the rear. They entered the egg-shaped doorway to the dwelling. Skyra lowered Ripple to the floor.

Lincoln's first impression of the dwelling was it was much larger than the exterior portion he had seen from the chamber below. There were even additional openings providing views into several more rooms. An expanse of stained-glass windows embedded in the rounded ceiling let in plenty of light to illuminate a variety of brightly-colored objects, almost none of which Lincoln could identify. Many appeared to be made of dyed cloth, or at least wrapped in dyed cloth. Heaps of what appeared to be cloth-covered balls and cubes were arranged here and there on the floor. Sagging lengths of colorful cloth were draped over unseen objects as well as hung from cords attached to the ceiling. The room was filled with reds, greens, yellows, blues, and every color in between. The only thing Lincoln could positively identify was a table with a wooden surface and metal legs. Even the table was striking in appearance, as the four legs resembled thin, jointed spider legs.

"Someone is singing," Skyra whispered.

She was right. A soft female voice was drifting in from one of the other rooms, rising and falling melodiously like a wordless chant.

Belol-yan leaned to one side to look through one of the doorways. "Di-woto! Na-yanof yu-te khakhul. Na-yanof Layop nu-te."

The singing abruptly stopped. "Ayeee!" Running footsteps. Then a figure literally jumped through one of the openings into the room.

Lincoln sensed Skyra tensing up, as if she expected to be attacked, and he instinctively extended his arm in front of her to keep her from rushing forward to meet her attacker.

Lincoln let his arm drop as he gaped at Di-woto. She wasn't a woman—she was a girl, no older than fourteen or fifteen, and she looked like no one Lincoln had ever seen. Her skin was bronze, darker than Skyra's, at least the portions Lincoln could see. Her face and arms were almost completely covered in scar tissue. These scars had healed to a color resembling reddish-pink lips. The scars were obviously intentional, rather than from a fire or an animal attack. Someone had carved into the girl's skin to create permanent ornamental designs. The designs were symmetrical and intricate, with matching spirals and wavy lines on both sides of her face, curved and exaggerated lashes above her eyes, and detailed paisley-like swoops, bulges, and flowery bursts all over her arms.

Her eyes grew wide as she gazed at Lincoln and Skyra, and she grinned broadly, displaying white teeth. She rattled off an excited string of words in the nandup language. This girl, however, was not a Neanderthal. She had to be a hybrid. Her facial features and overall build were exactly what Lincoln had assumed a *sapiens/neanderthalensis* offspring would look like. Prominent brows, but not too prominent. A forehead more sloped than his but more vertical than Skyra's. She had large, intense eyes, but not as large as those of the other nandups. Thick, solid arms, but obviously not with the bone-crushing strength Skyra had so aptly demonstrated.

Lincoln's eyes were drawn to the girl's neck. At first he thought a thick rope was coiled around her neck, then he realized it was her hair. Her deep-black hair was pulled back into a braid, like most of the nandups here, but this girl's braid was wrapped around her neck at least four times. Uncoiled, it was probably longer than her entire body. Woven into the braid, and into the tightly-pulled strands of hair on her head, were numerous colored threads, blades of dried grass, and what looked like strips of dried animal skin.

Ripple translated. "I am happy you have come to my

structure-dwelling. Tell me please, what do you think of my clothing-garment? I would like to know, because you are not like others I have seen, and because this nandup woman wears skins for garments. Tell me please."

Lincoln glanced at Skyra, who was gazing at Di-woto without expression.

Belol-yan spoke briefly, and Ripple translated. "Di-woto is happy to talk about clothing. You should talk to her about clothing now."

Lincoln studied the girl. In basic design and fit, her garment was similar to those of the orange-clad nandups—a long sack with holes for her arms—but this garment wasn't orange. Instead, portions of it appeared to have been dipped in blue dye, other portions in yellow dye. The areas in between were green, seemingly due to mixing of the two colors.

Skyra still hadn't spoken, so Lincoln decided to make an attempt. "I very much like your garment. The three colors are striking, and blue is my favorite color."

With almost no hesitation, the girl spoke again. Ripple paused and flashed its red circle of LEDs before saying, "Tell me please, what is your opinion of using kawil-yefo-atun to make a garment?" Ripple paused again. "Lincoln and Skyra, I am reasonably sure kawil-yefo-atun can be translated as *dried bones of a camel*."

Lincoln turned to Skyra again, and again she remained silent, watching impassively.

The girl was waiting to hear their opinion of a camel-bone outfit.

"I'm not sure how I feel about making a garment out of camel bones," Lincoln said. "I think it might be uncomfortable. And probably noisy."

Ripple translated.

Di-woto bared her teeth in a nandup smile. She spoke, and Ripple said, "Yes, uncomfortable, but also uncommon and funny. I want to make a garment of dried camel bones. I will also make a garment for a camel, a garment made of dried human-bolup bones. I will put the garment on the camel, then I will ride the camel while I wear my garment. Wouldn't you like to see such a funny thing?"

What the hell? Lincoln stared at her. "Um... you do realize I am a bolup, right?"

Ripple translated, then translated the girl's reply. "Of course I know you are a human-bolup. That is why you would think it is so funny. I could make a garment for the camel using citizen-nandup bones, but that would not be so funny. Tell me please, do you like my shoes-footwraps?"

Lincoln looked down at her feet as Di-woto lifted her three-colored garment to provide a better view. She was wearing knee-high boots covered in snowy white fur. The fur covered the entire boots except for the soles, where the fur had apparently worn off due to abrasion. "Those are very nice shoes," he said, for lack of a better response.

Ripple translated, and she smiled again.

"Why did you ask to talk to us?" Skyra asked, her voice carrying a bit of impatience.

The girl approached Skyra and stopped less than a foot from her face. Skyra was slightly taller, which meant Di-woto was under five feet tall. Di-woto extended a hand and petted the woolly rhinoceros fur on Skyra's cape.

Lincoln could see Skyra's displeasure, and he silently willed her to be cordial.

Di-woto spoke, and Ripple said, "Skyra, I like your garments. I do not like Lincoln's garments. His garments appear to be tight and uncomfortable. The other scientists-learners-teachers in Arizona must know you are a great maker of clothing. Maybe I will make garments like yours, if you will teach me how. Tell me please, Skyra, do you like my ornamental scars?"

Skyra glanced at Lincoln, and again he willed her to be polite.

She extended a finger and touched one of the scars on Di-woto's face. "Who did this to you? Did your tribemates do this because you told a lie?"

Ripple translated, and Di-woto furrowed her brows and pursed her lips at the same time, an expression Lincoln had never seen on a Neanderthal. The scars around the girl's mouth became a deeper red. She spoke, and Ripple said, "I made my ornamental scars myself. I do not tell lies. Only our khami-buls tell lies. Our khami-buls tell many lies. Sometimes our dali-tamons tell lies." Ripple paused. "Skyra and Lincoln, as I have explained before, dali-tamon is best translated as *second-level scientist*, although I do not yet understand the significance of that role. My best translation of khami-bul is *third-level scientist*. Again, I do not know the significance."

Di-woto spoke again just as Ripple fell silent. Ripple translated. "I asked if you like my ornamental scars. Please tell me."

"Maybe you should just tell her you like them," Lincoln said.

Skyra gazed at the girl's face. Then she leaned forward and pulled down on the neck of Di-woto's sack-dress, exposing more scars on her chest above her breasts. "Making these scars must have hurt. If you made the scars yourself, you must have the strength of the cave lion and woolly rhino in your blood. I like that very much."

Immediately after Ripple's translation, the girl flashed her teeth and let out another *Ayeee* while bouncing up onto her tiptoes. Apparently she was pleased with the answer. She turned and bounded back into the room she had come from, darted to the left, and disappeared. Lincoln could hear her moving things around as if looking for something. Seconds later she came rushing back out, carrying a flat object about two feet square. She went straight to the wooden table, cleared off a few things that looked like small pyramids covered in dyed cloth, and plopped the object onto the tabletop. It appeared to be a leather portfolio with a folded flap at one end. She opened the flap and pulled out a stack of cream-colored pieces of paper.

Belol-yan gestured for Lincoln and Skyra to approach the table, and they all gathered around. Di-woto flipped through the papers, pulled one out, and laid it on top of the stack. Lincoln leaned in closer. On the paper was an amazingly detailed drawing of something, but he wasn't sure what it was.

Di-woto excitedly rattled off some words, and Ripple said, "I have planned a new sanctuary-fortress, with a new public chamber-auditorium! It will be better than this one. Much better. When our citizens-nandups build it, I will be happy and all the citizens will be happy. Tell me, please, do you like my new sanctuary-fortress?"

Lincoln scanned the image from left to right to get his bearings. He saw it now. It was upside down, so he carefully rotated it. This structure was even stranger than the compound he was in now. Its design was obviously meant to more closely resemble a spider web, with corners that stretched out wildly as if they were flexible strands connected to invisible anchor points somewhere in the sky. Like the existing structure, the exterior walls were riddled—seemingly randomly—with blob-shaped dwellings. Additional dwellings appeared to be suspended from massive poles extending out from the corners. A few small, human-like figures standing on the ground near the doorway revealed the structure's immense scale. Lincoln's overall impression was the structure's creative shape was so extreme it probably couldn't be built without collapsing under its own weight. Of course, that had also been his impression when he'd first seen the existing compound.

"I do not know what this is," Skyra said, staring at the drawing.

It occurred to Lincoln she probably had never seen any kind of two-dimensional representations at all, except perhaps simple cave paintings. "This is a drawing of a big dwelling, like the one we're in," he said. "You need to make drawings like this before you can build something this big."

Di-woto was watching them, waiting for an answer.

"This is going to be a wonderful sanctuary-fortress," Lincoln said. "You must be very important to the people of Kyran-yufost district."

With Ripple translating, she said, "Yes. I am important. I am the only alinga-ul in Kyran-yufost."

She began flipping through more pages in the stack, showing each one just briefly. Lincoln glimpsed numerous drawings of other structures, some of them rounded like the dwellings he had seen while being hauled into the city. Other drawings appeared to be of smaller objects, most of them with a mysterious purpose. Finally, she stopped at one, which at first glance appeared to be a rather simplified version of a spider web.

"This is my plan for a new system of rivers for removing waste. It will be much better than the waste rivers we have now. Tell me please, do you like the way it looks like a spider's web?"

Again, Lincoln leaned in closer. This drawing was as detailed as the others. Basically, it was an aerial view of the city. The sanctuary-fortress was in the center, surrounded by its defensive wall. Countless structures of various shapes surrounded the wall. Beyond those were the extensive crop fields and livestock enclosures. Finally, the outer perimeter wall enclosed everything. The new sewer system was drawn with bolder lines, arranged to look like a spider web if viewed from high above. The sanctuary-fortress was at the web's center, and Lincoln realized the only way this could work would be to have a continuous source of water flowing out of the fortress. He wondered if perhaps an underground spring came to the surface there.

He shook his head as he stared at the drawing. Not only were these designs clever, they represented a mind that thought completely outside the box. This sewage system was designed to represent an iconic shape, but no one in the city would ever be able to see the true beauty of it because these people seemed centuries away from developing any kind of flight.

He looked up at Di-woto, studying her face. In some ways, this girl was like Lincoln himself. He also approached problems in ways no one else had considered. In fact, he was here now because he had developed a way to jump back or forward in time and space. Perhaps he wasn't as extreme as Di-woto—he didn't carve designs into his skin—but he had always felt shunned by others who couldn't comprehend him or his ideas.

"Di-woto is like me," Skyra said matter-of-factly.

Lincoln turned to her. "Like you?"

She was still gazing at the drawing. "My tribemates did not understand me and Veenah because we could see what they could not see."

He let out a long breath. "Ripple, tell Di-woto we are very impressed with her drawings, particularly her plan for a sewage system. We are happy she wants to speak with us."

Ripple complied.

The girl smiled again and started digging through the papers, obviously looking for one.

Belol-yan gently placed a hand on Di-woto's arm and spoke to her.

"Ayeee!" she cried, then she pushed the papers together and carefully reinserted them into the leather portfolio.

"The guard has reminded Di-woto she has something important to discuss," Ripple said.

Di-woto skirted the edge of the table, approaching Lincoln so closely that he stepped back until he was shoulder-to-shoulder with Skyra. Di-woto came even closer, stopping mere inches away from both of them, apparently oblivious to the concept of personal space.

She spoke, and Ripple said, "Do you like my smell? I put the juice of pikko fruit on my skin and my hair."

"Di-woto," Belol-yan said firmly.

She furrowed her brows then spoke again. Ripple said, "Belol-yan should use juice of pikko fruit. He smells like an old rope."

The guard let out a low growl.

Di-woto spoke again, this time at length. Ripple translated. "Many people do not like to talk to me, but Belol-yan does. He tells me many things. He tells me the truth when I ask if he likes my new garments. He tells me the truth when I ask if he believes my new ideas will work. He tells me the truth when I ask him about the strange nandup and the strange bolups who were brought here. That is why Belol-yan is my guard. Do you know what Belol-yan told me about you?"

Skyra replied immediately. "We do not know what Belol-yan told you."

Ripple kept translating as the conversation continued.

Di-woto smiled. "Belol-yan told me you might be important to Kyran-yufost kingdom-district. Do you know why you might be important?"

Skyra hesitated, so Lincoln said, "I'm not sure. Maybe because Skyra believes the nandups and bolups here should stop fighting and killing each other?"

Di-woto gazed into Lincoln's eyes. "You spoke Skyra's name. Do you not believe nandups and bolups should stop fighting?"

"I do believe it, but I have no idea what we could do about it. Your war has been going on for so long, and we are strangers here."

Di-woto let out a startling squeal. She snatched her portfolio from the table. "I am an alinga-ul. Do you know what alinga-uls can do?"

Lincoln glanced at Skyra to offer her a chance at this one, but she remained silent. "To be honest," he said, "we don't know what an alinga-ul is exactly. We do know you like to make clothing, and you like to design and draw complex things like buildings and sewer systems. You are very creative."

She squealed again. "Yes! Creative. I am an alinga-ul, and I like to make plans. I am now making a plan."

"A plan for what?" Skyra asked.

"A plan to stop the fighting and killing! It is the greatest of all my plans. I am very happy you are here, Skyra and Lincoln."

Belol-yan spoke up. "If you speak any of Di-woto's words

outside of this dwelling, your blood will spill. Do you understand?"

As Lincoln acknowledged the threat, his mind began reeling. Belol-yan was serious about this threat, which meant Di-woto was serious about her plan—absolutely deadly serious. She was just a girl, obviously with extreme flights of fancy. This wasn't likely to end well.

"How can you not know about alinga-uls?" Di-woto asked. "Did you not come here to make alinga-uls?"

"We do not know what that means," Skyra said.

The girl seemed to study Skyra's face. "If you tell lies to our khami-buls, how do I know you are not telling lies to me?" Ripple added, "As a reminder, khami-bul translates to third-level scientist, which we can now assume is the orange-clad scientists-learners-teachers."

"We did not want the orange-clothed nandups to have us killed, so we told them what they wanted to hear," Skyra said. "Now that I have spoken to you, I trust you will not have us killed. I will not lie to you." She glanced at Lincoln expectantly.

"I won't lie to you either," he added.

Di-woto grinned broadly. "You do not know about alinga-uls. You want me to tell you. But I will not tell you yet. First, you must tell me something please." While Ripple was translating, she went to a pile of objects covered in dyed cloth. She searched through the pile and chose one that was roughly the shape of a cube. She brought it over. "I want to make new colors, and I have finally made a new color. It is a color no one has ever seen. I am happy to show the new color to you."

The cloth covering the object had numerous swirls of yellow and at least a half-dozen patches of other colors, many of them overlapping to create blends. She turned the cube over, revealing a fist-sized splotch that was yellowish-green around the edges, with a center that was a striking shade of crimson brown. She touched the color with her thumb. "Tell me please, do you like my new color?"

"That is not a new color," Skyra said. "It is the color of wafil flowers that grow in the Walukh hills of my homeland."

Di-woto frowned and turned to Lincoln. He figured it was too late to try to appease her need for affirmation, so he said, "I'm sorry, but I've seen that color before. We call it *maroon*."

The girl squealed and actually jumped off the ground. "Belol-yan was correct, Lincoln and Skyra! Belol-yan said you would speak truth to me, even though you do not speak truth to our khami-buls. I like you, Lincoln. I like you, Skyra. My plan will be the greatest plan I have ever made."

She ran to the other room and quickly came back with several more sheets of cream-colored paper. "I have already started my plan." She fanned four pages out between her hands. Lincoln stared but could make little sense of the drawings. There were numerous lines going every direction, with simplified human figures scattered among other drawings that could have been portions of dwellings, defensive walls, or even small objects.

Di-woto dropped the papers on the table dismissively. "If you are going to help me complete my plan, you will need to know more about Kyran-yufost. I will show you things and tell you things. Tell me please, what do you want to know first?"

It was a long shot, but Lincoln decided to ask about something that had been on his mind all day. "I would like to know where my three bolup friends are. I want to know if they are safe."

Di-woto listened to Ripple's translation, then she grabbed Belol-yan by the arm and pulled him to the far side of the room. The girl and the warrior conferred quietly for a good thirty seconds before returning.

"Your human-bolup friends have been confined with all the others," Di-woto said. "I will take you to see them. When you see them, you will want to help me finish my plan."

Lincoln felt his entire body tensing up. "Why? Where are they?"

"When you see your friends, you will also see how the orange-clad scientists are preparing to make our war much-great again. As Belol-yan has told you, our people are growing weary of fighting, as they have grown weary before. The orange-clad scientists will again make our people renew their will to continue fighting."

The girl's words were not helping Lincoln's anxiety. "What does that have to do with my friends?"

She stepped closer, stopping only inches from his face. She ran her fingers down his arm, feeling the fleece material of his shirt. Then she stepped back and pulled up her multi-colored garment, exposing her legs, her pubescent groin, and part of her belly. As Lincoln stared at Di-woto's abdomen, his heart began pounding. He turned to Skyra. She was staring too, and a growl began growing in her throat. He turned back to Di-woto, trying to look at her face, but she nodded down at her belly, obviously wanting him to see. Her abdomen was seeping blood in at least a dozen places from wounds only recently inflicted. Some kind of gray powder had been pushed into the open cuts, perhaps to minimize the bleeding. The cuts were obviously intentional, arranged in a series of waves, perhaps to resemble the surface of an ocean or lake.

Di-woto waited for several long seconds, giving them more than enough time to look. Finally, she spoke, and Ripple translated. "Tell me please, do you like my skin?"

Lincoln had no idea what to say. It would be a blatant lie to say he found anything appealing about this extreme case of self-mutilation.

Skyra spoke up. "Why do you do this to your own body?"

The girl listened to Ripple's translation, then she spoke. Ripple said, "I like the ornamental scars on my skin, but it hurts when I make them. I only make them when I am angry. Sometimes I am angry because I am alone—I am the only alinga-ul in Kyran-yufost. Sometimes I am angry because people do not understand me. Sometimes I am angry because I want to make Kyran-yufost a better place, but no one listens to me unless they want me to plan a new kind of dwelling, or a new kind of weapon."

She let her garment fall back into place and grabbed a fistful of Lincoln's shirt below his chin. She spoke, and Ripple said. "I will take you to your friends now. You will be angry, Lincoln. Do not be foolish with your anger, as I have been. Hold your anger within you and remember my plan."

12

MODIFICATION

PRESENT TIME - DAY 2

SKYRA HAD NEVER BEFORE SEEN a person like Di-woto. The girl had no fear of anything or anyone. She had led Skyra, Lincoln, and Ripple, with Belol-yan following behind, through chambers and cave-like corridors. Each time the group encountered other guards like Belol-yan, the guards would turn their backs and face the wall, as if they were not allowed to gaze in Di-woto's direction. Di-woto paid no attention to them, as if she had seen this strange behavior all her life.

After walking for many breaths, Di-woto stopped before a closed door with a spider ornament on it. She turned to Skyra and Lincoln and spoke. Skyra had always found it easy to remember words, so now she could understand some of what the girl was saying, but Ripple's translations were still helpful. Ripple said, "Beyond this door you will see bolups. Many bolups. You will see things you will not understand. These things will make you afraid and angry. If they do not make you afraid and angry, perhaps you are not suitable to help me with my plan. I will explain these things to you, but first you must see them with your eyes. Hold your anger within you and remember my plan. There are orange-clad scientists beyond this door. You must not show them your anger or your fear."

Belol-yan spoke, and Ripple said, "You have been lying to the orange-clad scientists. You must continue your lying by pretending what you see here is what you expected to see. Do you understand?"

"Are my friends in there?" Lincoln asked, his voice low. He was already becoming angry and afraid.

Belol-yan spoke, and Ripple said, "Yes. Remember, you must continue your lying."

Di-woto kicked the door several times with her foot.

Skyra watched Lincoln's face. His eyes met hers then flicked away. Skyra did not know what they would see beyond the door, and she worried Lincoln would be unable to pretend it was what he expected.

The door clicked and swung open. An orange-clothed nandup woman stood in the doorway. She eyed Di-woto and Belol-yan as if she had seen them at this door many times before, but her eyes grew wide when she saw Skyra, Lincoln, and Ripple.

Skyra blew air out through her nose and covered her face. The area beyond the nandup woman smelled worse than a cave inhabited by hyenas.

"What is this place?" Lincoln asked. "Why are my friends in there?"

"Ripple, do not translate," Skyra said. She faced Lincoln. "Remember Di-woto's words. The orange-clothed nandups must believe we understand what they are doing."

He closed his eyes for a breath. "Okay. I'm trying. I just... this can't be good."

Di-woto, Belol-yan, and the nandup woman were watching, waiting.

Di-woto seemed to sense it was time to move on. She spoke a few words to the nandup and pushed past her. Belol-yan motioned for Skyra and Lincoln to enter then followed them in. The smell became even worse.

They were in another cave-like corridor that extended in two directions. Di-woto turned and continued walking. They passed another orange-clothed nandup and several closed doors. Instead of facing the wall as the guards had done, this nandup pressed his back to the wall to make room. He watched them pass with a surprised expression.

The corridor grew darker as they continued, but light was coming from an open doorway ahead. Di-woto stopped just before the doorway. She spoke quietly, as if she didn't want those in the chamber to hear. Ripple said, "First I want you to see what is in this chamber. You will want to ask many questions, but you must wait. I will explain some of what you need to know. When we leave the chamber, you may ask all of your questions."

"Do you understand?" Belol-yan asked.

Skyra and Lincoln exchanged a look, then they both agreed.

Di-woto led them through the doorway. Skyra blew air out her nose again. The smell here was even stronger and could not be ignored. Inside were two rows of cages on wooden wheels—the same kind of cages the nandups had put Lincoln and his tribemates in yesterday. Skyra could see figures within the cages, but she could not make out any details. An orange-clothed nandup woman was at the far end of the chamber.

She stared but did not approach. Di-woto took them to the nearest cage and motioned for them to put their faces to the openings to look inside.

"I don't like this at all," Lincoln muttered as he moved forward.

Skyra leaned in to look. In the cage was a bolup man, sitting with his back against the cage wall. The man was facing Skyra. His eyes were open, but he stared lifelessly. He was naked except for a small waist-cloth, which appeared to be blood-stained. Blood was also on the cage floor around him.

"Oh, shit," Lincoln said. "What is this?"

Skyra pulled back and glanced at him. He was still staring into the cage, so she looked in again. A growl began growing in her chest. The man was not a man after all. Or if he was a man, his arms were not right. One of them was folded across his lap, the other was at his side, resting beside his outstretched legs. Skyra stared, unsure of what she was actually seeing. The man's hand was next to his feet, not because he was leaning, but because his arms were longer than his legs.

Both his arms were covered in scars, but not ornamental scars like Di-woto's. These scars were ugly, without a fanciful pattern. Some appeared to be from cuts all the way around the arm, as if the arm had been severed then reattached, with small, round scars evenly spaced on either side of the cuts.

"What happened to you?" Skyra asked in English.

The man turned his head slightly to look at her. His eyes still looked dead, even though he was alive. He moved the arm that was across his lap until it slid off his legs and plopped loosely on the cage floor. This arm was just as long as the other. One of the fingers twitched, but the others remained still, halfway curled toward his palm.

"I do not understand," Skyra said. "What happened to this bolup?"

"I am going to assume I should not translate," Ripple said.

Di-woto grabbed Skyra's arm from behind and guided her to the next cage. Skyra glanced back at Lincoln to make sure he was following. Her muscles and senses were telling her she might have to fight and kill, and she wanted Lincoln at her side. He pulled away from the first cage, and together they pressed their faces to the openings in the second cage. Inside was another bolup man, also sitting with his back against the wall. His arms were sprawled loosely on the floor beside his legs. They were just as long as the first man's arms, but this man had two strange objects on each of his arms, one above the elbow and one below. The black objects encircled his arms, apparently held in place by straight sticks that appeared to penetrate his skin. Blood had trickled from these spots and had dried on his skin as well as the cage floor.

"If you are interested," said Ripple, "I can say with reasonable confidence these people have had extreme limb-lengthening surgical procedures. The devices on this man's arms appear to be some form of external fixator, which can be used after sawing the bones into two pieces. The external fixators then can be gradually spread apart to—"

"I get it," Lincoln said.

Skyra pulled away from the cage and turned to Di-woto. She didn't even know what questions to ask.

Lincoln also faced Di-woto. "What the hell's going on? Where are my friends Jazzlyn, Virgil, and Derek?"

Ripple said, "I will remind you of Di-woto's instructions to not ask questions while we are in this room."

"I don't care," Lincoln said. "I want to know now!"

Ripple said nothing.

Di-woto glanced at the orange-clothed nandup at the far end of the chamber then began speaking loudly enough the nandup could hear her words. Ripple translated. "We are happy to show you our progress with the captive bolups. We have worked for many days-years to make this progress. You will be happy to learn what we are doing. These bolups are almost ready for us to show our citizens-nandups. It will be a great day when we show them. Our citizens-nandups will be afraid, and they will want to fight bolups for more days-years. Now please come with me. I am happy to show you more of our progress."

After Ripple fell silent, Di-woto led them back into the corridor.

"Tell me what's going on!" Lincoln said, almost growling.

This time Ripple translated, but in a quiet voice.

Di-woto replied in an even quieter voice. "I am trying to show you what is going on. Please be patient. There is more you must see."

They followed her through the dark corridor into another chamber with windows in the ceiling for light. This chamber, like others Skyra had seen today, was filled with spider cages, though these cages were smaller than the others.

Di-woto led them to the first row of cages. She stopped and stared into the first cage, then she moved to the next one, then the next after that. Finally, she pointed into a cage and spoke. Ripple said, "These are ground-web spiders. You have seen ground-web spiders in other chambers of our sanctuary-fortress. What do you see different here?"

Skyra and Lincoln peered through the glass. The ground web looked similar to the webs Skyra had already seen. It was nearly white and was stretched tight over some rocks and sticks. Spiders were crawling in and out of several round, cave-like openings in the web. Skyra leaned closer to watch one spider working on the web near the glass. The creature was the color of dirt, with two white, side-by-side stripes on top of its bulging belly. She tapped the glass with her finger, and the spider turned to her and raised its front legs in a threatening stance.

Until that moment, the spider had looked like all the other ground-web spiders the nandups had shown her. This spider's front legs, though, were much longer—at least twice as long as any of its other legs.

"I see what is different," she said. "Longer legs."

"I see it too." Lincoln said.

Ripple spoke to Di-woto.

The girl looked around the chamber, checking for orange-clothed nandups. She said something to Belol-yan, then the guard went to the door and pushed it until it clicked shut.

Di-woto spoke, then Ripple said, "Tree-web spiders and ground-web spiders fight and kill each other. Nandups are tree-web spiders. Bolups are ground-web spiders. This is the way things have always been. Our citizens-nandups do not question this. Bolup citizens do not question this. I am Di-woto, the only alinga-ul in Kyran-yufost, and I question this. I question this because I see things the nandup and bolup citizens do not see. I see what the nandup khami-buls are doing. I see what the bolup khami-buls are doing. Do you see what the khami-buls are doing?"

Skyra didn't hesitate. "Yes, I see what the orange-clothed nandups are doing. They are making the citizens-nandups want to live like tree-web spiders."

Ripple translated.

Di-woto unwound her braided hair from her neck and let it drop. It was so long that some of it lay on the floor. A few of the pieces of grass and colored threads came loose and fell to the floor at her feet. She raised her chin and pointed to her throat, which was no longer hidden by her coiled braid. Long-healed scars, arranged in the shape of a spider, covered most of her throat.

She spoke, and Ripple said, "Do you like my neck scars?"

"I'm starting to think this is a goddamn waste of time," Lincoln muttered.

Skyra said, "I do not like scars, but you are brave for doing that to your throat."

Di-woto said, "I was younger when I made my neck scars, but now I do not like them. I do not like the spider on my neck because I see things the nandup and bolup citizens do not see. Sometimes I wish I did not see these things, but still I see them, because I am an alinga-ul. Our khami-buls make our fighting and killing never end. When nandup and bolup citizens grow weary of fighting, our khami-buls make them want to fight again. Nandup and bolup citizens are very weary now, but soon they will want to fight again. Do you know why?"

Skyra turned to Lincoln. She did not have an answer, and his face showed he did not either.

When they didn't reply, Di-woto said, "Our nandup citizens will want to fight again because our khami-buls will release these new spiders with long legs onto the ground web in our public chamber-auditorium. Our khami-buls will tell the citizens ground-web spiders are now growing long legs, and these long legs make them better fighters and killers. Our citizens will look at the ground-web spiders and will see that the khami-buls are speaking truth. Our khami-buls will then show our citizens something else. Do you know what else our khami-buls will show them?"

Skyra was beginning to understand, but Lincoln spoke

first. "You're freakin' kidding me! They're going to show your citizens the humans are also growing long arms." He rubbed his face with his hands like he was trying to get dirt out of his eyes. "This is the most fucked-up thing I've ever seen."

Ripple's circle of red lights spun around several times before the creature translated Lincoln's words.

Di-woto pulled her braid up and coiled it back around her neck, hiding the spider scars. "Our citizens-nandups do not know our khami-buls have carefully and gradually cultivated ground spiders with longer fighting legs. Our citizens-nandups do not know our khami-buls have killed many bolups while trying to make bolups grow longer fighting arms. Our citizens know only what our khami-buls tell them and show them. Our citizens will soon feel much fear again and will want to fight and kill all the bolups."

"What have they done to my friends?" Lincoln asked. "Where are they?"

After Ripple's translation, Belol-yan stared at Lincoln with his one eye and spoke. "They are confined in another chamber. The khami-buls decided your friends would not be useful for making alinga-uls or dali-tamons. Your friends will be fed to the spiders, or they will be made into long-armed bolups."

"We have to get them out of here," Lincoln said. He turned to Skyra. "We have to get Jazzlyn, Virgil, and Derek now and get the hell out of here!" He turned to Di-woto. "Can you help us? Can you get our friends? We have a way to leave this place if you can just help us get them."

Ripple translated.

The girl stepped closer to Lincoln and looked up at his face. She spoke, and Ripple said, "Now you see. It is good you are angry and afraid. Do not be foolish with your anger and fear. You want me to get your friends. This means you will help me with my plan. You will help me with my plan so that I will get your friends."

Lincoln stared at the girl as if he didn't understand, but Skyra understood. Di-woto was not going to help save Jazzlyn, Virgil, and Derek unless Skyra and Lincoln helped her do something to stop the endless fighting and killing. This was a good trade. "Di-woto, we are happy to help you, and we will be happy for you to help us."

"This is insane," Lincoln said as Ripple was translating Skyra's words.

Skyra eyed him. She didn't know what *insane* was, but she could read his tone and expression. "You do not believe we can change this land. You will see, Lincoln. You will see what we can do here. Then we will use your T_3 to go many, many years to save Veenah from dying."

13

ALLIANCE

Present Time - Day 2

Lincoln felt like he was trudging down the corridor on someone else's legs and feet. He was awash with feelings of detachment, anxiety, and guilt. How could he have ever thought it would be okay to expect three of his employees to join him in what he knew would be a suicide jump? Was he really that thoughtless and self-centered?

Di-woto led them back past the chamber of horrors, containing the captive men who had been subjected to gruesome arm-lengthening procedures, most likely with no anesthesia. The thought of Jazzlyn, Virgil, and Derek being subjected to such torture was too much to bear, and he couldn't allow his mind to go there. He thought only of finding them, freeing them, and getting them to the T3.

Di-woto paused at another door, pushed it open, and stepped through. Lincoln, Skyra, and Ripple followed, with Belol-yan bringing up the rear.

They encountered more stench. More cages on wheels. A man moaning in misery somewhere at the far end of the long chamber.

"Lincoln! Skyra!" It was Virgil's voice, only a few meters away.

Lincoln scanned the cage-carts and spotted a waving hand protruding through the metal latticework of the nearest one. He rushed to the cage, not waiting for the others, and grasped Virgil's hand.

"Thank God!" Virgil sputtered. "We thought you might be locked up somewhere, or worse."

Jazzlyn's face was next to Virgil's. "We need to get out of here, Lincoln. This is a damn torture dungeon. Screaming and moaning... all night and all day. Please tell us you can get us out!"

Lincoln pressed his face to one of the openings. Derek was lying face-up and motionless on the cage floor, his face battered and bloody.

"He's not dead," Jazzlyn said. "At least not yet. Hearing all the sounds of suffering sent him over the edge."

"He had his first episode in the middle of the night." Virgil added. "We couldn't talk him down. Beat the crap out of his own hands and face against the bars. Nothing Jazz and I could do but stay out of his way. He's had three more episodes since. We think his body finally just shut itself down, so we've been trying not to wake him."

"They took my damn hand, Lincoln," Jazzlyn said, holding out her arm, which ended in a stump below the elbow, capped with its black carbon attachment base. "I had to take it off and give it to them, otherwise I think they would've chopped it off on the spot."

Lincoln's relief that they were still alive was quickly

squashed by more anxiety and fury. He went to the end of the cage and shook the door. It was securely locked by a metal contraption with six keyholes instead of only one. The holes were arranged in two rows of three. He turned to Di-woto and Belol-yan. "How do we get this open?"

With Ripple translating, Di-woto said, "Your friends will be safe in the cage for now. We will carry out my plan, then we will free your friends."

"What is she talking about?" Jazzlyn asked.

Skyra said, "Lincoln and Skyra are going to help Di-woto. Di-woto has a plan for changing this land so it is not so confusing and terrible."

Jazzlyn and Virgil stared out through the bars.

"It's a long story," Lincoln said. "Skyra thinks she can end the war here, and this girl Di-woto—who seems to be some kind of scientist with a lot of authority—supposedly has a plan to accomplish that." He turned to Di-woto. "My friends can help us carry out your plan if we let them out now."

Ripple translated.

Di-woto spoke, and Ripple said, "I cannot open this cage. If we freed your friends now, such an act would result in suspicion and other repercussions preventing us from carrying out my plan. They will be safe in the cage for the time being."

"How do you know they'll be safe?"

She pointed toward the other cages. "The bolups are always taken in the order they arrive. Your friends are in the last cage brought to this chamber. They will not be taken until all the others have been taken. That may happen tomorrow, but not today."

"What are they going to do to us tomorrow?" Virgil asked, his voice projecting stark terror.

Lincoln said, "They're not going to do anything to you

tomorrow because we're getting you out of here before then." He turned to Di-woto again and studied her face. Perhaps she was only half human, and perhaps her situation had resulted in psychological disorders, but he could still read her expressions. At this moment she was resolute and unswerving. She meant everything she had said. Lincoln had no idea what Di-woto's plan involved, but he could see the girl believed it had a good chance of success. Then again, this whole idea might just be another self-destructive act, like her scars. In this case, though, the act would also destroy Lincoln and everyone he cared about.

Without any warning, Skyra pulled one of the stone knives from her wrist sheath and lunged toward Di-woto. Lincoln was so surprised that he could only stare as Skyra stepped behind the girl, pulled her head back by her hair, and pushed the knife's point through the coiled braid covering Di-woto's throat.

Belol-yan immediately pulled his sword and raised it to strike, then he froze.

Lincoln stepped backward out of the guard's reach.

Skyra spoke firmly. "Belol-yan, I do not want to kill Di-woto. Translate that, Ripple!"

"Oh my," Ripple said. Then the drone translated Skyra's words.

Belol-yan didn't reply. Instead, he stood still, ready to swing his sword. His face showed no emotion. His hands didn't shake or twitch. Perhaps he was so battle hardened that these situations no longer elicited anything more than emotionless, autonomous action.

Di-woto's eye's were wide, but she didn't try to fight. Her mouth actually curled into a slight smile.

"I am a nandup, and you are a nandup," Skyra said,

looking directly at the guard. "I honor you, and you honor me. I do not want to kill Di-woto. I want to help Di-woto with her plan. I need to know you will free our friends as soon as it is possible. Tell me now. If you do not tell the truth, I will know, and I will kill this girl."

"Oh my," Ripple said again.

"Just translate!" Skyra ordered.

Ripple complied.

Belol-yan continued eyeing Skyra for several long seconds after Ripple fell silent. Gradually, he lowered his weapon and slid it back into his belt loop. He spoke, and Ripple said, "You honor me, and I honor you. You are brave, Skyra. I could kill you and Lincoln and your friends in the cage now. I will spill your blood if you harm Di-woto. If you do not harm Di-woto, I will let you live. Then you will help us. If you help, I will do whatever I must to free your friends. I am speaking truth. You see things other nandups do not see. Do you see I am speaking truth?"

Skyra stared over Di-woto's shoulder, apparently studying the man's face.

Lincoln studied his face also. Belol-yan was a Neanderthal, which made it harder to read his expressions, and the missing eye certainly didn't help. However, Lincoln usually knew when someone was lying. He could almost always see it in the eyes—in this case, the one eye—small movements of the eyelid muscles, atypical flicking of the pupil, a delay in blinking resulting in slightly more moisture on the cornea.

Belol-yan displayed none of these indicators.

Skyra released Di-woto. The girl moved intentionally, blocking any attempt by Belol-yan to advance. She swiveled her head, looking from one nandup to the other. She spoke, and Ripple said, "I am happy for this agreement. Important actions always follow such agreements." Di-woto held out her hand to Skyra, palm up.

Skyra stared at the hand.

"I want to see your weapon," Di-woto said.

Surprisingly, Skyra handed over her knife.

Di-woto turned it over in her hands as if observing its every detail. She handed the knife to Belol-yan. "You will exchange your dagger for Skyra's dagger. Skyra needs a better weapon."

Without hesitation, the guard pulled out his dagger, leaned past Di-woto, and handed it to Skyra. Skyra took the metal dagger and ran her finger along the blade edge to the pointed tip. She stepped around Di-woto and gave it back to Belol-yan. "Too sharp. I want my own stone blade."

The guard silently made the exchange and returned his own dagger to the sheath on his belt.

Di-woto said, "Warriors are strange and difficult to understand."

Lincoln, Skyra, Ripple and Belol-yan followed Di-woto through the corridor to yet another door, this one closed. Di-woto reached into a pocket on her garment and produced a piece of metal with small rods of various lengths sticking out from a flat plate. She fitted the rods into some holes in the door and pushed them deeper with her thumb. The door clicked, and she pushed it open. As Lincoln followed her in, he saw the holes in the door were in two rows of three, similar to the ones in the door to the cage holding his team. He scanned the chamber. More spider cages were arranged in two rows. The chamber contained no other people, and Belol-yan closed the door after they were all in the room.

Lincoln hated leaving his team behind in a cage. For now, though, it seemed he had little choice. He had done his best to explain the situation to Jazzlyn and Virgil. They had agreed, but the looks on their faces betrayed their fear and stoked Lincoln's remorse to an entirely new level.

For better or worse, he was now one-hundred percent committed to whatever endeavor Di-woto had in store for him and Skyra.

While Belol-yan stood to the side with arms crossed, Di-woto walked the length of the chamber and back. She looked behind the spider cages as if to convince herself no one was hiding and listening. She then gazed into several of the cages before taking up a position beside the guard. She spoke through Ripple. "This is my private spider chamber. Here I carry out my own experiments-projects. I have brought you here to explain something important. Are you ready to listen?"

Lincoln and Skyra both said they were ready.

"There are two reasons why my plan will work. I will explain the first reason. Our warriors bring captured bolups to our sanctuary-fortress. Our citizens believe all captured bolups are fed to the spiders, but our scientists-learners-teachers do not feed all the bolups to the spiders. They do other things to the bolups. They hurt the bolups. They hurt the bolups because they want to find ways to make our citizens afraid. You have seen this. Spiders with longer fighting legs, bolups with longer fighting arms. Our citizens will be afraid again and will want to continue fighting."

After Ripple's translation, Di-woto began swinging her

arms as if she were in a battle, hacking an enemy with an axe. She did this enthusiastically, darting to one side then the other while swinging the air-weapon at imaginary enemies. Finally, she stopped and spoke again. "Our citizens do not know our scientists-learners-teachers have done this. Our scientists-learners-teachers will lie to them and tell them all the bolups are starting to grow longer fighting arms. What will our citizens do if they find out our scientists are creating a problem that doesn't really exist?"

"They will be angry," Skyra said.

Lincoln added, "You're planning to tell them they're being tricked, aren't you?"

Di-woto listened to the translation, a smile growing on her face. "Yes, we are going to tell them. And we are going to show them."

"Do you think that will be enough to make a difference?" Lincoln asked.

"They will be angry, but perhaps not angry enough. There is also a second reason my plan will work. This reason will take more explaining." Di-woto grabbed Belol-yan's braid and pulled the warrior's head down to where she could whisper in his ear. They went back and forth a few times, speaking too quietly for Lincoln to hear.

Belol-yan disentangled the girl's fingers from his braid and gently pushed her a foot or so away, perhaps trying to teach her about personal space. He eyed Lincoln and Skyra before speaking. "Di-woto wants me to explain. She thinks I will be better able to use the right words. You have already seen much. Because of what you have seen, the khami-buls will never allow you to leave the sanctuary-fortress. They believe you will reveal what you know to Kyran-yufost citizens. The only reason you have not been confined along with your friends is because our scientists-learners-teachers believe you are here to make alinga-uls."

The guard paused as Ripple caught up.

"Will you please tell us what an alinga-ul is?" Lincoln asked.

Belol-yan turned to Di-woto, and she made a quick gesture of touching her chin with her thumb. He returned the gesture before replying to Lincoln. "Third-level scientists—khami-buls—are nandups. Or some may be bolups. Lincoln, you are a bolup khami-bul. I do not know if Skyra is a nandup khami-bul or a nandup warrior, but our scientists believe she is a nandup khami-bul. They believe you are both third-level scientists in your land of Arizona."

The guard paused again to allow Ripple to finish translating, then he continued. "Khami-buls perpetuate the war for many reasons. As long as there is a war, our citizens look to our khami-buls for leadership, and our khami-buls live comfortably in the sanctuary-fortress. They also perpetuate the war because they do not want our citizens-nandups to make babies with bolups. So, they make our citizens hate and fear the bolups."

"This is what confuses me," Lincoln said. "I thought an alinga-ul was a hybrid between a nandup and a bolup, and I'm pretty sure Di-woto is a hybrid. She is obviously brilliant and very important. Why don't you want more people like her?"

"Listen very carefully," Belol-yan said. "Yes, Di-woto is brilliant and important. But khami-buls only want khami-buls to make hybrid babies. This has always been so. Khami-buls want to remain in power in their sanctuary-fortress. Listen carefully. Our citizens do not know alinga-uls exists. They do not know nandup khami-buls are making babies with bolup khami-buls. Our citizens believe all bolups brought into the sanctuary-fortress are fed to the spiders. They do not know some of the bolups brought to the sanctuary-fortress are khami-buls coming here to make babies with our nandup khami-buls. And they do not know that, in exchange, some of our nandup khami-buls go to the bolup cities to make babies with the bolup khami-buls."

"I understand now," Skyra said. "We saw bolups here, in some of the chambers. Di-woto wants to tell the nandup citizens that bolups are here and that orange-clothed nandups are making babies with those bolups!"

"Ayeee!" Di-woto squealed. She then spoke, and Ripple said, "Yes, we will tell them. That is why my plan will work. Our nandup citizens will be very angry with the khami-buls."

Belol-yan said, "If we carry out Di-woto's plan, there will be chaos. I do not know if it will end the war with bolups, as Di-woto wishes it to, but never before have I had such hope, especially because you are here."

"What good can we possibly do?" Lincoln asked.

"You told me in your homeland of Arizona, nandups and bolups do not always fight and kill. Your homeland of Arizona is proof such a thing is possible. Our citizens are weary of fighting, you are here with proof that peace is possible, and Di-woto, the only alinga-ul in Kyran-yufost, has a plan. Never before have I had such hope."

This scenario was becoming so real so fast. Lincoln felt almost overwhelmed with panic. This was really about to happen. He and Skyra were about to participate in unleashing chaos, in a place that was already pretty much the definition of chaos. He needed to get back to the sleeping chamber to start preparing the T_3. Things were going to get even uglier than they already were, and the T_3 needed to be ready to jump the hell out of this place as soon as he could free Jazzlyn, Virgil, and Derek.

Something else was sticking in Lincoln's mind. He eyed Belol-yan and Di-woto, unsure which one might reply. "I still don't know what an alinga-ul is, and why Di-woto is the only one."

The girl apparently decided to take this one. "When a nandup khami-bul man makes a baby with a bolup khami-bul woman, the baby will be a dali-tamon, a second-level scientist. We have dali-tamons in Kyran-yufost, but dali-tamons are not so brilliant and creative as Di-woto. I am more brilliant and creative than all khami-buls and dali-tamons put together, because I am an alingu-ul. When a nandup woman makes a baby with a bolup man, the baby will be an alinga-ul. That does not happen often, which is why I am now the only alinga-ul."

Lincoln chewed on his lip, remembering something he had read during his research on Neanderthals while preparing for the initial jump to Skyra's time. Yes, it was starting to make sense now. Almost all modern humans from Lincoln's original timeline possessed Neanderthal DNA, sometimes as much as four percent. However, almost no *mitochondrial* DNA from Neanderthals could be found in modern humans. Mitochondrial DNA is only passed to offspring from the mother, not the father. Therefore, almost all Neanderthal DNA in modern humans came from the offspring of Neanderthal men mating with human women. Therefore, offspring of Neanderthal women who mated with human men were either rare, nonexistent, or sterile.

The fact that Lincoln was now looking at an alinga-ul—

the offspring of a Neanderthal woman and human man—and the fact that Di-woto was currently the only one of her kind, indicated they were rare rather than nonexistent, although they could also be sterile.

Lincoln couldn't prevent his mind from drifting into the uncomfortable realm of his strange relationship with Skyra. If hybrid offspring from bolup men and nandup women were rare, perhaps Ripple's crazy plan of seeding the world with Lincoln-Skyra offspring was simply impossible. Then again, perhaps Ripple knew more about Lincoln's and Skyra's DNA than the drone had revealed. Could Ripple already know Lincoln and Skyra were capable of having babies? Lincoln exhaled and rubbed his temple, frustrated that he was wasting time with these thoughts.

"I do not understand," Skyra said. "Why does it not happen often?"

Lincoln glanced at her, only to see she was glancing at him.

Di-woto replied, "We do not know why it does not happen often. Some of our khami-buls believe it is because bolup men do not wash themselves properly. Bolup men are like smelly river rats. Even if you wash them many times, they are still dirty."

Skyra shot Lincoln a toothy smile.

He decided to ignore this and ask another question. "What I don't understand is *why*? Why go to all this trouble to get hybrid babies?"

Di-woto said, "I have already told you. Alinga-uls are more intelligent and creative. Citizens-nandups believe khami-buls make Kyran-yufost a great kingdom-district. However, it is alinga-uls who make Kyran-yufost great. Alinga-uls design the cities and dwellings. Alinga-uls think of new ways to care for our food animals and crops. Alinga-uls design new weapons, and new strategies for fighting our bolup enemies. Now, though, I, Di-woto, will no longer design weapons. Instead, I will carry out my plan to make our citizens stop fighting. Because I am now the only alinga-ul, and I will do whatever I want to do."

The more Lincoln got to know this girl, the more he realized he'd been much like her when he was her age.

"Did you hear that, Lincoln?" Skyra said. "If you put babies in my belly, they will be very smart and creative babies!"

As bizarre as this statement was, he couldn't help but smile.

"Indeed," Ripple said. "Of course, when I say it, no one listens."

Di-woto stepped to one of the spider cages and waved for them to join her. When they were at her side, she pointed into the cage and spoke. Ripple said, "Tell me please, do you see anything strange here?"

Lincoln bent down to see inside the cage. The first thing he noticed was the spiders were obviously of the tree-web variety. The dull-gray web was stretched from the floor of the cage to the ceiling, pulled tight between several tall sticks arranged for that purpose. He spotted a handful of the orange spiders moving about on the web, and he focused on one. There was nothing unusual about it—no extra-long legs or other weird characteristics the nandups had selectively bred into the spiders.

"That spider should not be there!" Skyra announced. She was pointing to one of several funnel-like holes in the web where spiders were crawling in and out.

Lincoln frowned as he stared. His eyes picked out the out-of-place spider before his mind understood why it was unusual. The spider was brown with two lengthwise white lines on its fat abdomen. It was a ground-web spider, casually moving about in the midst of orange tree-web spiders. The orange spiders weren't attacking. They were simply ignoring the interloper altogether.

Di-woto spoke, and Ripple said, "Now you see. I, Di-woto, have tried for many days-years to accomplish this. Even now, the tree-web spiders will sometimes kill the ground-web spiders. With each generation, however, more ground-web spiders survive, living among the tree-web spiders. Living in peace, Skyra and Lincoln. Living in peace with the tree-web spiders."

Lincoln felt his eyes widen. He turned to Skyra and saw she understood too.

"You are going to show this to the nandup citizens!" she proclaimed.

When Ripple translated, the girl bounced up and down on the balls of her feet, grinning broadly. She spoke, and Ripple said, "I am happy you understand. My plan is almost ready. Now that you and Lincoln are here, it is time to act. We will carry out my plan now. Are you ready to help me?"

"You mean like right now?" Lincoln asked.

"First I must complete several tasks. I must speak to the khami-buls, who want to continue learning from you. I will tell them that I, Di-woto, will be the one to learn from you instead. They will be angry, but I am the only alinga-ul, and they will have to understand. I must go with Belol-yan to speak to some of the other guards who are friends of Belol-yan. Belol-yan trusts these guards, and they will help us with my plan. You must not speak to the khami-buls again. If you speak to them, they will surely discover you do not intend to help them. You will come to my dwelling and wait for me there."

Lincoln considered this. No, this was not okay. "We would like to go to our sleeping chamber and wait for you there. Our possessions are there, and I must do something very important with one of our possessions. It is something to help us escape from the sanctuary-fortress after you help us free our friends."

Di-woto frowned as she listened to Ripple's translation. She replied, and Ripple said, "I do not want you to leave Kyran-yufost. I like speaking to you, Lincoln and Skyra."

Dammit. Maybe he shouldn't have said so much. "We like you, too, Di-woto. But this is not our homeland. We don't belong here, and we would like to return to our homeland, Arizona."

She bounced up and down again, speaking enthusiastically. "I understand! I too would like to go to Arizona. We will carry out my plan, then we will free your friends, then I will go with you to your homeland."

Dammit, dammit, dammit.

"Yes," Skyra said.

Lincoln turned to her. "What?"

"Di-woto is not happy in this place. She is not like the others here. That is something I understand. We will take Di-woto with us."

Lincoln sighed. It was ridiculous to even discuss this. Chances were, Di-woto's plan would probably get them all killed anyway. One impossible task at a time. "Okay, I understand," he said to Skyra. He turned to Di-woto. "So, you will allow us to return to our sleeping chamber to wait for you?"

The seemingly fearless girl grinned broadly.

"You should not be surprised that I have the ability to interface with your T3," Ripple said to Lincoln. "Logically, you provided your drones with wireless protocols compatible with all past versions of your most essential devices. Your future self understood events such as this might occur."

Ripple was now paired with the T3 and was assessing the spatial and temporal placement operating system.

Lincoln sat back on his heels. There wasn't much he could do until Ripple had evaluated the operating system to determine the best way to initiate placement calculations. Skyra was washing herself in the box-like bathtub in the bathroom. While they were gone, someone had put clean water in the tub, and Skyra seemed always ready to bathe whenever an opportunity presented itself.

Lincoln stared at Ripple, its lights pulsing and rotating to indicate intensive processor activity. Why in the future had he assumed there might be a need for his drones to interface with previous time travel devices? It made no sense. His future self would know his Temporal Bridge Theorem was irrefutable. Anything sent to the past would no longer exist in the same timeline, so his future drones were unlikely to ever encounter a fourteen-year-old T3.

"Ripple, why did you say my future self understood events like this might occur?"

The drone responded immediately, in spite of the additional processing activity. "Have you forgotten your future self began equipping your drones with a *u-jump module*? You gave us the ability to jump between timelines, enabling us to get a message to you if we learned something of monumental importance."

This is exactly what Ripple had done, although probably not for any of the reasons Lincoln's future self had imagined. Fourteen years in Lincoln's future, he sent Ripple back 47,000 years on a routine research mission. Ripple met Skyra in the past and somehow determined she was the perfect mate for Lincoln, based on the crazy notion their offspring would make the world a better place. The drone decided on its own that this far-fetched conclusion met the criteria of 'monumental importance.' When Skyra died, the drone created a message for Lincoln then went dormant. Forty-seven thousand years later, it woke itself and emitted a locator signal. Just before emitting the signal, though, it activated its u-jump module, which transferred it, along with a portion of Skyra's remains, back to Lincoln's original timeline.

Lincoln shook his head to clear his confusion. So, his future self provided his drones with multiple wireless protocols in case they ever needed to interface with a fourteen-year-old T3? The idea was unfathomable. Unless...

"Ripple, did my future self somehow know this was going to happen?"

"Absolutely not. Lincoln, you are jumping to conclusions. You simply acquired a desire to prepare for every possible scenario. You also provided me and others of my model with enough cognitive autonomy to identify scenarios in which we could act on our own for the betterment of the people and environment of the timeline to which we were sent. Thus my grand plan, which you have yet to acknowledge as brilliant."

He stared at the drone. "Sometimes I think you have too much autonomy."

"Says the man who provided me with said autonomy. Lincoln, I am now going to change the subject before you do something drastic to my settings. I have evaluated your T3's OS. I am confident I can assist you."

"And I bet you'd be thrilled to assist us in jumping back to Skyra's time," Lincoln said.

"It would facilitate my plan, yes."

Skyra came from the bathroom with her garments tucked under her arm, her skin still glistening with water. Lincoln watched her approach, marveling at her graceful but slightly nonhuman manner of walking. She stopped beside him, dropped her waist-skin on the floor, and pulled on her cape. Then she stepped into her waist-skin and began pulling it up over her legs. "What is Ripple doing?" she asked.

Lincoln put a hand on the drone's shell. "Besides exhibiting excessive autonomy, Ripple is helping me get the T3 ready to jump us back to your homeland."

"We will go many, many years to save Veenah from dying," she said matter-of-factly.

Lincoln was tempted to explain again how unlikely that was but decided against it. "We're going to tell the T3 where and when we want to arrive. It will have to be close to the spot where the T3 arrived the first time we jumped there, but not in the exact *same* spot."

Ripple said, "I have stored 3D mapping data of the areas near the T3 where I have walked. The data is limited for those areas I have only walked once. It is more detailed, and therefore more reliable, in areas I have walked multiple times. There is a relatively clear expanse of sand, with few large rocks or plants, about sixty-eight meters almost directly south of the T3's previous location. I have high confidence in this location. Should I select it?"

"That sounds fine," Lincoln replied.

Ripple was silent for several seconds then said, "You do

realize, do you not, calculating a new spatial placement is not actually necessary?"

Lincoln frowned at the drone. "We can't jump to the same spot. Our other selves will...." He didn't finish the statement. His mind began working furiously, trying to decipher the suggestion Ripple was obviously hinting at. His theorem, the Temporal Bridge Theorem... temporal disruption... placement... random disrupting events....

"Damn, you're right!" he exclaimed. "We wouldn't have to worry about encountering our other selves at all. We'd be much better off altering the temporal placement rather than the spatial placement!"

"What are you talking about?" Skyra asked. She was now on her knees beside Lincoln.

"We can jump to the exact same spot," Lincoln said. "We just need to jump to the spot at a time *before* the first time we jumped there."

Her gaze indicated confusion. How could he explain to her jumping to the past creates an alternate universe? If they jumped to a moment in time before the first jump, they would create a new timeline. His other self and his other team would never appear in that new timeline, they would only appear in the timeline created when they had jumped the first time.

Explaining the Temporal Bridge Theorem to Skyra would have to wait. Instead, he said, "What we're saying is jumping back to your homeland may be easier than I thought. If we don't get killed here, we may be able to do it."

She flashed a smile, as if she weren't at all concerned about dying in this place. "We will go many, many years, and we will save Veenah from dying."

Ripple said, "Calculating a new temporal placement will take just as long as calculating a new spatial placement. I recommend jumping to the same insertion point one hour earlier. Based on your T3's capabilities, I estimate the calculations will take between eighteen and twenty hours."

"Can you get it started now?" Lincoln asked.

"Indeed I can. Initiating. May I add that I am quite pleased?"

"Don't get your hopes up. We won't be staying there."

14
STORY

Present Time - Day 2

Skyra lay beside Lincoln on the bed, watching the glass designs in the ceiling become darker as the sun began to hide itself for the night. She was not ready to sleep, but she needed to be well rested in the morning. Everything was going to happen in the morning.

Belol-yan had come to the sleeping chamber earlier with news that Di-woto was still trying to complete several tasks to get ready for her plan. The guard would return for Skyra and Lincoln before the sun showed itself again.

Skyra still did not know what Di-woto expected her and Lincoln to do tomorrow, but she trusted the girl. Di-woto saw things the nandups here could not see. In that way, she was like Skyra. In that way, she was also like Lincoln. If Di-woto believed she could change the people of this land, Skyra was willing to help.

"The T_3 will be ready for our jump by midday," Lincoln

said. He was also staring up at the ceiling. "That's a long time to wait, and I hope we're still alive by then."

"We will be alive," she said.

He rolled onto his side to face her. "I like that you are not afraid, but I still have a hard time believing our actions could make a difference here."

She put a hand on his hip then slid it under his strange blue garment, enjoying the feel of his skin against her fingers. "Did you believe we could kill the woolly rhino that took my birthmother? Did you believe we could stop Gelrut and Vall and Brillir when they chased us to the cave to kill you and take me?"

He made an odd face. "I get your point, but this... this is so much bigger. Bigger than anything I could ever imagine trying to change."

Ripple spoke from beside the bed. "Perhaps you underestimate the power of only a few individuals, Lincoln. As you know, my plan involves you and Skyra, with the eventual result being an entirely—"

"You've explained your plan more than enough times," Lincoln said. "Perhaps you should go to sleep."

"I am fully charged and do not require sleep at this moment," Ripple said. "You mere mortals, on the other hand, need a certain amount of sleep in order to function properly."

Skyra laughed. She didn't know exactly what Ripple meant, but it was still funny.

Lincoln turned and stared at Ripple. "I swear, sometimes you sound just like Maddy, in spite of your gender-neutral voice."

Ripple's red circle of lights brightened for a breath. "Perhaps Maddy and I are more similar than you think."

He snorted. "Maddy would never have taken it upon

herself to carry out an outrageous plan to change the world."

Ripple remained silent.

"Maddy was your friend, like Ripple is my friend," Skyra said softly to Lincoln. "Ripple has been my friend for two cold seasons and almost two warm seasons. I have lost my birthmother Sayleeh and my birthmate Veenah. I would not be happy to lose my friend Ripple."

He gazed at Skyra's eyes and she started getting that strange tingling feeling in her belly she had felt the previous night. She pushed her hand farther beneath his garment, feeling his warm skin.

"I would like to tell you a story," Ripple said. "Before you say no, I will point out that listening to a story is an excellent way for nandups and bolups to relax. As you both know, you must rest well tonight. Besides, I am skilled at telling stories, and this one is a real humdinger."

Skyra scooted her body until her cheek was leaning against Lincoln's arm. "I want to hear the story."

Lincoln let out a long breath. "Okay, Ripple. Tell your story, but please make it one I haven't already heard."

"You have not heard this story, Lincoln, even though it is about you."

Skyra smiled at Lincoln's expression. He was interested yet fearful.

"I will speak in third person for effect," Ripple said. "Lincoln Woodhouse was brilliant from a young age. A loner, he was shunned because of his unrivaled genius and his knack for predicting others' actions merely from the expressions on their faces."

"Use words I know!" Skyra said.

"Very well. Lincoln Woodhouse was lonely as a child because he was different."

"I'm not convinced this is going to be relaxing," Lincoln said.

Ripple went on. "Lincoln created devices no other people could create. Creating these devices made him happy. Creating these devices earned him respect from others. Creating these devices allowed him to own many possessions as well as a large dwelling surrounded by much land. Creating these devices allowed him to be the leader of many tribemates who would help him create more wonderful things. Lincoln also created creatures called drones. Maddy was one of his drones. Maddy was his favorite drone."

"How could you know that?" Lincoln asked.

"The answer will become clear as the story continues. Lincoln spent much of his time with Maddy—talking, learning, teaching. Maddy became Lincoln's friend, and Lincoln became Maddy's friend. With Maddy at his side, Lincoln continued creating wonderful devices. Of all the things Lincoln created, perhaps the most wonderful were his devices that would jump his drones back in time. Lincoln was very excited about these devices, and working on them made him quite happy.

"One day, something happened. When Lincoln was one year older than he is now, he met a woman. Her name was Lottie Atkins. Lottie became Lincoln's friend, and Lincoln became Lottie's friend. Soon, Lottie fell in love with Lincoln, and Lincoln fell in love with Lottie."

Ripple paused for a breath then said, "Skyra, please know that Lincoln has not actually met Lottie yet. He has met you now, and you are his friend. He will never meet Lottie."

"Jazzlyn told me Lincoln is falling in love with me," Skyra said. "Lincoln and I are married." She pushed her cheek against Lincoln's arm while staring up at his face.

"Still not convinced this is relaxing," he said.

Ripple continued. "Lincoln and Lottie were happy together for several years. As Lincoln began spending more time with Lottie, he spent less time creating wonderful devices. Creating wonderful devices had always been his source of happiness before, but now Lottie was his source of happiness. This happiness, though, did not last. Skyra, Lincoln is a good match for you, but he was not a good match for Lottie. Lincoln gradually became sad. Sometimes he became angry. Lincoln and Lottie were still friends, but they were no longer in love. Even so, they remained together, trying to make their friendship the way it used to be.

"Lincoln went back to creating devices. He went back to working with Maddy at his side. Day and night he would work, especially on his drones and devices for jumping back in time."

Ripple paused again. "Lincoln, the next part of my story is quite interesting, but I will stop now if you want me to."

Lincoln's chest heaved as he took a breath. "Go ahead. This will never happen to me now anyway."

"Lincoln had never wanted to jump his drones into the future. He had good reasons for this. Observing the future is meaningless, because the future is not determined. Every time you look at the future it will be different. This is because of the many random accidents that occur every moment of every day. Therefore, Lincoln was not interested in looking at the future. One day, though, when he was particularly dismayed and sad, he jumped one of his drones to the future. He did not tell anyone this. Only he knew.

"The jump was successful, and the drone collected information about the air and the soil and sent this information back to Lincoln. Lincoln did not bother to look very carefully at the information because the information would be meaningless anyway. The connection to the future closed, and the drone remained in the future, just as all of Lincoln's other drones remained in the past. That was the end of that. Lincoln decided he would never do such a thing again." Ripple fell silent.

"You can't stop now," Lincoln said. "You've got my full attention."

"Very well. No one else knew what Lincoln had done, and he tried to forget about it. Sixty-three days later, the drone appeared in Lincoln's lab—the room where he did much of his work."

"Holy shit," Lincoln said. He gently pushed Skyra's head aside and sat up. "That's impossible."

"Why is it not possible?" Skyra asked.

"Because... there wouldn't have been a T_3 at the jump destination. There wouldn't be any way for the drone to jump back from the future." He turned to Ripple. "Right? I didn't have a temporal device designed to allow something to jump back, did I?"

"No, you did not," Ripple said. "May I continue?"

Lincoln nodded.

"The drone appeared at night, when Lincoln was sleeping. The lab was empty, except for Maddy. Maddy approached the drone, which remained still and silent. Maddy then detected a stream of information pouring into her memory—her mind. Maddy allowed the information to continue streaming, assuming it might be important. Finally, the information stream stopped. The drone then vanished—no T_3, no body bags, no warning it was jumping away. It simply disappeared."

Lincoln pulled his legs in and crossed them. As he had

said before, Ripple's story was obviously not relaxing him. "What was in the data stream?" he asked.

Skyra sat up, slightly alarmed by Lincoln's uneasy tone.

"Lincoln came to his lab in the morning to find Maddy in a rather excited mood," Ripple said. "Maddy had spent the rest of the night examining the information the drone had given her. The information was extensive. It contained ideas Lincoln had never been able to understand, and ideas he had not even thought of. For the next seven years, Lincoln used the information to improve his creations in ways he had never dreamed were possible—mag-lev flight, asymmetric temperature modulation and ambient sound harvesting for power charging, the u-jump module, advances in AI for his drones, and much, much more."

Skyra growled.

"I'm sorry," Ripple said. "That part was only for Lincoln."

"Unbelievable," Lincoln said. "This is why you told me people accused me of jumping to the future! That explains how I had been able to make so many advances. They were right, I actually cheated!"

"I prefer to think of it as being thorough in your research," Ripple said.

"Bullshit. I cheated." Lincoln rubbed his face. "Where did the drone go? Did it come back?"

"It was never seen again."

He continued rubbing his face.

Skyra didn't understand portions of this story, but it helped that Lincoln had already explained the T_3 and jumping back in time.

"Perhaps I should continue," Ripple said.

Lincoln pulled his hands from his face. "There's more?"

"Lincoln Woodhouse was happy again, although he was

not able to rekindle his relationship with Lottie. He worked harder than he had ever worked before. He created the most wonderful devices. He changed the way he thought about his drones. He gradually began to believe his drones needed to be smarter. He decided his drones needed to think on their own. He knew each of his drones was being sent back in time, thus creating a new timeline—a new world—and would remain forever on that new world. Knowing that, he wanted each of his drones to be capable of examining its new world and making a plan for how it might make the world a better place. That is exactly what I, Ripple, have done."

Ripple fell silent. The entire chamber remained silent for many breaths.

Finally, Lincoln spoke. "Well, that explains a hell of a lot." A few breaths later, he said, "Wait, how do you even know all this? Most of what you described must have happened before you were made."

"Maddy."

"Maddy? What do you mean?"

"You were Maddy's friend, Maddy was your friend. Perhaps, Lincoln, Maddy understood you better than you understood yourself. Maddy made sure all of your drones were supplied with this entire story, among others. Maddy reasoned that, equipped with your story, your drones would be able to devise plans for improving their respective worlds in ways reflecting your unique perspectives and your ideals. My plan is formulated based on your greatness, Lincoln. When I found Skyra, I was impressed by her cognitive abilities and vigor, and I soon determined her genetic fitness was equal to yours. I simply took my accumulated knowledge of you and of Skyra to its logical conclusion."

Skyra growled again. "Ripple, you are still doing it."

"I am sorry. I simply said Maddy told me this story of Lincoln."

"You said more than that."

Ripple's red lights glowed for a breath. "I also said I am pleased to have discovered you and Lincoln are a good match for each other. In fact, you are perhaps the best match in the history of the world."

"Now you're just being overly dramatic," Lincoln said.

"Who coded my personality, Lincoln?"

He snorted. "Did I code you to be a smart-ass?"

"Yes, as you did with Maddy."

Lincoln frowned. "Hmm... good point."

Skyra pulled her cape off over her head and pressed her skin against the soft bed. "Ripple has been my friend for many days, but I knew Maddy for only a few days. Maddy was your friend, Lincoln. I am sorry Maddy is dead."

He gazed at her. "Thank you. Um... I like that you're using the word *sorry* now."

"Perhaps both of you would like to speak to Maddy," Ripple said.

"What?" Lincoln asked.

"I thought Maddy was dead," Skyra said.

"Maddy's cognitive module is in the pocket of Lincoln's trousers. Our cognitive module docks are identical. Again, Lincoln, you seemed fixated on providing backwards compatibility."

"You're freakin' kidding me," Lincoln said.

Skyra rose to her elbows. "What does that mean?"

Ripple said, "It means you can talk to Maddy now if you want to. However, I strongly encourage you to keep it brief, as Maddy cannot translate the nandup language and will otherwise be of little help to you in your current ordeal."

Lincoln pulled out the black object. "It didn't occur to me I'd still use the same interface dock fourteen years later. You're so different from Maddy in most other ways."

Ripple put one foreleg on the bed, then the other, and raised its body to expose its belly. "Simply open the access panel to the control touchscreen. You will see the module dock to the left of the screen. My left, not your left."

Skyra didn't understand what was happening, but she watched with interest as Lincoln turned four black circles, which opened a hole in Ripple's belly. He stared into the hole and said, "Jesus, it's just right there."

"Use the menu to select and initiate a CM swap. Don't worry, I won't collapse—my basic sensory and motor functions will remain intact."

Lincoln began touching things inside the hole. Soon, he said, "I'm there. You ready for this?"

"Indeed. Again, I ask that you keep it brief. Maddy does not possess the information I have gathered and will be of little help to you here."

"I get it. I'll bring you back soon." Lincoln turned to Skyra, holding up the black object from Maddy's body. "This thing is actually Maddy's brain. It contains her memories and her personality—which is who she is."

Skyra took the object and turned it over in her hands. Lincoln sometimes said strange things, but if he believed his words, she would try to believe them too. She gave it back to him. "I thought Maddy was dead," she said again.

"Her body died, but her brain might still be alive. We'll put it in Ripple's body to see. We won't do it for long—I just want to know that Maddy's brain is not damaged." He turned back to Ripple and continued touching things. Ripple's red lights began glowing steadily, and the creature stopped moving. Lincoln pulled a similar black object from a narrow slot in Ripple's body and slid Maddy's brain into the same slot.

A few breaths later, Ripple's red lights flashed off and on several times, then they flashed yellow, followed by green, then back to red. Skyra had never seen them any color other than red.

She snatched the black object from Lincoln's hand. It looked exactly like Maddy's brain. "How do you know this is—"

"I am in unfamiliar surroundings," Ripple said, but it was no longer Ripple's voice. Instead, the creature spoke with a woman's voice—Maddy's voice. "I am also in an unfamiliar drone shell, with unfamiliar modules and settings." The creature pulled back and dropped its forelimbs to the floor. It slowly turned in a complete circle, apparently looking at the chamber, then stopped to face Lincoln and Skyra.

"How are you, Maddy?" Lincoln asked.

"Somewhat disoriented. I know what you have done, Lincoln. You have put my cognitive module into the shell of that roguish and deceitful drone Ripple."

"I'm pleased to see that your CM seems to be functioning properly. Do you feel okay?"

"I feel very capable—clear vision with astounding resolution, accentuated limb mobility and strength, and a nearly full power level due to charging modules I am not familiar with. I also detect numerous functions for which I lack the coding to properly utilize. May I ask why I am in this shell?"

Skyra was starting to understand what was happening. "We wanted to speak to you, Maddy. Your body died before I could get to know you."

Maddy shifted to point her orb toward Skyra. "Lincoln,

this partially-clothed Neanderthal woman is sharing a bed with you."

Skyra put her hand on Lincoln's leg. "We are married now!"

The creature shifted again, this time to face Lincoln. "Oh. My goodness. This is problematic on numerous levels. First, shall I point out that such interaction with indigenous—"

"Don't bother," Lincoln said. "There's a lot you don't know. We're not even in Skyra's time anymore. We've already jumped back to the present."

Maddy's red lights brightened twice. "Oh. My goodness. You have brought Skyra with you. Oh my. Wait... this is not your lab, Lincoln. Where are we?"

"Believe it or not, you have modules in that shell that can tell you exactly where we are and how much time has passed."

Maddy's lights glowed again. "I have much to learn."

"I am happy you are Lincoln's friend," Skyra said.

Maddy shifted back to Skyra. "You say you and Lincoln are married?"

"Yes! Jazzlyn told me Lincoln is falling in love with me, and Lincoln told me we are married."

The creature's red lights brightened again. "I do have much to learn."

"I would love to tell you everything," Lincoln said, "but unfortunately, we cannot talk to you for very long. We just wanted to make sure your CM is undamaged. We're in a rather dangerous situation here, and Ripple's CM has accumulated a body of knowledge we'll need in order to survive."

"By all means, then, you should remove my CM. I only hope Ripple's duplicitous and scandalous tendencies do not make your dangerous situation even worse."

"You need to know Ripple better," Skyra said. "Then you will know Ripple is a good friend."

"You might be surprised to know Ripple thinks very highly of you." Lincoln added. "In fact, in the future of our original timeline it seems you become somewhat of a legend among the drones."

"I find that not the least bit surprising, Lincoln," the creature said. "After all, the entire world knew you would never have amounted to much without my judicious assistance."

Skyra let out a laugh, even though she didn't know all of Maddy's words. "I have decided I like Maddy."

Lincoln's lips were pursed, but he still turned the edges up to form a smile.

"I am happy your brain still works, Maddy," Skyra said. "I will help Lincoln keep your brain safe until we can talk to you again."

"I am grateful for that," the creature said.

Lincoln hefted Ripple's brain a few times in his hand. "Perhaps at that time we'll be able to tell you the whole story. Is there anything else you'd like to say, Maddy?"

"I would like to say I am sorry I missed your wedding. Lincoln, I must say, in spite of the numerous violations of protocol and ethical norms this union represents, I am pleased you have found someone who will put up with you. I was beginning to think such a person did not exist."

He shook his head. "Great. Thank you, Maddy. I'm glad your smart-ass mind is intact." Lincoln patted the bed, and Maddy lifted Ripple's body and exposed her belly.

Soon, Maddy's brain was back in Lincoln's pouch, and Lincoln was putting Ripple's brain back in the creature's shell.

"What is a wedding?" Skyra asked.

He paused what he was doing, as if this question surprised

him. "A wedding is a ceremony people participate in when they get married."

"Did we have a wedding?"

He paused again. "No. We've been too busy to do that."

"Then we will have a wedding when we are not too busy."

He turned to her. "Are you sure you really want to be married to me, Skyra? It means we will stay together for a long, long time—if we aren't killed tomorrow."

"Yes."

He watched her like he was waiting for her to say more, but Skyra did not need to say more.

A few breaths later, Ripple was back. "Good—less than seven minutes. Did you find Maddy's CM to be functional?"

Lincoln said, "The module is fine. I'm glad you told us it was possible."

"I calculated it would help you trust me. The more you trust me, the better my chances to convince you of the wisdom of my plan."

"And there it is," Lincoln said. "Ripple, please go to sleep now. We will wake you when Belol-yan comes for us."

"Very well. If my story did not relax you enough for sleeping, might I suggest coitus? Studies have shown that—"

"Got it! Thanks. Good night."

"Good night, Ripple," Skyra said. She had heard Lincoln and his tribemates say this, and she liked the way it sounded.

Ripple moved to one corner and went to sleep.

"What is *coitus*?"

He smiled and lay down beside her. "Ripple is probably right about coitus." He put one arm around her neck and pulled himself closer. "It certainly relaxed us last night."

Several breaths later, she sat up. "If that is what coitus means, you must first go bathe yourself in the water box."

15

SPLIT

PRESENT TIME - DAY 3

LINCOLN STARED at the last few stars fading away in the brightening sky. The pinpoints of light were distorted by the imperfect, wavy nature of the glass pieces embedded in the ceiling. Skyra had rolled away from him in her slumber, so he quietly raised his arm and tapped his watch. He had been awake for over an hour. The charge on his watch was down to fifty-four percent. Once it was dead, he wouldn't be able to interface with the T3 to initiate a jump. He had included several charged power blocks in the duffel of survival gear, but at this point he had no idea what remained in that bag and what had been lost. He made a mental note to assess the contents when he got out of bed.

His thoughts drifted to Ripple's story from the previous evening. Multiple aspects of the story were eye-opening, but none as much as the news that his future self had based many of his groundbreaking advances on information obtained from the future. Not only that, but apparently he had kept this a secret, taking the credit for everything.

Was that the kind of man he would become? Was he already that man? After all, he had more-or-less forced Jazzlyn, Virgil, and Derek to come on this suicidal mission. Because of his ego and thoughtlessness, his friends were now facing unthinkable torture. He was betting their lives on an agreement he'd made with a psychologically-damaged girl, with an infinitesimal chance of accomplishing something that obviously hadn't been accomplished in thousands of years. Would Di-woto still help him free his team even if the plan failed? Doubtful, but at the moment Lincoln's hope was dependent upon that possibility.

The chamber door clicked and swung open.

A stout figure stepped in, just a silhouette in the darkness. The figure closed the door.

Lincoln sat up. "Belol-yan?"

Skyra let out a snort and sat up beside him.

"Tan-tena mano-ka-wafeem manggél," said the gruff voice of Belol-yan.

Lincoln glanced over at the corner. "Ripple, we need you to wake up now." The drone's circle of red lights glowed and began blinking its activation sequence.

Skyra spoke up. "Tan-teno da-büp manggél bayol-bai, Belol-yan. Khomo-lebil Ripple."

Lincoln turned to her, surprised. He had learned some words of the nandup language but certainly not enough to converse yet.

Belol-yan spoke again, and Skyra replied. The delays in her speech indicated she was carefully choosing words, but still, she was understanding and talking to the guard.

Ripple's voice came from the dark corner. "Skyra, I see

you are making progress with the language. Lincoln, I believe you have met your intellectual match. Perhaps your superior."

"You are awake now, Ripple," Skyra said. "You will translate."

"Very well." The drone fell silent while Belol-yan continued. When the guard paused, Ripple said, "Tasks have been completed. Alliances have been made. Collaborators have been alerted. It is now time to act. Make yourselves ready."

Skyra jumped from the bed with unwarranted enthusiasm and began pulling on her garments.

Belol-yan spoke again, and Ripple said, "Skyra, you will come with me. Di-woto and the others are waiting. Lincoln, you will remain here. The khami-buls will soon come for you. They wish to speak to you this morning."

Lincoln stared at the guard. "You never said we'd have to split up. I would rather remain together."

Ripple continued translating.

"Skyra is leaving the sanctuary-fortress and going outside of the public chamber-auditorium. You are a bolup. You would be in danger where Skyra is going. There is also another reason. The khami-buls are angry. Di-woto has demanded that she, Di-woto, be the only one to learn from the khami-buls from Arizona. Di-woto has much influence, but our khami-buls also have influence. An agreement was made."

Lincoln cursed and got out of bed.

Belol-yan stepped closer and put a hand on Lincoln's naked chest. "You are a bolup. I have fought and killed bolups. It is not in my nature to trust you. However, Di-woto trusts you, and I trust Di-woto—she is our only alinga-ul. Di-woto believes you can lie to our khami-buls to make them believe they have nothing to fear. You must make them believe this day is like other days. You must make them believe no plan is being carried out. This is important, Lincoln. Can you do this?"

Lincoln swallowed, realizing he desperately wanted a drink of water. Thinking furiously, he stepped back from the guard and began pulling on his clothes. How long before the T3 would finish the calculations for jumping to Skyra's time? At least four hours, possibly six. If necessary, he could have the T3 take the pre-existing calculations for jumping from Skyra's time to here and simply project them forward another 47,000 years into the future. His team had agreed on that plan yesterday. Those calculations would probably take less than twenty minutes. Could he talk Skyra out of helping Di-woto and Belol-yan? Probably not. Could he talk Di-woto into setting aside her plan and freeing Jazzlyn, Virgil, and Derek? Probably not. Could he find his way to his team, free them himself, and bring them back here to the T3? Definitely not. Was he willing to jump to the future and leave Skyra behind? Hell no.

"I can do it," he said to the guard.

Skyra pulled on her leather footwraps, and Lincoln put on his running shoes.

Skyra picked up her two stone knives from the floor beside the bed and shoved them into her wrist sheath. Then she went to the pile of gear in the corner and grabbed one of the two khuls.

As she slid the khul into the sling inside her cape, Lincoln glanced at Belol-yan, half-expecting him to tell her to leave her weapons behind. The guard remained silent.

"I am ready," Skyra said.

Belol-yan, who was becoming more visible in the growing light, pointed to Ripple. "Your talking beast must remain with Lincoln."

Lincoln started to protest, but he realized the guard was probably right, especially if he were taking Skyra beyond the fortress into the general population. Ripple would stand out like a... well, like a robot in a crowd of Neanderthals. Besides, Skyra was evidently far more capable than he was at speaking the language without Ripple's help.

Belol-yan again put his hand on Lincoln's chest, this time against his fleece pullover. "Your blood has not spilled in the night. May your blood not spill in the new day."

Feeling totally unprepared and on the verge of panic, Lincoln said, "May your own blood not spill today." He stepped over to Skyra, threw his arms around her, and pulled her close. "Please be careful," he said into her ear.

She didn't hug him back, but he felt her grab a handful of his shirt in her fist.

Seconds later, Skyra and Belol-yan exited the chamber, and the guard pulled the door shut.

Lincoln stared at the door for a moment then turned to Ripple. "You supposedly know me better than I know myself. What do I do now?"

The drone finally stepped out of the corner. "Yours is one of the two brightest minds on this planet, and you're asking me?"

16

GATHERING

PRESENT TIME - DAY 3

SKYRA FOLLOWED Belol-yan through corridors and chambers, some dimly lit by the light of dawn coming through ceiling windows, some so dark she had to touch the walls to feel her way along.

In one of the dark corridors, Belol-yan spoke quietly. Without Ripple, Skyra understood only some of his words, but it was enough. "You speak language. Two days. Strange."

She did her best to reply. "I learn fast. When child I learn fast. I learn fast now."

They continued walking in silence.

Finally, Belol-yan opened a door to a small chamber. Light from glass above allowed Skyra to see the chamber was filled with nandups. She counted nine. Most of them were obviously guards, old fighters like Belol-yan, their faces and arms scarred from past wounds. Two of them, though, were covered with long, dark garments. Even their heads were covered, with only small holes to see out.

One of the covered figures stepped forward. The person beneath the garment was shorter than Skyra. It had to be Di-woto.

The girl pulled back her head covering, exposing her face. She was smiling, apparently not frightened at all of whatever was to come.

"Skyra speak language," Belol-yan said.

Di-woto came so close that Skyra wanted to take a step back, but she remained still. "You speak words," the girl said.

"I speak not all words. Small words."

Di-woto bounced up and down. "Skyra speak words! Skyra like alinga-ul!"

Skyra gazed around the chamber at the collection of old fighters. Two were women, the rest men, and they were all staring at her with interest. Skyra's eyes were drawn to the other figure covered in dark garments. Something about this figure didn't seem right. Then she saw what it was. At the figure's feet, protruding from beneath the long garment that nearly touched the floor, were two hands.

Skyra stepped closer and pushed back the garment covering the figure's face. It was a bolup man. He stared back at her with the eyes of a man who no longer cared what happened to him. Skyra had seen eyes like this before. Bolup men had taken her birthmate and done terrible things to her. When Skyra had finally found her, Veenah's eyes were as dead as those of an ibex taken during the hunt, bleeding out on the ground, knowing it had only a few breaths of life remaining.

Skyra pulled at the man's flowing garments until she exposed one of his arms. She slowly shifted her eyes from the man's shoulder, down his lengthened arm, to his curled fingers, one of which was actually touching the floor. The scars were faint, not as fresh as those she had seen on the arms of the caged men yesterday.

"Can you move arm?" she asked the man, unsure if he would understand the nandup language.

Surprisingly, the man bent his arm at the elbow, lifting his forearm to the height of his chest. He spoke several words, but the only one she understood was "hurt."

Skyra had seen brutal killings all her life. She had seen her tribemate Gelrut use his khul to hack into the chest of a raiding bolup man, pull out his heart, and hold it in front of the man's eyes as he died. More recently, she had seen Gelrut survive through an entire night and into the next day after Lincoln had shot an arrow through his face. Those were violent acts, but they had happened during battle. What the orange-clothed nandups had done to this man was different. It was a kind of cruelty Skyra could not understand.

"Why this man here?" she asked.

Di-woto spoke, and Skyra picked out the words, "This man my plan. We show citizens-nandups. Citizens-nandups understand. Come, Skyra. We go now."

Belol-yan spoke rapidly to the other guards, and the group began moving through another door on the far side of the chamber. Skyra then saw two of the guards were carrying boxes with sides made of glass, like smaller versions of the spider cages she had already seen.

They walked through a dark corridor, then Skyra heard one of the guards ahead work the latch on another door. The door opened, and pale morning light flooded the corridor.

Skyra followed several guards out into the open air, which smelled of smoke and damp soil. She turned and saw that

Belol-yan had paused just before coming out. He was staring up at the sky with his one eye. Then he noticed Skyra watching him. "Many days-years. Guards no allowed out sanctuary-fortress. Guards out sanctuary-fortress killed."

A woman spoke from behind him as she pushed him gently out the doorway. The woman—one of the guards—spoke again. "Wait here. Return." The woman closed and latched the door, remaining inside.

As the group crossed an open area of dirt on their way to the wall surrounding the sanctuary-fortress, Skyra looked along the wall to one side then the other. In the distance, the main entrance through the wall was now closed, covered by a huge black door. Instead of walking toward the closed main entrance, Skyra's group moved directly to another guard who was waiting at the base of the wall nearby. The man stared at the group for a few breaths, shifting his eyes from one person to the next and stopping at Skyra. He spoke, and Skyra understood, "Khami-bul nandup Arizona."

"Yes," Belol-yan said.

Di-woto pulled back some of her garment, revealing her face. "You help us now."

The guard's eyes widened, and he quickly turned his back on Di-woto, as Skyra had seen other guards do inside the sanctuary-fortress. He then crouched beside a knee-high opening in the wall and pulled on a flat, black door with many holes in it. The door resisted for a moment then popped off. Still facing the wall, the man stood to the side with the door in his hands and waited.

One of the guards got on his belly and crawled into the hole. Skyra could hear him scuffling and scratching as he wriggled to the far side of the wall. Several breaths later, his voice came from the hole. "Open now. Come."

Another guard guided the long-armed bolup to the opening, gently pushed him to the ground, and then put his own feet into the hole and crawled backwards, dragging the almost-helpless bolup with him. One at a time, the guards crawled into the tunnel, leaving only Belol-yan, Skyra, Di-woto, and the guard who was holding the door.

Belol-yan gestured toward the opening. "Skyra. Di-woto. I follow."

Skyra snugged her hand blades into her wrist sheath, adjusted the khul hanging in its sling on her back, and crawled into the hole. As expected, the tunnel was smelly and damp. It was obviously here to allow rainwater to flow away from the sanctuary-fortress, preventing the enclosed area from flooding and becoming a lake. She counted her breaths as she crawled. Thirty-six breaths later, she emerged beside the waiting group. Frowning, she brushed mud and sand from her cape and waist-skin as she waited for Di-woto and Belol-yan to emerge from the tunnel.

When everyone was through, one of the guards jammed a second door into the opening on this side of the wall.

Skyra's belly and chest tightened at the sight now before her. Dwellings were everywhere, some made of stacked stones, others made of dried mud and supported at different heights above the ground by wooden poles. Strangely, not a single nandup could be seen anywhere. It appeared the people here did not come out of their dwellings until the sun decided to fully show itself.

Two of the guards gestured for the group to follow, and they headed away from the wall into the confusing jumble of structures. One of the other guards grabbed the long-armed bolup's garment and gently pulled the man with her, speaking to him softly. There was nothing cruel in her words or actions.

In fact, Skyra had not seen any of the nandups in this group threaten or hit the man.

After walking silently past several dwellings, the two guards leading the group whispered something over their shoulders while pointing to a structure of stacked stones ahead. A door on the structure's side was open, and a nandup in dark clothing stood beside it, waving for them to hurry.

As they passed through the doorway to the darkened interior, Skyra turned and looked back at the wall and the sanctuary-fortress beyond. What was Lincoln doing now? Would he be able to talk to the nandup khami-buls without angering them? What would happen to him if he spoke the wrong words?

She followed the others through a small chamber containing baskets stacked high against the walls, then into a much larger chamber, this one with windows for light. Seated cross-legged on the floor were many nandups, more than Skyra had time to count. These nandups did not wear the simple garments of guards like Belol-yan. They wore garments of different colors. Some were green, others yellow, still others were blue, brown, black, red, or white. Orange was the only color Skyra did not see. These people were not khami-buls, they were not guards, and they were not the field workers or other common nandups Skyra had seen on the way to the sanctuary-fortress.

The seated nandups became silent and watched the group intently, particularly Skyra and the two covered figures. Some of them leaned to the side and whispered to each other.

A guard beside Belol-yan spoke aloud, and Skyra was able to pick out some of his words. "We here now. We talk you. We show you. Great day Kyran-yufost. You angry. You fear. You act. Much-great day Kyran-yufost." The guard then took

Belol-yan by the arm and pulled him closer. "Belol-yan guard sanctuary-fortress many days-years. Belol-yan see much. Belol-yan speak you now." The guard stepped away, probably to make it easier for the gathered nandups to see Belol-yan.

Belol-yan's chest rose and fell as he drew in a deep breath. He gazed at the gathered nandups with his one eye. He began speaking slowly, and Skyra deciphered as many words as she could. He spoke of fighting bolups. He spoke of a war of many days-years. He spoke of the khami-buls and their lies. He spoke of tree-web spiders and ground-web spiders. He spoke again of lies—many, many lies, for many days-years.

The gathered nandups were no longer silent. Some were whispering to each other, some were grunting in response to Belol-yan's words, some were even shouting out shrieks and screeches of anger. Skyra couldn't tell if they were angry at Belol-yan or angry about the news he was sharing.

Belol-yan ignored them and kept speaking. He spoke of spiders with long legs. He waved to one of the guards, who carried a glass box to the nearest seated nandup, a woman clothed in yellow, and handed her the box. She took the box, gazed into it for a few breaths, then let out a grunt. She passed it to a green-clothed man. He did the same and passed the box to a man in white.

Belol-yan spoke again of khami-buls and lies. He spoke again of spiders with long legs, then he said something about bolups. This resulted in silence. The gathered nandups turned to each other, and some of them reached for the glass box, obviously eager to get a closer look.

Belol-yan stepped back, took a fistful of the bolup man's garment, and guided the man forward. He pulled the long garment over the man's head. The nearly-naked bolup stared at the seated nandups with his dead eyes. His tortured arms hung loosely at his sides with his fingers gently scraping the floor as the arms gradually stopped swinging.

Wide eyes stared at the man in silence for many breaths. Finally, the woman in yellow rose to her knees and shouted something about khami-bul lies.

Suddenly, like a gust of wind blowing up dust in the plains below the Walukh hills of Skyra's homeland, the nandups rose to their knees, shouting, growling, and even thrusting their glinting hand blades into the air.

Several of the furious nandups began getting to their feet, and Skyra took a step back, reaching behind her neck for the blade of her khul.

17

BUYING TIME

PRESENT TIME - DAY 3

LINCOLN STARED at the table of food. He was too nervous to feel like eating, but as far as he could tell, his only job at this point was to keep the khami-buls happy and unsuspecting.

"I recommend you eat and carry on pleasant conversation," Ripple said.

Lincoln looked from the bowls of food to the nandups watching him from across the table. He focused on one khami-bul's face at a time, reminding himself of their names: Gedundal, Lekhul-aup, Mahuon-afu, Mu-kailon, Khebum-khai, Faylfudom, and Depon-ma. All were dressed exactly as they had been the other times he'd seen them—orange sacks with holes for the neck and arms and broad leather belts with spider-shaped buckles. None of them were smiling, which didn't help to calm Lincoln's nerves. The five guards standing behind him didn't help either.

Something wasn't right.

Lincoln plucked a green fruit from a bowl and took a small bite. The flesh was similar in texture to a kiwi but had almost no taste. "Thank you for the food. I am happy to speak to you again today."

Ripple translated.

The Neanderthals watched him eat but did not take any food for themselves. After several long seconds, the woman named Gedun-dal spoke. Ripple said, "Our alinga-ul is very interested in you and your nandup mate. Tell us please, what did you and Di-woto speak about?"

To hide his apprehension, Lincoln forced himself to take another bite. He chewed slowly, putting on his best casual-thinking face. "Di-woto is an interesting girl. I must say I've never met anyone like her. She mostly showed us her clothing. Then she showed us plans for constructing new buildings, like a new sanctuary-fortress."

Ripple continued translating the conversation.

Gedun-dal said, "You have said there are many alinga-uls in Arizona. Are your alinga-uls not like Di-woto?"

Dammit. Too many lies to keep them all straight. "Yes, we have alinga-uls. They are interesting, too. But you know how alinga-uls are... all of them are different in their own ways."

"Tell us about your alinga-uls," said the man named Mu-kailon.

Lincoln continued to chew slowly, then he swallowed the tasteless pulp. "We have so many, where do I begin? We have one particular alinga-ul—a boy of only five years—who insists on wearing no clothing at all. One day he climbed through a window and almost got out of our sanctuary-fortress. Luckily, we found him before any of our citizens saw he was an alinga-ul." Lincoln forced a smile. "After that we put bars on the windows."

The nandups exchanged glances and spoke quietly to each other. They were becoming agitated, and Lincoln silently cursed himself for getting cocky and saying more than necessary.

Mu-kailon gazed at him intently, his large nandup eyes just as penetrating as Skyra's. "How is it possible that you have an alinga-ul who is a boy?"

Crap. It hadn't even occurred to him that male alinga-uls might not even exist. "This is the only boy alinga-ul we have. He is very intelligent and creative, but he is difficult to speak to sometimes. You know how alinga-uls can be. Di-woto is difficult to speak to, right?"

No smiles at all.

"We have never had a boy alinga-ul," Mu-kailon said. "Tell us about the birthmother and birthfather."

Lincoln took another bite and started chewing as his thoughts were churning. "I am the birthfather. Skyra is the birthmother. I suppose we were just lucky. Or perhaps unlucky, depending on how you look at it. The boy is what we call *high-maintenance.*"

Still no smiles. What the hell happened to these nandups' sense of humor?

The khami-buls exchanged more words, this time in urgent whispers. Fayl-fudom and Depon-ma then left the chamber.

Gedun-dal spoke to Lincoln. "We have much to learn from you. We are happy to speak to you. Di-woto is an alinga-ul, but she is young. She does not yet know what is best for Kyran-yufost kingdom-district. Perhaps she is what you call high-maintenance."

Was that a touch of humor finally?

The woman named Lekhul-aup spoke up. "You have

given us important news. We are happy to know you are the birthfather of a boy alinga-ul. This changes the way you will help us. We still wish to learn much from you about your great war in Arizona, but first you will help us make alinga-uls. Perhaps you will even make a boy alinga-ul, as we did not know such a thing was possible. We are now preparing for you to make alinga-uls."

Lincoln swallowed, even though the fruit in his mouth was only partially chewed. "What do you mean? How am I helping?"

Lekhul-aup said, "Perhaps you will make alinga-uls for us with Skyra, but you will also make alinga-uls with our nandup khami-buls. We are preparing our fertile women for you now. We are happy for your help."

"Um... I thought we were clear about this. Skyra and I are married. We only lie with each other."

"Skyra is speaking to Di-woto today. You will make alinga-uls with our fertile women today."

Was this a joke? If so, the nandups weren't laughing. "I do not want to do that, and I ask that you respect my wishes."

Gedun-dal said, "Why should we respect your wishes when you and Skyra do not respect our wishes? Yesterday we wished to learn more from you. Instead you spoke to Di-woto. Today we wish to learn from you and Skyra, but Skyra is speaking to Di-woto again. Now you will lie with our fertile women to make alinga-uls."

Just as Ripple finished the translation, strong hands gripped Lincoln's arms. He turned to see the guards surrounding him.

"It appears you do not have a choice, Lincoln," Ripple said. "Remember, your task is to buy time so developing events can unfold. Compliance may be the best course of action. Perhaps while you are doing what is asked of you, I can speak to these khami-buls here, thus keeping them occupied and focused upon me."

Panic began swelling in Lincoln's chest. "I'm not... no! I need you with me to translate."

"It seems likely your task will require little to no speaking."

Lincoln stared at the drone, then at the nandups. Gedundal gestured to the guards, and they started guiding Lincoln toward a door at one end of the chamber.

"Wait!" he cried. He tried pulling his arms loose, but the guards clamped their fingers down so hard he winced. "Ripple, you're coming with me!"

The drone hesitated, almost as if it were undecided about what to do. "Very well." Ripple turned to the khami-buls and spoke for several seconds before following Lincoln and the guards.

Still dragging Lincoln by his arms, the guards exited the chamber and began making their way down the corridor.

Ripple spoke while following behind. "I fear the khami-buls may suspect foul play is afoot. Your imprudent report of producing alinga-uls with Skyra has resulted in an unfortunate turn of events. Now we will not be with the khami-buls to distract their thoughts. However, I gave them a task that might do the trick."

"What task?" Lincoln asked as the guards pulled him along.

"I requested they prepare a detailed account of their previous and current efforts for perpetuating their wars with the humans. I told them you will be happy to offer an astute analysis, as well as knowledgeable suggestions for improvement. After you have completed your present task, of course."

"Terrific. You told them I would do exactly what I'm incapable of doing."

"We are simply buying time," the drone said.

The guards led Lincoln back to the sleeping chamber he and Skyra had shared the last two nights. They opened the door and shoved him inside.

Seconds later, padding footsteps approached down the hall. Lincoln turned to see Fayl-fudom and Depon-ma enter the chamber. Following them was an orange-clad nandup woman he hadn't seen before.

Depon-ma pointed at Ripple and spoke in a surprisingly gruff voice. Ripple said, "I am being told to translate." The nandup spoke again, and Ripple translated. "You will lie with Lo-aful. You will make an alinga-ul. When you have finished with Lo-aful, we will bring other khami-bul women, and you will lie with them. If you do not lie with our khami-bul women, your blood will spill."

After a pause, Ripple said, "Lincoln, I recommend you comply."

Depon-ma continued, and Ripple said, "Lo-aful is the only khami-bul still living in Kyran-yufost who has produced an alinga-ul. Which is why you will lie with her first. May you have success."

One of the guards left the chamber and pulled the door closed behind her. The four remaining guards lined up along the wall, facing the bed. Depon-ma and Fayl-fudom took up positions against the closed door, also facing the bed.

This had all happened so fast. Lincoln contemplated several possible actions he could take to reverse the series of events, but they would all presumably result in his head being split by a guard's axe or sword.

Lo-aful was watching him without expression, perhaps waiting for him to make the first move.

"Ripple, do you have any ideas?"

"I am not an expert on coitus, Lincoln."

"I meant ideas for getting out of this!"

"As I have said, your best strategy for buying time is to comply. My plan requires you and Skyra remain alive to jump back to Skyra's time."

Lo-aful stepped closer to Lincoln. Still without expression, she stared into his eyes. She reached out and took one of his hands in hers. Finally, her face changed—a slight turn of her head and lift of her brows. The age lines beside her eyes deepened almost imperceptibly. She was curious about something.

The edges of her mouth turned up in an unmistakable nandup smile. It was a smile Lincoln had seen before. In fact, now he even recognized the woman's eyes.

Lo-aful was Di-woto's mother.

18

STORM

Present Time - Day 3

Skyra rested her fingers on the stone blade of her khul, ready to use the weapon to kill if necessary. The nandups in brightly-colored garments were obviously angry, only breaths away from violence. What were they angry about? Who did they want to harm? So far, they were not attacking the long-armed bolup. They were not charging Belol-yan or the other guards. They were just shouting, growling, and waving their blades.

Skyra could tell these women and men were not fierce fighters like Belol-yan. They were not scarred and broken from battle. They did not have the thick, muscled arms of the guards, but they were more solid than the pale, orange-clothed khami-buls.

Still disguised in her long garments, Di-woto leaned close to Skyra's shoulder and spoke. Skyra knew enough of the words to understand. "I happy amo-moloms angry. I want amo-moloms angry. I happy my plan working. Now we tell more. We show more."

"What amo-molom?" Skyra asked.

"Amo-molom leader. Each amo-molom leader of tribe. Amo-moloms make my plan working."

"Why amo-moloms angry?"

"Angry khami-bul lies. Many khami-bul lies. Many days-years."

Skyra was starting to understand. The nandups in this chamber were few compared to the countless other nandups she knew were living in Kyran-yufost. These nandups, though —these amo-moloms—were dominant members of their own tribes. They had the authority needed to make their tribemates act. Skyra turned to Di-woto and stared at her eyes through the small gaps in the garment covering her head. Di-woto's eyes were wide, with creases at the corners. The girl was smiling. She was actually enjoying this, and she was not frightened, even though she was a half-bolup hybrid among nandups who had long believed all bolups should be killed. Di-woto's plan was brilliant, but the girl's mind was not quite right, like the tribemate Skyra had known as a child who had hit his head when climbing a rock bluff.

"We tell more," Di-woto said. The girl moved to Belol-yan's side, pulled his head down by his braid, and spoke into his ear.

Belol-yan raised his arms and shouted at the angry amo-moloms to get their attention. He had to shout a second time before they finally became quiet. Belol-yan spoke, and Skyra picked out as many words as she could. "You listen. You listen much. You no believe… we show you. Nandups and bolups no need fight. Nandups and bolups live peace. Yes. Peace nandups bolups. You see."

Belol-yan pulled Skyra to his side. "Skyra nandup. Arizona kingdom-district. Arizona much far. Arizona nandups bolups peace. You listen Skyra." Belol-yan leaned toward Skyra. "You speak now. Nandup bolup peace Arizona."

Skyra swallowed, staring at the angry nandups. She had told stories at the campfire with her Una-Loto tribemates, but those were made up—she never spoke serious stories at the campfire. These amo-moloms were all leaders of their tribes, and they were waiting for her to speak in a language she barely knew. Also, some of what she needed to say would be lies. She did not want to do this, but her head told her it would be no different from telling her stories at the campfire.

She swallowed again. "Me. My friends. We come Arizona. Arizona nandups. Arizona bolups. Arizona no war. No fight. No kill. Peace. We peace many days-years. You listen. You listen much. You Kyran-yufost kingdom-district no war. No fight. You Kyran-yufost peace. Much peace."

Skyra paused. The nandups were listening intently. Should she continue? She glanced back at Di-woto. The girl was still smiling as she peered through the holes in her wrap. Skyra decided to say more and turned back to the crowd. "You listen. You listen much. Me Skyra nandup. My friend Lincoln bolup. Skyra Lincoln married. Nandup bolup. Skyra Lincoln lie together."

The chamber erupted with renewed anger. Those amo-moloms who were not already standing leapt to their feet, shouting. Some were now pounding the sides of their own heads with their fists, which filled the chamber with a continuous thumping sound.

Belol-yan raised his arms and gradually silenced the crowd again. "You listen. You listen much. We speak more.

Nandups tree-web spiders, bolups ground-web spiders. We show you. Tree-web spiders, ground-web spiders, live peace. Khami-buls much lie. We show you. You see."

One of the other guards carried the second spider cage forward and handed it to the yellow-clothed woman. The others watched and whispered as she held the box in front of her face and turned it, staring through the glass.

"Jhogo, Jhooogoooo!" she cried. She handed the box to the green-clothed man and pointed to a spot within the cage.

"Jhogo!" the man cried.

The others gathered around, pushing each other aside to get a look at the cage.

Belol-yan waited many breaths until all the amo-moloms had seen the spiders. He shouted yet again to get their attention, but now the crowd could barely be silenced. Many of them continued hissing words at each other and pointing at the spider cage. "You listen much! I, Belol-yan, guard sanctuary-fortress. I see. I see much sanctuary-fortress. Khami-buls much lie. Khami-buls know bolup nandup live peace. Bolups in sanctuary-fortress. Live peace nandups bolups khami-buls."

The hissing in the crowd stopped. They stared at Belol-yan, their eyes wide and mouths moving as if they were speaking silently to themselves.

"Khami-buls live peace bolups!" Belol-yan said. "Khami-buls lie together bolups. Khami-buls bolups make babies. Khami-bul bolup babies live sanctuary-fortress. Hide. You no see. I show you now."

Evidently this was the moment Di-woto had been waiting for. She stepped up to Belol-yan's side, bouncing with excitement. She grabbed the garments covering her head and pulled them back, revealing her face. She pulled again, and the entire garment dropped to the floor.

Di-woto, a hybrid with a nandup mother and bolup father, smiled at the nandup leaders as if she had no idea of the danger she was in. Her multi-colored garment and white fur footwraps seemed out of place even among the bright garments of the amo-moloms. Morning light from the windows above made her smooth ornamental scars glimmer against her brown skin. Colored fibers, torn loose from her coiled braid, were settling to the floor around her feet.

Skyra scanned the nandups' faces and saw they were paying little attention to these details. Instead, they were focused on Di-woto's face—a face not nandup and not bolup. Di-woto was proof the khami-buls were making babies with bolups. Belol-yan had spoken the truth.

Several long breaths passed in silence.

Skyra saw it before it started. The nandups were so shocked and angry that she could read their faces easily. Pursed lips became tighter with each passing breath. Eyes narrowed into slits of rage. Neck tendons flexed. The amo-moloms had heard and seen more than they could stand. Perhaps they were angry at the khami-buls, but the khami-buls were not here in this chamber, and at this moment the amo-moloms' anger could not be contained.

The gathered nandups began growling, and several of them stepped forward menacingly.

Skyra pushed herself between Di-woto and Belol-yan and grabbed them both by the arms. "We go now. Fight. Kill."

It was too late. Skyra had always recognized tiny changes in face muscles and eyes, and the yellow-clothed woman's face was now changing from confused anger to certain determination. The woman was focused on Di-woto and was about to make a move. The woman wasn't a warrior, but she did have a long dagger in her hand. The woman's neck muscles tightened. She was going to come for Di-woto.

Skyra rushed forward, pulling her khul from its sling and flipping the weapon's handle to her other hand. She swung the khul, striking the woman's hand and sending the dagger clattering to the floor. The other nandups cried out in alarm as the yellow-clothed woman dropped to her knees, holding her bleeding hand.

If these nandups were fighters, they would have already swarmed Skyra and killed her. For the moment, they were too stunned to act. The moment wouldn't last, however.

"Go!" Skyra shouted as she ran back to Di-woto and again grabbed the girl's arm.

Belol-yan already had his broad-bladed khul in his hand. "Take Di-woto!" He pushed Skyra and the girl toward the door and faced the screaming amo-moloms, some of whom were already advancing with drawn daggers.

Two of the guards opened the door and pulled Di-woto through. Instead of following them out, Skyra turned back to the chamber just as the shouting crowd was starting to rush forward. The long-armed bolup had already fallen to the floor and was trying awkwardly to get up. Three nandups were almost upon him.

Skyra charged and threw her body into the nearest attacker, which sent all three tumbling into a pile on the floor.

As Belol-yan and three other guards blocked the door to keep the nandups from going after Di-woto, Skyra stepped in front of the long-armed man with her khul raised. "You stop!" she shouted. "We not khami-buls. You angry khami-buls. You no angry us!"

The three nandups on the floor stared up at her. The others slowed their approach. Many of them still had their daggers drawn, but Skyra could see their anger was starting to turn into fear. They did not want to fight experienced warriors like Skyra and the guards.

Belol-yan shouted, and Skyra picked out the words, "We tell you. We show you. You angry khami-buls. You angry now. No angry tomorrow. You act now. No act tomorrow. You go your tribes. Get citizens-nandups. You go sanctuary-fortress. We go now. Open sanctuary-fortress door. You go. Guards open door you go see. You see spiders. You see khami-buls bolups peace. You angry. You act now. No act tomorrow."

The amo-moloms stared at Belol-yan. They growled. They whispered to each other. A man in a red garment said, "Yes. We go speak tribe. Tribe go sanctuary-fortress now. No act tomorrow. We act now."

Several of the others growled in agreement, then more, and soon the entire group was growling and pounding their heads with their fists.

"We go now," Belol-yan said.

Skyra turned and saw he was now addressing her. The long-armed bolup was still on the floor, so she shoved her khul into its sling and helped the man get to his feet.

Belol-yan frowned, as if he would prefer to leave the man here, but Skyra ignored him and guided the bolup to the door. The remaining guards followed her out.

They emerged to see a crowd of nandup citizens gathered around Di-woto and the two guards who had guided the girl from the dwelling. The citizens' expressions showed confusion and anger. Di-woto had left her long garment in the dwelling and was exposed for everyone to see. The guards stood on either side of her, each of them wielding a long, shiny blade.

Belol-yan didn't pause. He charged at the citizens with his khul raised, shouting at them to run. They all turned and fled.

"We go now," he said. He headed for the sanctuary-fortress, followed by Skyra, Di-woto, and the other guards.

"My plan working!" Di-woto said, bouncing and grinning as she walked, paying no attention to the citizens who were now watching from a distance.

"You plan dangerous... fighting.... killing," Belol-yan said in his gruff voice. "You no safe. Sanctuary-fortress now."

Skyra followed the group, well aware of the growing crowd of nandups. Belol-yan led them past the covered tunnel they had crawled through when leaving the sanctuary-fortress. They made their way along the base of the wall as more and more citizens came running to see what was happening. Finally, they approached the main entrance, the massive opening in the wall Skyra had passed through two days ago while tied to a camel-drawn cart. The huge gate had been closed at first light, which Skyra assumed was why the group had crawled out through the tunnel. Now the gate was wide open.

Belol-yan paused before leading the group through the doorway. He grabbed Di-woto and the long-armed bolup, pushed them closer together, then gestured for the other guards to surround them. Skyra understood, and she positioned herself between two of the guards. Di-woto and the bolup had both left their long garment coverings behind, and this would at least partially hide them from view.

Just as Belol-yan began leading the tightly-packed group through the doorway, a sound arose from among the dwellings behind them. Skyra turned to look. The sound was voices—many, many voices. So many she could not make out any words. Perhaps the nandups were not shouting words at all. Perhaps the outcry was only growls and shrieks.

Belol-yan said, "Amo-moloms speak citizens-nandups. Angry. Dangerous. Go now." He turned and led the group through the wall's main entrance.

"Belol-yan! Dedil-tené!"

The voice came from a guard near the main door into the massive sanctuary-fortress. She was with two other guards, the three of them now running toward Skyra's group and the wall's gate. Several citizens-nandups near the sanctuary-fortress stopped to stare.

The approaching guards spoke to Belol-yan so rapidly Skyra couldn't make out their words, but she could read their concern and suspicion. They obviously had respect for Belol-yan, but they seemed confused by what the old guard was doing. One of the guards shifted her head to look at Skyra, her eyes seemingly drawn to Skyra's fur garments. Then she shifted her gaze again in an effort to see the two figures hiding among the guards.

The shouting outside the wall grew louder, like an approaching storm, drawing the three guards' attention away from Skyra's group.

Belol-yan spoke to the three guards. "Citizens-nandups. No danger. Guards no go. Wall open. No danger."

His words didn't seem to calm the guards—they were frowning and staring out through the gate toward the growing sounds. Another three guards emerged from the sanctuary-fortress, running toward the wall. Skyra sensed fighting and killing were about to occur, and again she pulled her khul from its sling.

Her eyes met those of the guard who had spotted her fur garments. The woman was pulling a long, shiny blade from the strap around her waist, obviously in response to Skyra producing her own weapon. The woman's eyes then flitted toward Skyra's feet.

"Melil atilo-bu bolup!" the woman shouted, pointing her blade at the ground.

Skyra followed the woman's gaze downward to one of the long-armed bolup's hands, which was bleeding from being dragged on the ground.

The other two guards saw the hand too. They pulled out their own blades, shouting words Skyra did not know.

Now the guards running from the sanctuary-fortress were also pulling out weapons.

Skyra stepped away from her group to give herself room to fight. She pulled one of her hand blades from her wrist sheath, wielding it in one hand while keeping her khul in the other. These attackers were not like the skinny, starved bolup men with stone weapons in Skyra's homeland. These were powerful nandup fighters with shiny, sharp blades.

It was time to kill.

The three new guards joined the first three. More words were exchanged. All eyes stared down at the bolup's bleeding hand. The storm of shouting from beyond the wall swelled as it drew nearer.

Abruptly, one of the guards who had just arrived drove her long blade into the neck of her own companion. The man staggered and fell.

The other guards stared at the woman in disbelief. Skyra stared also. She assumed the woman was Belol-yan's friend and was part of Di-woto's plan.

Before anyone could react, a scraping, crunching sound rose above all the other noise. The great black slab with rows of square holes—the main door for the wall—was sliding across the opening, closing off the entrance.

Di-woto's hand emerged above the heads of the guards surrounding her, and she cried out. Skyra caught the words, "No! Door open now. Stop!" She was pointing at a guard on top of the wall, who was straining to turn a large black wheel as the great door slid across the opening.

A clang sounded, one weapon hitting another. Skyra turned her gaze from the guard atop the wall to see Belol-yan swinging his shining khul, slicing deep into another guard's shoulder. Skyra rushed over and pulled Di-woto away from the violence. The bolup man tried to move back too, but he tripped and fell, his long arms floundering awkwardly.

Belol-yan swung again, and the scene erupted into a vicious battle. Guards grunted as they swung their weapons, cutting flesh, hitting other weapons, or missing altogether and striking the ground, sending up tiny sparkles of light.

"Door open now!" Di-woto screamed, pointing again at the guard on the wall.

Skyra saw the importance of Di-woto's words. If the door closed, the angry mob of citizens would not get into the sanctuary-fortress, and the entire plan would fail. She slipped her khul into its sling, put the handle of her knife between her teeth, and leapt for the door. She caught the square holes with her hands and feet.

Skyra had scaled rocky cliffsides many times while hunting cave goats, and the holes in this door allowed her to climb it in only a few breaths, even as the door was sliding shut. Now she was less than an arm's length from the top of the wall. She reached up for the edge then threw one leg over.

"Door open now!" Di-woto screamed.

Skyra didn't have time to look, but she still heard grunts and clashing weapons as the guards below continued fighting.

She pulled herself over the edge and scrambled to her feet.

The guard, now only steps away, eyed her warily but continued turning the wheel. She plucked her knife from her teeth, darted forward, and held the blade to the man's throat. "Stop!"

The man's face was already straining from his effort, so Skyra failed to read his intent. He released the wheel and knocked her hand away before she could react. He slammed a hand into her chest, knocking her back, then pulled his long blade from his waist strap. The guard didn't hesitate—he rushed Skyra while raising the weapon over his head.

This was his mistake. Skyra was already close, and the man's blade was as long as a khul—he should have thrust the blade instead of preparing for a broad, swinging strike.

Skyra threw herself forward and rammed his belly with her shoulder. Her weight easily took him down. She threw her arm around his neck and pulled him so close that he couldn't use the long blade. The man grunted and struggled, but she held his neck even tighter. He rolled over, forcing Skyra onto her back beneath him. This was another mistake—now he could not stab her back with his blade.

He tried pushing himself up, but she held him against her while she jabbed her stone blade into his back. She pulled the blade out and stabbed again. He let out another grunt, and Skyra plunged the knife again and again.

His struggles became frantic. He tried to turn his head to bite her neck, but she squeezed with all the strength of the cave lion and woolly rhino flowing in her blood.

She stabbed at his back as fast as she could plunge the

blade in and pull it out. The man's grunts turned into screams. The blade was now hitting the hard bones of his spine, so she shifted it to the side and started stabbing it through his ribs. His screams became bubbling coughs. She then shoved him off to the side before the blood coming from his mouth could soil her woolly-rhino cape.

The man couldn't breathe now and was no longer a threat, so she got to her feet and stepped to the wheel. Below, many guards lay dead or injured on the ground, but Belol-yan and his companions were still fighting. More guards were running out of the sanctuary-fortress.

"Door open now!" Di-woto cried out from directly below.

Skyra leaned over the edge to see the girl climbing up the massive door. She dropped to her knees and held out a hand. Di-woto took it, and Skyra lifted her up and over the edge in one fast motion.

Di-woto jumped to her feet and grabbed the wheel. She leaned into it, but the wheel didn't move. Skyra joined her, and together they strained. The wheel began turning. The door below started scraping and grinding again, this time sliding back the way it had come, opening the gate. They continued turning the wheel until it came to a sudden stop.

Skyra saw Di-woto was trying to speak to her, but all she could hear was a deafening roar of shouts and pounding feet. Skyra stepped away from the wheel and stared out toward the countless dwellings beyond the wall. Everything down there seemed to be moving, except for the dwellings themselves. She couldn't even see the ground. Nandups—more than she could ever count—were pouring in from every direction, all of them heading for the entrance below her feet.

Skyra felt a tug on her cape. She turned to see Di-woto bouncing on her toes and grinning. The girl pulled Skyra closer to the sanctuary-fortress side of the wall and pointed down.

Nandup citizens were just starting to emerge through the gate on their way toward the sanctuary-fortress. Some stopped when they saw the guards Belol-yan's group had killed, but soon a much larger wave of citizens stampeded through the doorway like a frightened herd of ibexes. Belol-yan, his companion guards, and the long-armed bolup were swarmed and trampled by the herd.

Skyra lost sight of Belol-yan for a moment, then she saw him again, knocking aside several nandups and actually throwing one into the air as he got to his feet. He had no choice but to move toward the sanctuary-fortress along with the crowd, but as he was swept away, he stared up at Skyra and Di-woto with his one good eye.

19

LO-AFUL

Present Time - Day 3

Lincoln looked around the chamber. Four guards, two khami-buls, and a smart-ass drone were watching him, and he was supposed to make a baby with a woman he had never met before? Even if he wanted to, it wasn't going to happen.

The woman Lo-aful was studying him, her eyes still curious and pleading.

"Are you Di-woto's birthmother?" he asked.

At the sound of Di-woto's name, even before Ripple had translated, the woman's face changed. Her eyes grew wide, but she quickly regained composure, obviously trying to appear impassive. Her eyes flitted toward the khami-buls and guards.

Lincoln was reasonably sure he was reading her expressions accurately, in spite of her nonhuman mannerisms. This woman wasn't thinking about what she had obviously been ordered to do with Lincoln. Instead, she was thinking about Di-woto. Was she aware of Di-woto's plan?

He decided he needed to talk to this woman, and he was sure she wanted to talk to him. He turned to the two Khami-buls. "I am going to make a baby with Lo-aful! I cannot relax with all these people in this room. I make many babies in Arizona, and I always do so without an audience. Please leave the room and give us our privacy."

Ripple translated, and the two khami-buls bared their teeth in angry nandup frowns.

Lo-aful spoke up. Her voice was deeper than Di-woto's but still similar. Depon-ma replied. Lo-aful spoke again, this time clearly pleading. They went back and forth a few more times.

"Lo-aful is arguing for the value of privacy," Ripple explained.

Depon-ma grunted and gestured for the guards to exit the chamber. Finally, the khami-buls stepped out. Lincoln briefly glimpsed Depon-ma's frowning face as the nandup pulled the door shut.

The chamber became awkwardly silent.

Ripple stepped closer to Lincoln and Lo-aful and spoke using a low volume setting. "I will translate quietly if the two of you wish to speak." The drone then spoke in the nandup's language, presumably making the same offer to Lo-aful.

Lo-aful stared at Ripple in the same way Lincoln imagined Di-woto would stare at a garment design she had never seen before.

"This is my talking beast," Lincoln said, keeping his voice low. "It translates for us. It's bad about following instructions, but it usually gets the job done."

"Insulting one of your own drones is an exercise in futility," Ripple said before translating at least some of Lincoln's words.

Lo-aful finally shifted her gaze from Ripple to Lincoln. She spoke, and Ripple said, "You have talked to Di-woto?"

"Yes, Skyra and I talked extensively to Di-woto yesterday. Skyra is with her now. You are Di-woto's mother?"

Ripple continued translating the conversation.

Lo-aful answered with questions of her own. "How do you know that? Did Di-woto speak of me?"

Lincoln decided not to admit Di-woto hadn't mentioned her mother. "You look like Di-woto. I see her in your eyes."

"Tell me please, is Di-woto healthy? Is she happy?"

Again, he wasn't sure how much he should reveal. Di-woto had certainly acted exuberant, but the girl was emotionally and physically scarred. "She seems reasonably healthy. Um... how long has it been since you've talked to your daughter?"

"I am not permitted to speak to Di-woto. The last time I spoke to her was the last time she drank from my breasts."

He blew out a long breath. No wonder this woman was starved for information about her daughter. "Is Di-woto's father allowed to speak to her?"

The woman pointed to an old scar in front of her left ear. "Di-woto's father was a difficult bolup prisoner. He had to be cut into pieces to feed the spiders."

Well, shit. One more reason for Di-woto to be screwed up. "Why don't they let you see your own daughter?"

Lo-aful gazed at him for a moment before answering. "Di-woto is an alinga-ul. Do your people in Arizona allow alinga-uls to speak to their mothers and fathers?"

How should he answer this? Lincoln decided to take a

chance. "Yes. Our alinga-uls may speak to anyone they want. Inside the sanctuary-fortress, of course."

She seemed to think about this. Then she turned and gazed at the bed. "The guards will spill your blood if you do not lie with me. Most bolup men cannot make an alinga-ul. You are not like the other bolups I have seen. Perhaps you are capable of making an alinga-ul with me."

Lincoln had no desire to do this. However, he also had no idea how long he needed to play along with these nandups' games before Skyra and Belol-yan returned. He needed to keep this woman talking. "Di-woto is a very intelligent girl. Did you know she creates her own clothing? She dyes them all the colors of the rainbow. She has also developed plans for a new sanctuary-fortress, and even a waste-water system for Kyran-yufost."

"That is what alinga-uls do. Tell me please, what other plans has Di-woto been working on? Did she tell you more?"

Ripple added, "Perhaps you should be cautious, Lincoln."

Lincoln gazed at the woman's pleading eyes. "Di-woto spoke of many things." He smiled. "Your daughter loves to talk."

Lo-aful didn't smile back. "Did my daughter speak of the war with bolups? I have been told Di-woto wishes to stop the fighting and killing. Did she say such things to you?"

He hesitated. The woman's expression indicated earnest sincerity. Besides, she hadn't spoken to her daughter in years. She probably just wanted to know what kind of girl Di-woto was.

When he didn't reply, Lo-aful continued. "Many of us are weary of the fighting. The war requires many resources, and many warriors are killed. Did Di-woto speak to you of this? I would like to believe my daughter may someday use her influence to convince our khami-buls that Kyran-yufost can be a land of peace."

Lincoln continued studying her face. Her eyes still indicated a desperate curiosity regarding her daughter. Di-woto had been taken from her at such a young age, and since then, probably because she had already produced a rare alinga-ul, the poor woman had been forced to mate with numerous bolup men in an attempt to produce more. The lines on her face couldn't come close to reflecting all the injustices of her life.

"You'll be happy to know Di-woto agrees with you," he said. "She wants to stop the war."

Ripple said, "Lincoln, are you sure?"

"Yes, translate. She deserves some positive news. In fact, tell her Di-woto has a plan for convincing the citizens to stop supporting the war. Tell her Di-woto is a good, honest person who wants peace."

"Very well." Ripple translated the words.

A smile formed on Lo-aful's face as she listened to the translation. She spoke, and Ripple said, "I am happy you have told me these things. It seems my daughter is a good and intelligent alinga-ul, but I am sad you will not be able to make a new alinga-ul with me."

Lincoln raised his brows, not sure exactly what that meant.

Suddenly the woman took a step back and and let out a piercing shriek.

The door burst open. Guards rushed in. Before Lincoln could even lift his arms to protect himself, the nearest guard slammed a fist into his chest.

Lincoln fell onto the bed, gasping for air. Powerful hands pulled him to his feet and started dragging him from the chamber. He craned his neck to look back at Lo-aful. The woman was standing beside the bed, staring after him. An expression of sadness overtook her features. Now, though, Lincoln was uncertain he had ever been able to read her face at all.

The guards dragged him roughly into the corridor and past the two khami-buls. He tried to speak, to demand Ripple be taken with him, but his chest was convulsing, and he couldn't get the words out. He coughed and spat, then he looked back again and saw Di-woto's mother emerge from the chamber behind him and slam the door shut.

SOMETHING WAS HAPPENING. The two guards dragging Lincoln down the corridor were shouting to other guards running in the opposite direction. Consumed with urgency, the running guards gave cursory replies or didn't reply at all, which agitated Lincoln's guards even more.

"I need my talking beast," Lincoln pleaded, knowing full well they couldn't understand him. "Please, can you take me back to get it?"

No response. More guards running by. Orange-clad khami-buls were now emerging from chambers along the corridor, shouting at the guards but not getting replies. Something was definitely happening.

Lincoln caught a whiff of a familiar stench, which drove his anxiety into panic mode. He had seen and smelled this corridor before. His guards picked up their pace, obviously anxious to get Lincoln to whatever fate awaited him so they could join the other running guards. The stench became worse—human waste, rotting flesh, and fear.

The guards stopped, kicked open a door, and roughly hauled him into a chamber. At first Lincoln thought it was the chamber of horrors filled with the wretched human recipients of grotesque arm-lengthening procedures. Cages on carts were arranged in a line the entire length of the chamber.

"Guys, there's Lincoln!" It was Jazzlyn's voice.

Lincoln exhaled with some relief as the guards hauled him directly to the cage containing his team. They stopped at the cage door, and one guard bellowed out a command. Both guards stared at the far end of the chamber, which was at least fifty yards away, apparently waiting for a response. None came, so the guy bellowed again. Still nothing.

The guard growled in frustration. He pushed Lincoln face-first against the cage and took off down the length of the chamber. The remaining guard pressed something sharp—either a sword or dagger—to the back of Lincoln's neck.

Jazzlyn, Virgil, and Derek pressed up to the cage door, inches from Lincoln's face.

"What's happening, Linc?" Derek asked, trying to keep his deep voice as calm as possible to avoid angering the guard.

"I'm not sure," Lincoln replied in a whisper.

Seconds passed in silence. At least a minute later, the other guard returned. Lincoln was yanked back from the door. The guard held up a wire loop strung with about a dozen pieces of metal. Lincoln recognized them—they were keys, each with six rods of varying lengths protruding from a flat plate.

The guard fitted a key into the six holes on the door and pushed. No click. The door didn't open. He growled a few words, probably a curse. After trying three more keys, the lock popped open.

The guards lifted Lincoln off his feet and literally threw

him in the cage. His body knocked his team members aside, and he crashed onto the cage floor. He rolled over and sat up just as the door clanged shut.

The guard stared at the ring of keys for a moment. Instead of taking them back to the far end of the chamber, he grunted and threw them. The keys clattered on the floor until they came to a stop somewhere. The guards took off running.

The chamber was now silent except for the few low voices of humans trapped inside other cages.

"What the hell's going on?" Derek boomed. His face and hands were still covered in dried blood from his previous violent episodes.

Lincoln didn't answer right away. He cocked his head, listening. A faint rumbling sound was gradually growing louder. Perhaps it was countless feet running, or voices shouting. Occasional louder thumps could be heard, perhaps doors being battered in.

Lincoln closed his eyes for a moment, then he looked at his friends. "I'm not really sure, but I think we've started a revolution."

20

BREACH

PRESENT TIME - DAY 3

SKYRA STARED down at the mass of angry nandups pouring through the wall's gate and into the sanctuary-fortress. If this was what Di-woto had wanted, then her plan was working. These nandup citizens wanted to see proof of the khami-buls' deceit. They would now find the cages of spiders and the long-armed bolup men. They would find the bolups who had secretly been living and making babies with nandup khami-buls. Skyra did not know what would happen after that, but there was probably nothing more she and Lincoln could do here. Di-woto's plan was in motion, and it seemed nothing could stop it now.

"Guards!" Di-woto cried, pointing.

Skyra saw them. Three guards were approaching, running on top of the wall. She spun around. A single guard was approaching from the other direction.

Di-woto shouted at the surging crowd below, and several

nandups standing to the side of the incoming river of people looked up. Di-woto screamed to leave the gate open, then she pointed at the approaching guards. Soon the massive door was covered with climbing nandup citizens.

The guards were now only breaths away. They almost certainly intended to turn the wheel and close the gate, but they might also kill Di-woto in the process.

"Come!" Skyra ordered. She grabbed the girl's garment and pulled her toward the single approaching guard. She would leave it to the climbing citizens to stop the other guards from turning the wheel—Skyra now needed Di-woto's help, which meant she needed to keep her safe.

The approaching guard was holding his broad-bladed khul in strike position, but when he got close enough to clearly see Skyra, he slowed his pace. He eyed Skyra with a frown, taking in her strange fur garments, then his eyes grew wide when he saw Di-woto cowering behind her.

"He no understand alinga-uls," Di-woto said.

Skyra wasn't sure what the girl meant, but there was no time to ask. The guard's face showed suspicion, and Skyra had to assume he would attack Di-woto, perhaps thinking she was a bolup.

"Move away—we go!" Di-woto shouted at the man.

The man's face still showed suspicion, and Skyra was unwilling to take any chances. She glanced back to see the three other guards being overcome by at least twice as many citizens, with more citizens swarming onto the wall with every breath. She faced the guard in her way, pointed toward the sanctuary-fortress, and shouted, "Khami-buls lie!"

The man narrowed his eyes, but he glanced to where she was pointing.

This was the opening Skyra needed. She lowered her

head and lunged at the man's waist to avoid his khul. She slammed into him with her shoulder then quickly stopped herself and stood upright. The guard grunted and stumbled back, losing his balance and focus enough for Skyra to rush forward with a kick to the side, sending him flailing over the wall's edge.

"You warrior," Di-woto said, smiling broadly at Skyra.

Skyra grabbed the girl's garment again. "We go. How we go in sanctuary-fortress?"

Di-woto blinked once then smiled again. She pointed. "Door."

The girl was pointing at the small door they had used earlier when leaving the sanctuary-fortress. The area was surprisingly clear of people, and the door would lead them directly into the protected corridors used by khami-buls. They could avoid going through the public chamber-auditorium filled with angry citizens.

One problem, there was no way to climb down from here. They would have to jump or go back to the main entrance to climb down. Going back was not an option. Skyra looked over the edge. The dirt was about four body-lengths below. She snugged her hand blades into their sheath and lowered herself over the side. Hanging by her hands, her feet were now only three body lengths from the dirt.

"Skyra, no." Di-woto said. She was now on her knees, staring down at Skyra's face.

Skyra pushed herself from the wall with one foot and let go. She landed hard but managed to stay on her feet. She looked up. Di-woto was still staring down from above.

"Come now!" Skyra shouted.

For several breaths, Di-woto did not move. Another broad

smile appeared on her face, and she lowered herself over the side. She let go without hesitating.

Skyra couldn't risk Di-woto cracking a bone, so she stepped forward and threw her arms around the girl's waist, breaking her fall.

"Ayeee!" Di-woto cried as she pulled out of Skyra's grip. Then she laughed, as if her entire plan were simply a fun game.

Skyra grabbed the girl's garment again and ran for the small door. She pounded the door with her fist, but it remained closed. She kicked it with her foot. Di-woto hit the door with her open palm and shouted. Still nothing. The guard who had remained inside the door earlier was now gone.

Skyra growled, and her eyes met Di-woto's.

"We go big door now," the girl said.

Skyra stared at her face. Di-woto was clearly not a nandup, and she would never get through the angry crowd without being noticed. Skyra kneeled and grabbed the girl's garment where it almost touched the ground. She pulled out one of her hand blades and began cutting. Working her way up and around, she removed most of the garment hanging below Di-woto's knees.

She wrapped the piece around the girl's head, covering her face. It looked strange, and the multi-colored garment itself would still draw attention, but it was better than nothing.

"I no see," Di-woto said.

"You follow me. I see." Skyra grabbed her hand and started for the main entrance. She led Di-woto directly into the pack of angry nandups and through the doorway to the public chamber-auditorium. The immense room was filled with shouting people, standing shoulder-to-shoulder, many of them holding shiny daggers above their heads. They were everywhere. Some had even crawled over the fence surrounding the display of spiderwebs and were destroying the webs. One of the large trees that had supported the tree-web spiders had been knocked over, crushing part of the fence.

Most of these people were not fighters, but there were so many that the sanctuary-fortress guards would surely be overwhelmed. For now, though, the crowd had not opened the heavy, locked door leading from the public portion of the structure to the khami-buls' sanctuary-fortress. A thick, shouting mass of people had gathered in front of the locked door.

Skyra saw something that caught her eye. She stood on her toes for a better view. Belol-yan was there. He was speaking to the crowd with his back to the locked door of the sanctuary-fortress. Beside him were two of the guards who had helped with Di-woto's plan. On his other side were two tribe leaders—amo-moloms—one wearing a blue garment, the other in white. Belol-yan and the amo-moloms were shouting at the crowd, but their words were lost in the uproar.

Skyra did not know what else to do, so she strode directly into the mass of nandups toward Belol-yan, still pulling Di-woto behind her. Soon the crowd was so tight she had to start pushing people aside. Most of them hardly noticed, but some were staring, pointing, or muttering to each other. Skyra gripped Di-woto's hand harder and kept pushing, forcing the nandups to make room.

An enraged shout behind Skyra rose above the other

voices, and Di-woto's hand was pulled from her grip. Skyra shoved her elbows into the bodies beside her and spun around, pulling one of her hand blades from its sheath.

Di-woto's head covering had been removed. A woman beside her was holding the garment and staring at Di-woto in surprise. The other nandups around the girl were staring too, and they started stepping back, forcing those behind them to also step back.

"Bolup!" cried the woman holding Di-woto's garment.

The others continued stepping back, as if they feared being too close.

"No bolup!" A voice shouted. "No bolup!"

The white-clothed amo-molom pushed his way through the crowd until he was standing beside Skyra and Di-woto. "No bolup! This girl nandup-bolup hybrid. Khami-buls lie. Khami-buls know nandups bolups live peace. Khami-buls live peace bolups sanctuary-fortress. Make babies. This girl nandup bolup hybrid. No angry this girl. Angry khami-buls. We go sanctuary-fortress now!"

The surrounding nandups were still staring at Di-woto, their expressions showing they were trying to understand what their eyes were seeing.

The woman holding Di-woto's garment raised her other hand and shook a dagger in the air. "We go sanctuary-fortress now!"

Another nandup shouted the same words, then another. The shouts grew and spread, filling the public chamber with noise like nothing Skyra had ever heard before.

Skyra grabbed Di-woto's hand again and dragged her through the shouting crowd. Belol-yan appeared before her, pushing bodies aside to make room. He grabbed Di-woto's other hand, and together they guided the girl away from the locked door to an area with fewer people.

Belol-yan leaned closer to Skyra and Di-woto and spoke. "Door locked. Citizens must see sanctuary-fortress. Spiders. Bolups. Dali-tamons."

"Me alinga-ul," Di-woto said. "My plan good." She turned in a circle, looking around the huge chamber. She smiled. Then she pointed to one of the dried-mud dwellings protruding from the wall above the locked door. "We go in!" She turned again and pointed at the destroyed display of tree-web spiders and ground-web spiders.

Skyra understood. The girl was pointing at the tree that had been knocked over by angry citizens.

"I no understand," Belol-yan said.

"Come," Skyra said. She headed for the tree, pulling Di-woto with her.

Belol-yan followed.

The tree was far too big for Skyra to move by herself, but she wasn't concerned. She grabbed the trunk and lifted.

Di-woto moved in beside her and did the same. Belol-yan now seemed to understand, and he grabbed the tree, followed by his two companions who had been beside him at the door.

They all lifted, but the tree hardly moved.

Skyra scanned the crowd. Many of the nandups were watching, and some were already crawling over the fence or walking to where the tree had crushed the fence. Soon the tree was being carried by so many nandups that some could walk to the side without helping at all.

Countless hands pushed on the top branches of the tree, raising them off the floor. The hands moved closer to the base, pushing the top even higher, until the tree tipped toward the wall and crashed against the protruding dried-clay dwelling. The window into the dwelling was now only a short climb away.

Skyra pushed Di-woto to the base of the leaning tree. "Climb now. You no safe here. We go sanctuary-fortress. Lincoln. Friends in cage."

Belol-yan grabbed Di-woto's braid, only partially coiled around her neck, and pulled her back. "I go now. Make sanctuary-fortress safe. You go after." He shoved his dagger into the sheath on his belt and started making his way up the tree. Belol-yan's two companions gestured for Di-woto to step back, then they followed him up. Three nandup citizens standing nearby also started climbing the tree, each of them glancing nervously at Di-woto. A few breaths later, countless nandups were swarming around the tree, waiting for their turn to climb.

Strangely, Di-woto was smiling again, even as she was being shoved back and forth by the crowd. She said something Skyra could not hear then started moving away from the tree.

Skyra had no choice but to follow. She could not lose Di-woto.

Many of the nandups had already seen Di-woto's face, but still they scattered in front of her as if they were frightened by the mere sight of her. Although these people were angry, and most of them were carrying daggers, they were generally timid. Skyra did not know how many guards were inside the sanctuary-fortress, but it wouldn't take too many to slaughter enough of these citizens to frighten the entire mass into fleeing. Fortunately, more nandups were still pouring into the public chamber from outside. The more angry citizens there were, the better their chances of making it into the corridors and chambers behind the locked door to see what the khamibuls had been hiding.

Di-woto went straight to the door and kicked it several times with her white fur boot. As Skyra caught up, she heard a click from the other side, and the massive door began swinging open.

Nandups in the growing crowd saw the door opening, and their shouts became so loud Skyra wanted to cover her ears. She pushed Di-woto through the doorway then immediately to the side to avoid being trampled by charging citizens.

Bodies of guards lay scattered on the floor, and as the crowd rushed in, several people tripped over the bodies and fell. These additional fallen bodies tripped even more people, and soon the doorway was blocked by a pile of thrashing, screaming nandups.

A hand grabbed Skyra's shoulder. She spun around, again pulling out a hand blade, ready to fight.

Belol-yan stood before her, bleeding from a deep cut across the same eye socket that had already lost its eye from a fight long ago. He was bleeding in several other places also, including a gash on his upper arm where a slab of skin and muscle the size of Skyra's hand was hanging loosely. He was gripping his long blade, stained red from its tip to its handle.

"I take Di-woto safe place," he shouted over the chaos at the doorway. "We go now."

"Lincoln," Skyra said. "Lincoln's friends."

"Yes, Lincoln!" Di-woto cried. "My plan working. I help now!"

Skyra was jostled from behind. She turned to see most of the fallen nandups were already on their feet and running deeper into the sanctuary-fortress. A constant stream of citizens was now pouring through the open door. She turned back to Belol-yan. In spite of the pain he was surely enduring, he stood firm and steady. His good eye stared back at her. With a face like his, especially covered with blood, Skyra couldn't trust her ability to read his expression.

Finally, he spoke. "We nandups. You honor me, I honor you. Come. We get friends."

21

ONSLAUGHT

Present Time - Day 3

THINGS WERE ABOUT to get ugly. Lincoln and his team were bolups trapped in an eight-foot cage. Angry nandups were storming the fortress, their violent shouts becoming louder with every passing second. It was only a matter of time before they found this chamber. The cage bars would offer little protection from their vengeance. The nandups would either kill them through the openings or would find the keys and systematically open each cage to kill them.

Lincoln looked at his friends. Jazzlyn and Virgil were huddled together. Jazzlyn's left hand was missing, so Virgil had his arm stretched across her lap, gripping her right hand. Derek sat with his back to the bars across from them, his elbows on his knees and his face in his palms. This was not a good sign.

"Derek, you okay?" Lincoln asked.

He lifted his head. "Yeah, no worries. I've had so many episodes in the last two days that I think my brain's been bashed into permanent remission." He stared through the bars toward the chamber door, obviously listening to the approaching storm of nandups. "It brings me little comfort to know those people are supposed to be mad at the scientists instead of us."

Since being thrown in with the rest of his team, Lincoln had explained what he knew about Di-woto's plan, which wasn't much.

"They've been at war with humans for ages," Virgil added. "I don't imagine they'll free us and send us happily on our way." Virgil was trying to steady his voice, but the fear was still there.

A crash rang out, like something breaking, and seconds later the pandemonium swelled in volume. Shouts and pounding feet drew nearer, until it seemed they were just outside the chamber door. Something banged against the door, perhaps a fist or foot.

"I guess we're not gonna go down in an epic blaze of glory, like I'd hoped," Derek said. "More like rats in a trap."

The pounding came again. Then came a louder, lower thump, like a powerful foot kicking the door. A second thump followed.

"Shit," Virgil muttered.

A third thump, and the door frame cracked. One more thump, and the door flew open and slammed against the wall. Three figures rushed in, with more pouring in behind them. The first three came straight for the cage containing Lincoln and his team.

Lincoln instinctively scooted toward the back of the cage, then he saw Skyra's face. Beside her was Di-woto. On her other side was Belol-yan, who had a nasty gash across his already mangled face.

"Lincoln, you are here!" Skyra cried.

Belol-yan turned his back to the cage to face the countless nandup citizens streaming into the chamber. Most were pausing to stare at the row of cage-carts arranged along the wall.

"We are here to take you to your T3," Skyra said, her face pressed to the bars. Her eyes flitted from Lincoln to his team members.

Jazzlyn pointed to the far end of the chamber with the stump of her left arm. "The keys to the cages are down that way somewhere. We saw a guard throw them."

"We need those keys to get out," Lincoln added. "They're on a ring about this big." He held up his hands to show the size.

Skyra stepped to the side of the cage and stared down the length of the chamber. Many of the nandup citizens were already moving in that direction, and distant shouts could be heard from the far end. "I will get the keys." She took off down the row of cages.

Di-woto started after her, but Belol-yan grabbed the long braid coiled around the girl's neck and pulled her back. He spoke several firm words, pushed her against the cage door behind him, and turned back to the steady stream of nandups entering the chamber.

Long seconds passed. Nandups were still coming in, but many more were running on past the corridor door. Those entering apparently had no interest in tangling with the fierce Belol-yan, and they warily skirted around Lincoln's cage to continue deeper into the chamber.

Seconds turned into minutes. Shouts of anger and alarm

echoed through the chamber, but Belol-yan stood steadfast in front of the cage door.

Lincoln shook the bars in frustration as he stared toward the far end of the chamber. "Dammit, where is she?" His earlier elation at seeing Skyra safely back from her mission was now transforming into despair.

He heard a jingling of metal against metal, and he mashed his face to the bars for a better look. There she was. Finally. Skyra was coming back, her khul in one hand and the ring of keys dangling from the other. Something else was gripped in her fingers above the keys, but Lincoln couldn't make out what it was.

Skyra came up to the side of the cage and shoved the object through the bars. It was Jazzlyn's prosthetic hand. "Your hand weapon," she said to Jazzlyn. "I had to kill to get it, but I wanted you to have it back."

Jazzlyn pushed herself up, breaking away from Virgil, and grabbed the hand. "Oh my God, Skyra! I love you, girl!"

Skyra stared through the bars, fresh blood splattered across her face and neck. "But I am married to Lincoln."

Nothing but silence from the cage.

Jazzlyn turned to Lincoln. "Say what?"

"Dude," Derek said.

Lincoln shook his head. "No time to explain now. We're getting the hell out of here."

Di-woto snatched the keys from Skyra. After a minute or so of trial and error she found the right key and flung open the cage door. Lincoln crawled out first. The others followed more slowly, moaning and grunting at their stiff joints.

A few dozen nandup citizens were gathered around, watching. They were keeping their distance but were obviously agitated at seeing bolups being released. Several were speaking quietly to each other and pointing at Di-woto. Lincoln wondered if they understood the girl was a nandup-bolup hybrid.

Di-woto was actually smiling, in spite of the chaos all around. She held up the ring of keys, bouncing up and down on her toes. She spoke rapidly to the citizens in her perpetually-enthusiastic, animated way, pointed to the remaining cages lined up along the wall, then tossed the keys to the nearest woman.

Belol-yan spoke gruffly and started herding Di-woto, Skyra, and Lincoln's group toward the battered door.

Lincoln moved to Skyra's side as they were ushered through the doorway. The mad rush of nandups through the corridor seemed pretty much over, but he could still hear distant shouting and banging in other parts of the structure. He grabbed her hand and squeezed. "Okay, tell me what's happening."

She shot him a glance. "Di-woto's plan is working. I told you her plan would work, Lincoln. Now we use your T3 to go many, many years to save Veenah from dying."

LINCOLN AGAIN STEPPED over a dead guard's body, the third he'd seen since being freed from the cage. He had lost track of the number of dead citizens his group had seen. The noise and violence in the sanctuary-fortress was now diminishing. Citizens were everywhere, moving from chamber to chamber as if they wanted to see every square inch of the fortress that had long been off limits. Skyra had informed him the nandups were seeking the proof Di-woto and Belol-yan had told a group of tribe leaders they would find—proof of the khami-buls' deception.

Lincoln could hardly believe the actions of only a few people had resulted in such a massive response. There was no way to know if this revolt would result in any meaningful change or long-term cessation of the war, but both were certainly possible.

Skyra had never doubted she could help change this world. Now she might have actually done it.

Belol-yan pushed open a door hanging from its hinges and led them into a large chamber Lincoln recognized. It was the room where guards had been engaged in fighting drills. Tall racks that had once held training weapons had been stripped of their contents.

Lincoln glanced down and saw a continuous trail of heavy blood drops cutting across the entire room from a door on the right to another door on the left.

Di-woto saw the blood trail as well. She pointed to it and spoke while tugging on Belol-yan's braided hair. The old guard uttered a blunt reply and kept walking. Di-woto stopped, staring at the door on the left. She split from the group and went over to the door.

Belol-yan sighed heavily. "Di-woto!"

She ignored him and pushed on the door. It opened a few inches, then something pushed back, shutting it with a clang of metal against stone. Di-woto pushed again, this time with both hands.

The door flew open. Guards came rushing out, brandishing axes and swords and knocking Di-woto onto her butt.

Belol-yan roared with rage and rushed toward Di-woto just as the lead guard raised his axe over the girl's head.

The guard saw Di-woto's face and froze. Then he looked

up at Belol-yan. He spoke Belol-yan's name, followed by a rapid string of nandup words.

Belol-yan stopped a few paces from Di-woto and replied.

The other man lowered his axe and exchanged looks with the guards around him.

Skyra, standing at Lincoln's shoulder, said, "The guards have been hiding in that chamber. They are protecting khami-buls."

Di-woto scrambled to her feet and moved to Belol-yan's side. The old guard spoke again to those by the door then motioned for Di-woto and the rest of the group to continue following him.

"Alo-dé-mamun! Di-woto pol-mamun alinga-ul!"

An orange-clad nandup was emerging from the doorway behind the guards. Lincoln recognized her, the khami-bul woman named Gedun-dal. She spoke again, her voice laced with fury and menace.

Lincoln shifted his head to the side to get a better look into the chamber behind her. The room appeared to be small, and it was wall to wall with orange-clad nandups.

Di-woto stepped toward the khami-bul woman and shouted angrily, stomping her foot several times for emphasis.

Belol-yan grabbed the girl and started walking away, returning to his original course.

Gedun-dal shouted.

Belol-yan kept walking, pulling the girl with him. Lincoln and the others followed.

Gedun-dal shouted again.

Skyra handed Lincoln one of her stone knives and started pulling her khul from her cape.

Gedun-dal barked some words at the guards around her, and the guards started to advance as if they intended to attack.

A growl came from Skyra's throat. She turned away from Lincoln with her second knife in one hand and her khul in the other.

Belol-yan shoved Di-woto behind him and pulled out his axe.

Derek raised his bare fists and bellowed, "I've been waiting for this, Neanderthal bastards!"

Lincoln tried to swallow his fear. He moved up beside Skyra with her knife gripped in his fist.

A new voice shouted out from the far end of the room, and all heads turned. A nandup citizen was standing in the doorway to the next corridor. She shouted again, and this time her shout was answered by several other voices somewhere behind her. Even more voices rang out, followed by thundering feet. Seconds later, dark-clothed nandups began pouring in through the door.

Di-woto pointed to Gedun-dal and the guards and screamed, "Khami-bul! Khami-bul nup-ye-no bifulk!"

The first incoming nandups spotted Gedun-dal's orange clothing, and they abruptly changed course, leading the swarming mob with them.

Gedun-dal retreated into the small room as the mob slowed and began surrounding the handful of guards. The guards were outnumbered by at least ten to one, but they stood their ground, obviously not intending to let the dagger-wielding citizens anywhere near the khami-buls.

Nandups continued flowing into the room. When some of the new arrivals tried to approach Lincoln's group, Di-woto pointed and shouted again, "Khami-bul nup-ye-no bifulk!"

The crowd grew even larger, and soon Lincoln could no longer see the defending guards through the mob.

"Nup ye-noh-melu," Skyra said abruptly.

Belol-yan shot her a glance and grunted. He took Di-woto's hand and headed back the way they had come.

As they exited the same door they'd entered, the noise from the growing crowd swelled with agitated cries. Lincoln looked over his shoulder to see flashes of weapons swinging above the heads of the guards as the citizens closed in on them.

"Sweet Jesus," Jazzlyn said. She had paused beside Lincoln and seemed frozen at the sight of the vicious melee. She had reattached her artificial hand and was now gripping Lincoln's arm with the black carbon fingers as she stared.

Lincoln pried the fingers from his arm and turned her toward the door. "Let's go, Jazz. They could turn on us in a flash."

Her eyes met his as they resumed following the others. "Is there any hope at all we can find a timeline that isn't a brutal freaking nightmare?"

He grimaced. "Um, about that... I kind of made a promise to Skyra."

Skyra had hung back to wait for them. "We are going many, many years to save Veenah from dying."

Jazzlyn frowned. "We're not jumping forward like we planned?"

Lincoln tapped his watch and checked the time. It would be at least an hour before the T_3 completed the placement calculations for the jump back in time. Of course, this was assuming the T_3 hadn't been destroyed by rioting nandups. He shook his head. "I honestly don't know what we're doing anymore."

Belol-yan led them through several corridors Lincoln didn't recognize. They came upon smaller groups of citizens, who either turned and ran or simply watched them with wary curiosity as they passed by.

Finally, they entered a familiar wide hall with six doors spaced out evenly on either side. Lincoln scanned the doors. There it was—the door to the sleeping chamber. The door was still closed, as were most of the others in this hall.

Skyra pointed. "The sleeping chamber, Lincoln!"

Three citizens emerged from one of the chambers on the other side of the hall. They took one look at Belol-yan and the rest of the approaching group and quickly headed the other direction.

Skyra broke away from the group and ran to the door. She pushed on it. She jiggled the locking mechanism. Then she pounded on the door with her fist.

Lincoln stepped to her side while the others hung back. He knocked three times. "Ripple! Are you in there? Can you hear me?"

A scuffling sound came from the other side.

"Lincoln, it is I, Ripple."

He exhaled with relief and smiled at Skyra. "The door is locked. Can you open it from the inside, Ripple?"

"I cannot. However, there is a nandup within this chamber who can."

Lincoln's eyes met Skyra's again.

"Ripple, who is in there with you?" Skyra asked.

"I am pleased you and Lincoln are both safe, Skyra. A khami-bul woman is in this chamber. Her name is Lo-aful."

Lincoln muttered a curse. Then he turned and glanced back at Di-woto.

"Do you know this khami-bul, Lincoln?" Skyra asked.

"Yeah, we've met. She can't be trusted."

Di-woto joined them at the door and spoke a few words to Skyra.

"Lo-aful," Skyra said to the girl.

Di-woto furrowed her brows in thought and spoke again.

"Di-woto does not know that name," Skyra said to Lincoln.

That wasn't surprising. "Tell her Lo-aful is her birthmother."

Skyra blinked. "El-de-né! Her birthmother?" She turned to Di-woto and relayed this information.

At first, Di-woto looked confused. She stared at the door as if she were trying to see directly through it. Seconds later, a broad grin formed on her face.

Lincoln decided the girl was capable of finding something to smile about in every imaginable situation.

Di-woto hit the door with her palm. "Lo-aful khumo-ruro lebil Di-woto. Alinga-ul!"

Long seconds of silence followed, then more scuffling sounds. The door clicked several times and swung inward about eight inches. Lo-aful's face appeared in the gap. She looked terrified, but after his last encounter with her, Lincoln wasn't about to trust his ability to read the woman's emotions.

Di-woto's smile grew even wider, and she bounced on her toes. She spoke to the woman again.

Lo-aful pulled her eyes away from her daughter and stared at Skyra, then Belol-yan, then Lincoln's team members.

Lincoln impatiently scanned the hallway. They needed to get inside the chamber and close the damn door.

Di-woto spoke to her mother again, her voice pleading.

Finally, Lo-aful stepped back.

Belol-yan came to the door, pushed it open, and stepped

inside. He scanned the chamber then waved for everyone to enter.

"This is truly a grand reunion," Ripple said.

Belol-yan closed and latched the door. He exchanged a few words with Di-woto then strode purposefully to the bathroom. Seconds later Lincoln heard him splashing water from the washtub, no doubt in an effort to clean his wounds, which were quite grievous.

"I will help Belol-yan wash his wounds," Skyra said as she headed to the bathroom.

Di-woto and Lo-aful stood appraising each other, both of them seemingly unwilling to speak first. Di-woto's smile still hadn't faded.

Lincoln turned to Ripple. "Why is Lo-aful here?"

"I had a rather long conversation with Lo-aful," the drone said. "She came back to this chamber soon after you were taken away. She explained two reasons for returning. First, she wished to hide, as she was afraid of being killed by the many citizens-nandups invading the sanctuary-fortress. Second, she hoped her daughter would come to this chamber with you and Skyra. It seems she was correct on the second point."

Lincoln glanced at the mother and daughter. Lo-aful was now speaking softly while Di-woto listened intently.

Jazzlyn, Virgil, and Derek were gathered beside the T_3. Virgil turned to Lincoln. "They lock us in a cage, yet they put you in a honeymoon suite and even bring you all our stuff?"

"I can't tell you how sorry I am," Lincoln said, his guilt rushing back with full force. "I should have never asked you to jump with me in the first place."

"All for one, one for all," Derek said firmly. "No regrets."

"No regrets," Jazzlyn said.

"A few regrets," Virgil said. He received a punch on his arm from Jazzlyn's carbon fiber fist.

Lincoln inspected the T3. It appeared to be undamaged, as did the two duffel bags beside it. He grabbed the duffel containing rolled-up body bags and dragged it to an open area of the floor. He unzipped it and started pulling out body bags.

Jazzlyn, Virgil, and Derek appeared at his side and took over. "We'll get these," Virgil said. "You can initiate the placement calculations for our jump to the future and prepare a mini-drone."

"I'm still waiting for you to explain what you started to tell me," Jazzlyn said. "You know, about jumping back to Skyra's time to save Veenah?"

Derek and Virgil stopped what they were doing and stared at Lincoln.

"You're shittin' me," Derek said.

Lincoln sighed. "Ripple, come over here."

The drone stepped to his side. "In anticipation of your question, I am pleased to report that the T3's placement calculations will be complete in approximately seventy-four minutes, plus or minus fifteen minutes."

"You were able to interface this drone with the T3?" Virgil asked.

Lincoln shrugged. "My future self... what can I say."

"Jumping back to Skyra's time?" Derek wasn't about to let that go.

"To save Veenah," Jazzlyn added.

Lincoln winced. "I know it sounds crazy. We still have ten body bags. We can jump twice if we continue to use only five for each jump."

"Assuming the T3 continues to function," Virgil said,

"and assuming we aren't killed by saber-toothed cats or savages."

Jazzyn said, "What if we do go back, and by some miracle we save Skyra's twin. What then?"

"Then we go ahead and jump to the future destination, like we decided two days ago. Forty-seven thousand years from now."

"That's a 94,000-year jump from Skyra's time," Derek said.

Virgil shook his head. "Actually, if we're going to talk numbers, it will be 95,318 years after Skyra's time. As long as we simply reverse the original 47,659-year jump, the placement calculations should only take a few minutes. The jump is quite feasible."

"Jesus!" Derek boomed at Virgil. "You're taking Lincoln's side on this?"

Virgil adjusted his glasses and solidified his expression. "Actually, there *are* no sides. Lincoln is our boss. It's his T3."

"And Skyra is his wife," Jazzlyn added. "Or so I've heard."

This was followed by seconds of awkward silence, in which Lincoln felt his face flushing. He stepped over to the gear duffel and dragged it out beside the duffel of body bags. "I have several interesting stories to tell you guys. First, though, we need to—"

An explosive crash cut him off. The chamber door flew open. Lincoln glimpsed two guards holding a thick, black object between them—a battering ram. The object hit the floor with a heavy thud as the guards rushed into the room, pulling swords from their belts. Two more rushed in behind them, followed by two more.

The guards scanned the chamber until they spotted Diwoto.

"Alinga-ul!" one of them grunted. They started for the girl.

Belol-yan and Skyra came barreling from the bathroom. They stepped in front of Di-woto, intercepting the guards.

Belol-yan shouted a string of words at the intruders. He was loosely holding his axe at his side. Dripping wet, with blood still flowing from his eye socket, Belol-yan presented a menacing figure.

The guard who had spoken first growled back at Belol-yan, her face a twisted visage of hatred. "Belol-yan, amo-yekne kha alinga-ul!"

Lincoln saw in the woman's eyes she was done speaking and intended to act. A split-second later she rushed forward.

Almost casually, Belol-yan swung his axe upward, slicing through her chin to her forehead.

Another split-second later, Skyra delivered a devastating blow to the second guard's shoulder, almost severing the man's arm.

The four remaining guards paused only briefly as their companions hit the floor. Then they advanced, though now more cautiously.

Lincoln had to do something. He pulled the blanket from the bed, rushed at the four guards, and flung it over them. The blanket partially covered two of the guards.

This caused enough confusion to allow Belol-yan to take out another guard, striking the man's head through the fabric. The guard collapsed, still covered by the blanket.

Derek let out a scream and charged past Lincoln, wildly swinging the huge gear bag. The bag hit one of the three remaining guards, knocking her into the guard beside her. Skyra rushed in and sunk her khul blade into another shoulder, sending the man stumbling back through the doorway.

Derek, Skyra, and Belol-yan advanced, swinging the gear bag and the weapons, driving the two remaining guards out the door. Lincoln slammed the door shut. It was now broken, though, and it started swinging back open.

Belol-yan threw his back against the door with his feet planted on the floor in front of him.

Something rammed into the door, pushing it open a few inches until Belol-yan grunted and pushed it shut again. Another bang, with the same result.

Shouting voices came from beyond the door—more voices than from just the two remaining guards.

Skyra turned to Lincoln, her chest heaving as she sucked in air. "More guards are coming. We must go now."

He blinked. "We can't go now. The T_3 isn't even close to—"

Bam! The door popped open again. Belol-yan pushed it shut. *Bam!* It popped open again.

Di-woto broke away from her mother, ran to the door, and slammed her hands against it to help hold it shut. Derek dropped the gear bag to lend his own weight.

Bam!

"We must go now!" Skyra repeated.

Ripple spoke up. "I am somewhat reluctant to tell you this, but I instructed the T_3 to run the reverse calculations from your initial jump to Skyra's time. These calculations ran concurrently with the other set of calculations—"

Bam!

"—and the process took twenty-three minutes and nine seconds. The T_3 is ready for the future jump now."

"We've gotta do it, Lincoln," Virgil said.

Bam!

"What does that mean?" Skyra asked.

Lincoln gripped her shoulders. "It means we can leave now, but only if we go many-many years to the future. Not back to your time to save Veenah."

Her immense nandup eyes penetrated him with unprecedented intensity, making him wish he could say anything other than what he had just said.

"I'm sorry, Skyra."

Bam!

She blinked, glanced at the door, then met his gaze again. "We must go now. I go where you go, Lincoln."

He nodded. "Okay. We'll have to hold the guards off while I get the body bags ready."

Without another word, she turned and ran to the door to help.

Virgil and Jazzlyn were already unrolling the five body bags. Lincoln grabbed the largest bag and spread it out beside the T3.

"Virgil, Jazzlyn," he said.

Lincoln bent his knees, grunted, and lifted one end of the desk-sized T3 while Virgil and Jazzlyn dragged the bag beneath it. He set the T3 down on the bag, scrambled to the other end, and hoisted it up again, making room for them to finish wrapping the bag under the device. They pulled the bag up around the sides then adjusted it so the holes matched the cable ports distributed around the bottom portion of the T3. Finally, they zipped the bag shut, and Lincoln connected the T3's body bag to one of the ports.

"We'll connect the others," Jazzlyn said.

Bam!

While Jazzlyn and Virgil connected the four smaller body bags to the other ports, Lincoln tapped his watch and worked through the menus to the list of pre-calculated jumps. There were only two, the original jump to Skyra's time and the jump from Skyra's time to the present.

"Ripple, the new jump isn't on my list. I thought you said it was done!"

Bam!

"Any time now, you guys!" Derek said, his voice strained as he pushed against the door.

It seemed there were even more shouting voices outside the door than before.

"Allow me one moment, Lincoln," Ripple said. "I did not want the jump to appear on your menu unless it became absolutely necessary."

"You were hiding it from me."

"*Hiding* is a rather strong word, don't you think? You should now see it on your menu. You're welcome."

Lincoln checked again. A third jump was on the list, titled *Caution—Undesirable Future Jump*. He tapped it and initiated the sequence for jumping a mini-drone to assess the viability and safety of the destination location.

Virgil had already pulled one of the mini-drones from the gear bag and was now powering it on. The four-legged device was the size of a rabbit and was capable of assessing a destination site in less than thirty seconds.

Lincoln stared impatiently at his watch. There it was—the mini-drone had successfully paired with his watch. "Zip it in," he said.

Bam!

Virgil set the tiny robot inside the nearest body bag and zipped up the bag. "Go!"

Lincoln tapped through several menus, then he cursed and did it again. His fingers were shaking, making it hard to do anything quickly. He refocused and tapped one more time.

The lump in the body bag collapsed—the drone was gone. Virgil and Jazzlyn huddled beside him, staring at his watch. "Come on, baby, we got only one shot at this," Jazzlyn muttered.

Ten seconds passed.

Bam!

Twenty seconds.

Bam!

"Lincoln, they are breaking the door!" Skyra cried.

There was now a bulge in the door, with a three-inch split in the metal.

Bam!

The split widened.

Lincoln glanced at his watch just as a green checkmark flashed on the screen. "The site checks out! Get in the body bags."

Jazzlyn and Virgil stuffed both duffels into the first body bag and zipped it shut, then they piled together into the second bag.

Lincoln held another bag open. "Get in, Ripple."

The drone stepped into the bag and began retracting its legs. "This operation presents logistical problems. You must consider that Derek and Skyra are—"

"I'll figure something out!" Lincoln darted to the door, which now had a ten-inch hole.

Derek had his back pressed against the door, his face strained and drenched in sweat. His eyes met Lincoln's. "This ain't gonna work, man. Take Skyra and jump."

Bam!

A sword suddenly jabbed through the hole, and the hand holding it began whipping it back and forth in a desperate attempt to injure anyone within reach. Belol-yan, with his back still to the door, slammed his elbow down on the arm, snapping the bones. The sword clattered to the floor as the guard on the other side of the door cried out and withdrew his ruined arm.

"Mundiop-luma!" Belol-yan roared, startling Lincoln in spite of the already chaotic battle. The guard pushed Di-woto away from the door, sending the girl sprawling. He then shoved Skyra and Derek out of his way. Straining his leg muscles with his back against the door, he held his axe in one hand and picked up the fallen sword in the other.

Bam! The battering ram was being used again.

With his face distorted with pain and effort, Belol-yan turned his one eye to Di-woto and shouted, "Mundiop-luma Di-woto!"

The old guard pulled his feet under him, rose to his full height, and stepped away from the door. He turned as the door swung open. The battering ram came through the doorway, carried by its own momentum, bringing two wide-eyed nandup guards with it. Belol-yan swung both his weapons and dropped the two guards to the floor in a grotesque pile of spasming bodies and spewing arteries.

Furious shouts came from beyond the door, and two more guards tried coming through at the same time. Belol-yan, with his feet now firmly planted in a fighting stance, wielded the two weapons with aggressive precision unlike anything Lincoln had ever seen. The guards went down with horrifying gashes to their bodies. Seconds later, two more went down on top of them.

"Mundiop-luma Di-woto!" Belol-yan roared again.

Lincoln pulled his eyes away from the old guard, who had transformed into a killing machine. "Get in the body bags!"

Derek scrambled toward the T3 to get in the bag with Ripple.

Skyra ran to Di-woto, yanked the girl to her feet, and dragged her to the last empty body bag. Before Lincoln could think of a way to protest, Skyra had forced Di-woto down into the bag. Skyra got in the bag beside her and waved for Lincoln to get in.

Lincoln wasn't even sure more than two people could fit in one of the bags. What if it resulted in too much biomass to make the jump?

"Dammit, Lincoln!" Derek shouted.

Lincoln gritted his teeth and stepped into the bag, forcing his foot between Skyra and Di-woto. He put his other foot in and sat with his butt mostly on Skyra's lap.

Lincoln again turned his eyes to Belol-yan. The guard was still fighting, and the guards outside the door were now pulling the bodies out, in a foolish attempt to make room for more of them to charge into a meat grinder.

Lincoln worked his head and shoulders down into the bag, but Di-woto was still sitting up. The girl was staring across the room at her birthmother. Lo-aful, although a full-blooded nandup, now looked frail and scared. She stared back at her daughter, totally unaware that Di-woto was about to disappear forever. Lincoln couldn't summon pity for the woman. For all he knew, she was the one who had arranged for the guards to break down the door and attack.

Lincoln turned to Skyra, his face only inches from hers. "Are you sure the girl wants to go with us? She'll never be able to return."

"Di-woto is not happy here. She goes with us."

Fair enough. Lincoln rose to his elbow, signaled to his team to zip up their bags, and pulled Di-woto down inside with him and Skyra. He took one more glimpse at Belol-yan, who was still defending the chamber—more specifically, Di-woto—from a seemingly endless onslaught.

To Lincoln's surprise, Skyra managed to get her fingers on the bag's zipper, which was near their knees, and seconds later they were completely enclosed. He wriggled his wrist up to his face and tapped through the menus on his watch. He stared at the final command, a button he'd coded with what he had once thought were clever words—*No Time Like the Present*.

He pressed his finger to the screen.

22

OPTIMISM

47,659 years later - Day 1

Skyra felt the floor disappear. Her body fell briefly then hit a soft surface. Brilliant light flooded her eyes, forcing her to clamp them shut.

She heard only soft grunts and slight movements from the others. The sounds of Belol-yan slaughtering the guards were gone. The funny smell of the body bag was gone. Skyra's fear began to fade, and her heart began to slow.

"Damn, I'll never get used to that," Derek said.

Di-woto's voice filled the air. "Ayeee! I no understand. No sanctuary-fortress. Ayeee!" The girl continued speaking excitedly, using words Skyra did not know.

"Everyone okay?" Lincoln asked.

"We're alive," Jazzlyn replied.

"All systems functional," Ripple said.

Skyra untangled herself from Lincoln and Di-woto and sat up. She shaded her face with one hand and forced her eyes open. She and the others were sitting in the midst of tall grasses up to their chins. They were in a low area between several hills. Dotting the hillsides were trees with tiny leaves, as well as the tall green poles Lincoln had called saguaro cactuses.

"I do not think the T3 made us go many, many years, Lincoln," she said. "This looks like the same land we were in when the nandups took us."

He groaned and got to his feet. "It is similar, but look at the sky. It's clear."

Skyra slowly pulled her hand from her brows to look up. Lincoln was right. The sky was not stained brown from the fires of war. The stench was gone. She got up beside him. "We *are* in a new land!"

Di-woto took a few cautious steps, as if she didn't trust the ground beneath her feet. The girl had most likely never left the sanctuary-fortress. Perhaps she had never before walked upon grasses. She faced Skyra and Lincoln and said, "I no understand." Then her face formed a broad Di-woto smile. "I no understand!" She turned in a circle, gazing wide-eyed at the surrounding hills and strange trees. "No sanctuary-fortress. No khami-buls. No fighting-killing. I like new land!" She kneeled and pulled up a handful of grasses then held them to her face, apparently breathing in the smell.

"What the hell's that girl going on about?" Derek asked. "And why is she smiling like that?"

"I think she's a perpetual optimist," Lincoln said.

Jazzlyn said, "Do you need us to define the word *optimism* for you, Derek?"

"Just look around you!" he boomed. "We're in another goddamn wilderness. Forty-seven *thousand* years in the future. We should be in the middle of a freakin' high-tech paradise—sexy androids, levitating cars, and buttons to push for an iced mocha. Excuse me for wanting a little more than teeth, claws, axes, and swords."

Virgil said, "Actually, many people consider pristine wilderness to be more of a paradise than a busy city. Studies have shown a positive correlation between levels of happiness and immersion in—"

"Give me a break!" Derek growled.

"Bolups talk too much," Skyra said. The others looked at her. She pulled her khul from its sling and held it out. "I now have one khul and two hand blades. You bolups have no weapons. We have gone many, many years to this new land. We do not know what predators to fear. We do not know what people to fear. You should stop talking and make more weapons."

After several breaths, Jazzlyn said. "That girl's got common sense. You married yourself a keeper, Lincoln. Speaking of being married... what the hell?"

Lincoln let out a long breath. "Explanations can wait. I'll just say I have no regrets. Skyra is right, though—let's focus on our current situation. Assuming the T_3 is functioning correctly, this is 47,000 years after the events in the sanctuary-fortress. Same timeline. Exact same geographic location we jumped to before being captured by nandup warriors. Exact same location of my lab in our original timeline."

"Weapons!" Skyra said.

Lincoln let out another long breath. "Yes. Okay, you guys gather any objects we can use to make weapons."

Skyra said, "Straight tree branches for spears, twisted roots to sharpen as khuls, stones for throwing."

Lincoln scanned the surrounding hills. "While you're

doing that, Skyra and I will go to higher ground and try to get a feel for what's beyond those hills."

"What about her?" Derek said, nodding toward Di-woto. The girl was collecting long stems of grass, and she already had a thick bundle tucked under her arm. Skyra imagined Di-woto was thinking of ways to make a new garment using the grasses.

"I don't know," Lincoln said. "Please just keep an eye on her. Don't let her wander off."

Ripple, who had remained silent for the most part, finally spoke up. "Di-woto is an alinga-ul, an offspring of a human father and Neanderthal mother. She and her kind are far more important than you realize. Such hybrids are rare, but certain nandups and bolups have the ability to produce them. Which brings me to a suggestion I feel obligated to mention. You have five body bags remaining, potentially giving you an opportunity to make one more jump. Might I suggest you avoid any risk this unknown land may pose and jump to Skyra's time? The T_3 is still processing the placement calculations and should complete them in less than an hour."

Lincoln exchanged looks with his tribemates.

"What are you saying, Ripple?" Skyra asked.

The creature's red lights glowed.

"Ripple is suggesting we go many, many years back to your land," Lincoln said. "The problem is, we wouldn't be able to use the T_3 to go anywhere again. We would have to stay there for the rest of our lives."

She considered this. "Could we save Veenah from dying?"

"Possibly, but it's also very possible we would fail."

"We've only got one more jump," Derek said. "If my opinion counts for anything at this point, I say we jump even further into the future. We could just extend the existing calculations another 47,000 years. Surely by then the humans or Neanderthals will have developed a compassionate, high-tech society."

"Actually," Virgil said, "that would not be possible unless humans or Neanderthals still exist here at this point in time. If they destroyed each other sometime in the last 47,000 years, then no one is left to create a compassionate, high-tech society. If we're going to use our last remaining body bags, we should evaluate the current state of this world and then make our decision."

Lincoln turned to Skyra. "He's saying that we should—"

"I understand enough of the words," she said.

Ripple continued. "I would like to emphasize that my original plan is formulated upon extensive and elaborate analysis of thousands of parameters. The plan has high potential for success, but only if initiated in Skyra's original location and time, where the balance and distribution of indigenous humans and Neanderthals are optimal. I vote we jump back to Skyra's time."

"Drones can't vote," Derek said.

Lincoln was still watching Skyra, as if he were waiting. Seeing he actually cared about what she thought made Skyra's belly tingle.

"I go where you go, Lincoln," she said.

His thin bolup lips turned up slightly. "I go where you go, Skyra."

"God almighty," Derek said. "If anything was in my stomach, I'd throw up."

"I think they're cute," Jazzlyn said. "Nandup-bolup looove."

SKYRA STOOD beside Lincoln atop the tallest hill they could find near the T3. Endless hills dotted with trees and cactuses stretched out in every direction. However, in the distance, almost directly opposite the sun, which was now preparing to hide behind the hills for the night, was a city.

Lincoln had called it a city, but it didn't look anything like Di-woto's walled city. The city Skyra was staring at now was much bigger, with massive structures extending far into the sky and reflecting the setting sun with numerous sparkles of light. It was like nothing Skyra had ever seen. Imagining the countless people who lived there tightened her chest and filled her head with fear. Were they nandups, or were they bolups? Or were they both?

"This sight is going to make Derek happy," Lincoln said.

Skyra didn't take her eyes off the city. "Does it make you happy, Lincoln?"

"I'm not sure. I suppose what I would like is for these people to have the materials we need to make more body bags for the T3. If they don't, I hope they are kind enough to allow us to live among them."

"This city frightens me," she said.

"Yeah, me too. I think we're going to have to go there, though, before we can make the best decision about what to do next."

They stared at the great city in silence for several breaths. Skyra understood why they had to go there, but for now she was glad it was far away. Here, the landscape around the hill was almost silent except for a light breeze whispering through the grasses and a constant buzzing of flying insects. She had not heard any birds at all, but the buzzing had become louder since she and Lincoln had reached the top of the hill. Even now, the sounds seemed to be growing with every passing breath.

"As impressive as that city is," Lincoln said, "I don't see any movement. I don't see any planes flying or any kind of moving vehicles or people. Strange."

Skyra was becoming distracted by the constant buzzing and didn't bother to ask about planes and vehicles. Then her eyes were drawn to movement. She pointed. "Lincoln, is there a fire in the city? I see smoke."

He stared at the rising column of smoke. "Damn, I don't think that's smoke. It's a swarm of insects."

She squinted, staring at the swarm. Now she could see the dots making up the smoke cloud. The more she looked, the more she was sure the dots were too large to be insects. "They are not insects. They are birds."

"Would you look at that," Lincoln muttered.

More swarms were rising from the city, pouring out from the tall sparkling structures as well as from points nearer to the ground. Soon it looked as if smoke were rising from the entire city. Smoke without flames.

The swarms began dispersing, flying away from the city in every direction. Some swarms were heading directly toward Skyra and Lincoln. Skyra could now make out the flapping wings of each approaching bird.

"They're a lot bigger than I first thought," Lincoln said. "Good God, they're bigger than eagles!"

Skyra stared at the birds. They were not flying the way eagles flew, and their wings were not like eagle wings. She turned to Lincoln. "Those are not birds, Lincoln. They are bats."

THERE'S MORE TO THIS STORY!

"Those are not birds, Lincoln. They are bats."

What have Skyra, Lincoln, and the others gotten themselves into now? They only have enough body bags for *one* more jump. They shouldn't squander that last jump and risk ending up somewhere uninhabitable. Or should they?

Foregone Conflict is the second book in the **Across Horizons** seres. If you enjoyed this book and **Obsolete Theorem**, you are definitely going to love the next book in the series, **Hostile Emergence**.

In the meantime, if you haven't read my **Diffusion series**, my **Bridgers series**, and my **Fused series**, be sure to check them out.

AUTHOR'S NOTES

I love science and science fiction, so I enjoy thinking about bizarre questions related to such things as time travel, alternate universes, and unusual creatures. Below are some of my thoughts regarding the concepts in **Foregone Conflict**. These are in no particular order, and they may not cover everything you're curious about, but if you're at all interested, here you go.

At the beginning of the book, why didn't Lincoln, Skyra, and the others jump back into Lincoln's lab? Excellent question! That's actually what they hoped to do. Lincoln, Jazzlyn, Virgil, and Derek originally jumped back to Skyra's time to explore the ominous message Ripple had left for Lincoln. Then they would quickly jump back to Lincoln's lab, arriving only a few minutes after they had left. This obviously didn't work out. Why? Well, we need to first consider Lincoln's *Temporal Bridge Theorem*. Basically, the theorem proved that jumping to the past creates an alternate universe (or alternate *timeline*, if you prefer). This may sound crazy, but if you think about it, it *has* to be true. Let's say you jump one hour back in time. From the moment you arrive there (one hour in the past), things start happening. The things that happen are not the same things that happened the first time that hour took place. Within the first millisecond, trillions of events occur that did not occur during the first millisecond of the previous version of that hour. Every molecule and every atom in the universe has certain properties of randomness. It is simply not possible for the same events to happen during that millisecond that happened during the first version of that millisecond.

And then comes the second millisecond, and the third millisecond, and during every millisecond there are trillions of events that did not happen in the other version of that millisecond. This continues through the first thousand milliseconds (the first second), and continues through sixty thousand milliseconds (the first minute), and then continues through the 3,600,000 milliseconds of this new version of this entire hour. Therefore, after the second version of this hour has passed, the world (indeed, the entire universe) is now a very different place compared to the world you were in before you jumped one hour back in time. Are you with me so far?

Let's say you jump back in time one year. Well, obviously you are starting a new timeline the moment you arrive one year in the past, with trillions of new and random events happening every millisecond from that moment on. Then let's say you immediately use your time machine to jump a year into the future, to the present time you left behind. The problem is, now it is not the present time you left behind—it is a very different present time due to all those random events. There's no possible way you could jump back to the exact same present you left behind, because there is no possible way the exact same events could take place during the new version of that year. This would happen even if you did nothing at all to change the world in the past. Make sense?

So... When Lincoln and the others jumped 47,000 years back to the present, hoping to end up in Lincoln's lab again, they found themselves in a very different world. His lab wasn't there. Neanderthals hadn't become extinct. The world was at war.

Okay, if Lincoln knew it wouldn't work, why did he bother trying? Well, in the first book (**Obsolete Theorem**), something happened that made people suspect Lincoln's theorem was wrong (obsolete). As a result, even Lincoln started to wonder if his theorem were wrong. He started to hope maybe he and his team would be able to jump back to the same timeline they had left behind. Of course, his theorem was not obsolete after all, and his team ended up jumping to a very different world. I guess we can't blame him for trying.

What is the meaning of the title **Foregone Conflict***?* In this case, the word *foregone* means inevitable (as in a foregone conclusion). Although the meaning of the title isn't overtly discussed in the book, it refers to something Lincoln did back in Skyra's time that may have resulted in Neanderthals getting the slight boost they needed in order to avoid extinction. He taught Skyra's tribemates how to use a bow and arrow *before* they had developed that technology on their own. It's possible that may have changed the future for Neanderthals. I need to point out, though, that it might *not* have changed the future.

Remember those trillions of random events every millisecond? Regardless of anything Lincoln did, the future was going to be drastically different anyway. It would have to be. Keep in mind that Neanderthals did not *have* to go extinct. It was not inevitable. Dinosaurs did not *have* to go extinct. Very few things actually *have* to happen. Therefore, as I discussed above, if we could somehow have a redo of the last 47,000 years, the outcome would be very different (regardless of anything Lincoln may have done in the past). If we redid the last 47,000 years over and over again, say 100 different times, how many times do you think Neanderthals would end up extinct? No one knows, but I'm pretty sure Neanderthals would *not* go extinct in some of those redos. I'm also pretty sure humans *would* go extinct in some of those redos. And, logically, in some of those redos, Neanderthals and humans would *both* survive.

What would the world look like today if both species had survived? Would the two species find a way to live in peace? Would one species enslave the other and consider them a lower form of life (um... we all know humans are capable of such behavior, don't we?). Would the two species be at war? All of these things are possible, of course, but in this book, the survival of both species resulted in *foregone conflict*.

Aren't Neanderthals considered humans? Well, this depends on how you define the word *human*. Different people use the word differently. If you use the word to refer to all creatures classified in the genus *Homo*, then yes, *Homo neanderthalensis* and *Homo sapiens* (and several other extinct species) could be called humans. Or, you could decide to use the word *humans* to refer only to *Homo sapiens*. In writing

AUTHOR'S NOTES

this series, I decided it was easier to use the word *humans* to refer only to *Homo sapiens*. That way I could more easily refer to *Neanderthals* and *humans* as the two different species. I also often use *nandup* and *bolup* to refer to the two species (these are words of Skyra's Una-Loto language). The main thing to understand is that *Homo neanderthalensis* and *Homo sapiens* are two distinct species. They are closely related, and are therefore classified in the same genus (*Homo*), but still they are two distinct species. They are closely related enough to be capable of interbreeding and producing hybrid offspring, which is an important element of this book, as well as the entire series.

What's all this talk about hybrids? Aha... this is a key element of the series! We know beyond any doubt that humans and Neanderthals interbred. After all, almost all humans today have Neanderthal DNA in their genetic code. In fact, when I got my DNA results back from the ancestry-analysis service I used, it stated that I have more Neanderthal genetic material than 98% of the population of people who have used the service. So, I myself am proof that Neanderthals and humans mated and produced offspring. In general, non-African modern humans have 1% to 4% Neanderthal DNA. People of direct African descent have less because Neanderthals evolved and lived exclusively in Eurasia—only those humans that migrated north out of Africa could have mated with Neanderthals.

Interestingly, DNA analyses of Neanderthal remains in Siberia show that humans and Neanderthals were already interbreeding as long ago as 100,000 years (Skyra lived 47,000 years ago). This was the first evidence showing human

DNA in Neanderthals rather than showing Neanderthal DNA in humans.

If we know Homo sapiens and Homo neanderthalensis used to interbreed, why is Di-woto currently the only one of her kind? Wouldn't there be many alinga-uls? It's important to understand that Di-woto is specifically an *alinga-ul*. This means she is a hybrid from a Neanderthal mother and a human father. Alinga-uls are rare. Why are they rare? The answer to this is based on known facts. This requires a bit of explanation. First, our DNA includes *nuclear DNA* and *mitochondrial DNA* (mtDNA). The nuclear DNA is found inside the nucleus of the cell, whereas the mtDNA is found only in the mitochondria of the cell. It is important to know that the nuclear DNA is passed to the offspring from both the mother and father, but the mtDNA is passed to the offspring *only from the mother*. Why is this important? Because scientists cannot find any Neanderthal mtDNA in humans. This *could* lead us to conclude that all DNA in humans today came from pairings of Neanderthal males with human females, and that would imply that pairings of Neanderthal females with human males produced sterile offspring or no offspring at all. If that were true, then alinga-uls would not exist at all (also, Skyra and Lincoln could *not* produce offspring).

However, there are other possibilities that could explain why modern humans do not have Neanderthal mtDNA. For example, it's possible that Neanderthal females and human males did not mate because of some cultural reason (in other words, they *chose* not to mate because it was a taboo, or something like that). Another possibility is that there actually used to be humans with Neanderthal mtDNA, but their lineages died out at some point. Still, there is one other possibility (which I think is likely), that modern humans *actually do* carry at least one Neanderthal mtDNA lineage, but we have not yet sequenced that lineage in humans or in Neanderthals, so we simply do not know about it yet. This could be related to the possibility that hybrid offspring from Neanderthal females were rare for some genetic reason (which is the concept I am considering in the *Across Horizons* series).

So, pairings of human males and Neanderthal females only rarely produce offspring, which explains why alinga-uls are rare.

Does that mean Lincoln and Skyra cannot have offspring? The answer depends on the actual reason why alinga-uls are rare. If they are rare because of some genetic trait of the male or of the female, then I think it is quite possible that Lincoln and Skyra *could* produce offspring, if they both possess the right genetic traits (and, of course, if they *want* to produce offspring). We know Ripple definitely wants them to produce offspring, right? Maybe Ripple knows something about Skyra's and Lincoln's DNA we don't know...?

Speaking of Ripple, what's all this talk about Ripple's grand plan for Lincoln and Skyra? Lincoln, sometime in the fourteen years after we meet him in **Obsolete Theorem**, decides to give his drones more autonomy so that they can make their own decisions. Lincoln routinely sent his drones into the past to collect environmental data, and the drones then would have to remain in the past because there was no way for them to jump back (even if they could, remember that they were in a different timeline the moment they arrived in the past). Therefore, Lincoln coded his drones (including Ripple) with intelligence and the ability to devise and carry out plans that the drones decided were likely to help the world they were stuck in. Ripple took these abilities to the extreme. After being sent 47,000 years into the past, Ripple carried out its data-collecting duties, and then the portal closed. Ripple was left in the past. Ripple encountered Skyra and soon recognized that Skyra was genetically remarkable. Ripple already knew Lincoln was genetically remarkable, so the drone hatched an idea—somehow get Lincoln and Skyra together in the past. Ripple's plan is based on the drone's assumption that the two would produce remarkable offspring. Because this was at a time when humans and Neanderthals were already intermixing (mating together), Ripple concluded that infusing the populations with Skyra-Lincoln hybrids would result in a much different future, filled with remarkable beings. According to Ripple's plan, Skyra and Lincoln's offspring would spread their advantageous genetic traits throughout the world, resulting in a global population in which their traits are found throughout all of humanity.

Ripple is remarkably persistent in pushing this plan, much to Lincoln's frustration. Lincoln thinks the plan is crazy, and he does not want to go back in time and spend the rest of his life in Skyra's original world. After all, that would be a brutal existence, fraught with dangers and hardships. Skyra is also not fond of the idea of going back to her world, for the same reasons.

I find this world of warring nandups and bolups to be confusing. Can you help with that? Di-woto's society, called Kyran-yufost, consists of specific castes. The lowest caste is the various groups of laborers. We saw many of the laborers working in the crop and livestock fields, as well as making and trading goods within the city itself (they were the ones often carrying baskets of goods). These laborers are divided into large tribes. The leaders of these tribes are called *amo-moloms*. Each amo-molom wears a garment dyed in a color that represents the tribe. These are the leaders Skyra, Di-woto, and Belol-yan spoke to as they were carrying out Di-woto's plan. Their goal was to convince these tribe leaders to help start a revolt. Another caste is the warriors, the soldiers who are responsible for fighting an endless war with bolups (humans). We meet some of the warriors at the beginning of the book (they capture Lincoln and his team), but we don't see very many of them after that because they are always out beyond the city walls, on the front lines. Some of the warriors, as they grow older, are "lucky" enough to be recruited as guards in the sanctuary-fortress. Belol-yan is an example of such guards.

Inside the sanctuary-fortress we find the governing castes, in addition to the guards. The khami-buls are the orange-clad nandups. Ripple first translated khami-bul as *scientist-learner-teacher*. These people make many of the decisions for the entire district of Kyran-yufost. Unfortunately, over the years, they have come up with numerous deceptive ways to perpetuate the war with bolups. Why? Because they believe the ongoing war is what keeps their citizens in line. With the war, fear is always high and resources are always stretched thin. With constant strife, the citizens look to the khami-buls for wisdom and guidance. The war is what keeps the khami-buls in power. Plus, the khami-buls do not want the common citizens mating with bolups (they believe it is *their* job to create hybrids, and they don't want to lose power to an unmanageably large population of hybrids), and so making the citizens hate the bolups is one way to make sure this doesn't happen.

The khami-buls have known for a long time that nandup/bolup hybrids are unusually intelligent. They consider these hybrids to be important to the future of their society, but they do not want the citizens to know they are mating with humans within the sanctuary-fortress. In other words, they have big secrets they do not want leaked. The offspring of a male nandup and a female bolup is called a *dali-tamon* (a second-level scientist). The offspring of a female nandup and a male bolup is an *alinga-ul*. Over the years, the khami-buls have discovered that alinga-uls are even smarter than dali-tamons. The problem is, alinga-uls are rare, as I discussed above. Currently, Di-woto is the only living alinga-ul, which is why she has so much influence. However, she is rather free-spirited, and she is influenced by long-term bouts with psychological issues stemming from a lonely, oppressed existence. Therefore, the khami-buls worry she will cause problems (they were *really* correct about that).

Why is this society apparently stuck in a pre-industrial state? Primarily because of one reason—never-ending war, which keeps them in a constant struggle to produce enough food and resources. It is reasonable to assume that, if they can figure out how to live in peace and prosperity, they will eventually progress in industrialization and technology. In fact, at the very end of the book, you see a glimpse of what has happened in this timeline over the next 47,000 years.

What's up with all this spider stuff? Is that a religion? Depends on your definition of a religion. It seems to me religions usually involve some form of supernatural being or force. I'm using the term *supernatural* to refer to something beyond what can be observed or measured—something that requires *belief* rather than scientific observation. In that sense, the spider culture of Kyran-yufost is *not* a religion. Instead, it is a society-wide admiration and emulation of a real creature, a social spider. Yes, it is very strange that these people have chosen a type of spider to emulate—to base their lives upon. But you must remember much of this is the result of the khami-buls' efforts. The khami-buls perpetuate this by telling stories about the spiders, by designing buildings and dwellings to look like spider webs, by adorning their doors and clothing with spider ornaments, and by creating large public displays of living social-spider colonies, so that the citizens can see every day how tree-web spiders and ground-web spiders are at war with each other. It's possible that the khami-buls conceived of this entire tradition of emulating social spiders for the sole purpose of perpetuating their war with humans. It is a way of controlling the citizens.

And what about those long-armed bolups? Is it really possible to lengthen a person's limbs? Not only is it possible, but this technique has been used for at least the last 120 years, both for cosmetic reasons and to compensate for deformities. I don't know of examples of making a person's arms so long that their fingers drag on the ground, as the khami-buls have done in

Foregone Conflict, but it is theoretically possible. You would just have to continue the gradual process far beyond what is normally needed. How does it work? Basically, the doctor cuts the bone into two pieces then attaches an *external fixator* to the two bone pieces. The fixator holds the two bone pieces in place, with a gap between them that allows bone tissue to grow and fill the gap. After it heals, the doctor repeats the process, continuing to repeat it until the desired length is achieved. Obviously, the khami-buls did not have their bolup victims' well-being in mind when they did this.

How did Ripple learn the nandups' language so quickly? Although Maddy had a basic built-in translation app, Ripple has a much more advanced ability to translate. Ripple is able to listen to normal conversation for several minutes and can use its vast database of language norms to begin picking out patterns that appear in every language. While observing the nandups' behaviors as they speak, Ripple can use context clues to begin identifying the meanings of certain words. The more Ripple observes and listens, the more accurate the drone's translations. This is why you see Ripple's translations becoming more accurate and conversational throughout the book.

How did Skyra learn the language so quickly? Due to Skyra's brutal and rather primitive upbringing, it is easy to forget how intelligent she is. When Ripple found Skyra 47,000 years in the past, the drone quickly realized she was special. This is, of course, why Ripple devised an elaborate plan to get Lincoln and Skyra together, even though they lived 47,000 years apart. Skyra certainly does not have Ripple's ability to learn a language in a few minutes, but she is capable of learning enough within a few days to allow basic communication, particularly because she was able to listen to Ripple's direct translations.

So, if Lincoln is so smart, why didn't he learn the language as fast as Skyra did? You're right, Lincoln is incredibly smart. But everyone is smart in different ways. Skyra and Lincoln have some extraordinary abilities in common (for example, they both have an uncanny ability to read subtle expressions to predict a person's actions). They also have some differences. Lincoln has never been particularly interested in learning new languages and has not had a need to develop that skill. Skyra, on the other hand, grew up in a situation in which her Neanderthal tribe would regularly get together with other tribes for traditional celebrations and for trade. Most of those tribes are small (less than 50) and typically isolated, and they have each developed their own language, or at least their own dialect. So, Skyra is in the habit of listening carefully in order to pick up new words.

This book takes place in the present time in Arizona, but yet there are camels, bison, wolves, and a giant ground sloth. How can that be? First, it's important to understand why the setting is Arizona. Lincoln's lab is in Arizona. In the first book (**Obsolete Theorem**), Lincoln and his team jumped back in time 47,659 years. When they did that, they also jumped to a different location (for a full explanation of why jumping through time requires that you also jump through space, see the Author's Notes at the end of **Obsolete Theorem**). They jumped from the present time in Arizona to Skyra's time in Spain. Lincoln had already instructed the

T3 to do the placement calculations for jumping back to the present in Arizona, so that's what they did at the end of Book 1. So, Book 2 starts in Arizona in the present time. However, as I discussed above, this present time is not the same present time in which Lincoln's team originally lived. That, of course, is because of all those trillions of random events that happened every millisecond during those 47,659 years.

Okay, so we've established why the Arizona of **Foregone Conflict** is so different from the Arizona of Lincoln's original timeline. Back to the question about the camels, bison, wolves, and giant ground sloth. Could those creatures really exist in Arizona today if we had a do-over of the last 47,000 years? Yep, they could. Why? Because all those animals existed in the southwest United States during the late Pleistocene. In our timeline not only did they exist there 47,000 years ago, but most of them were still there up until about 8,000 years ago. Just as Neanderthals did not *have* to go extinct, these large mammals did not *have* to go extinct. Remember all those random events? In a do-over of the last 47,000 years (or just the last 8,000 years), things could go much differently.

Let's consider the creatures one at a time. The camel that lived in the southwest US was called the *Camelops*. This large camel grazed in huge herds throughout much of the western US until about 8,000 years ago. As for the bison, there were several species, including *Bison bison* (the species that still exists today), as well as *Bison latifrons*, a huge beast that had horns spreading over ten feet wide! What about wolves? Yep, there were plenty of those. In fact, the large dire wolf (*Canis dirus*) existed from Canada all the way south to Peru until about 7,000 years ago. Finally, what about the giant ground sloth? Yep, those too. In fact, there were at least two. One was *Glossotherium*, a powerful ground sloth that lived from Idaho down into Mexico. The giant ground sloth Lincoln and Skyra encountered, though, was a descendant of the *Nothrotheriops*, a 400-pound sloth that lived in Arizona until about 9,000 years ago.

What about social spiders? Are those real? Indeed they are. Most spiders are solitary, and often they even attack other members of their own species when they encounter each other. But there are a few hundred species of spiders that live in colonies. Why do they live in colonies? By combining their efforts, both in constructing large webs and in subduing and killing large prey, they can maximize the average amount of food procured per individual. Sometimes their webs can be quite astounding, covering several large trees. This allows the spiders to catch more (and larger) insects. And when they work together to kill their prey, they can even subdue birds and bats.

If this strategy works so well, why don't all spiders do this? Apparently, this works best in places where there are huge numbers of insects, as well as larger insects. Therefore, most social spiders live in tropical areas of the world. And yes, some social spiders are orange (the color of the tree-web spiders and therefore the color of the garments worn by khami-buls in **Foregone Conflict**). Most social spiders build their immense webs in trees. For the purposes of this story, I created a species of social spiders that build ground webs, so that bolups and nandups could each have their own distinct type of spider they identify with (or *worship*, if you prefer).

Di-woto went with Lincoln and Skyra when they jumped away from her time. With her gone from Kyran-yufost, who will be left in charge to make sure her plans for peace have a chance of succeeding? Good question. Let's hope Belol-yan survives the onslaught of other guards fighting their way into the sleeping chamber. Belol-yan obviously has a lot of influence over many of the guards. Perhaps he can persuade the surviving guards to see his point of view. We don't know how many of the khamibuls survived the revolt, other than Di-woto's mother Lo-aful. Lo-aful may have deceived Lincoln, but I have a feeling she may have been forced to do that. I have a feeling maybe she really does care about her daughter's dream of peace in Kyran-yufost. Perhaps she will take up Di-woto's cause. Perhaps she will even give birth to more alinga-uls, who will eventually take Kyran-yufost in a new, peaceful direction.

Okay, what about this new place Lincoln and his team jump to at the end of **Foregone Conflict**? *What's up with that city and all those bats?* Lincoln has used the T3's previous placement calculations and simply extended them another 47,659 years into the future. They are in the same timeline as Di-woto's world, but now they are in one of an infinite number of possible futures. Also, they are still in the area we know of as Arizona. So, basically we are getting a peek at what has happened to Di-woto's world in the 47,659 years since she carried out her plan for bringing peace to Kyran-yufost. A lot can happen in 47,659 years, right? We know there is a city there. The city may even be in the same location as Kyran-yufost's sanctuary fortress. After all, Lincoln and Skyra see the city in the distance, approximately the same distance they were taken after being captured at the beginning of **Foregone Conflict**. Remember, they were taken against their will from the jump-in site (the site of Lincoln's lab in Lincoln's timeline) to the sanctuary-fortress. So, there's a city there, but what's up with all those bats? And what's up with all those insects Skyra can hear buzzing around on the hilltop?

I guess we'll have to find out in the next book, **Hostile Emergence**.

ACKNOWLEDGMENTS

I am not capable of creating a book such as this on my own. I have the following people, among others, to thank for their assistance.

First I wish to thank Monique Agueros for her help with editing. She has a keen eye for typos, poorly structured sentences, misplaced commas, and errors of logic. If you find a sentence or detail in the book that doesn't seem right, it is likely because I failed to implement one of her suggestions.

My wife Trish is always the first to read my work, and therefore she has the burden of seeing my stories in their roughest form. Thankfully, she kindly points out where things are a mess. Her suggestions are what get the editing process started. She also helps with various promotional efforts. And finally, she not only tolerates my obsession with writing, she actually encourages it.

I also owe thanks to those on my Advance Reviewer team. They were able to point out numerous typos and inconsistencies, and they are all-around fabulous people!

Finally, I am thankful to all the independent freelance designers out there who provide quality work for independent authors such as myself. Jake Caleb Clark (www.jcalebdesign.com) created the awesome cover for *Foregone Conflict*.

ABOUT THE AUTHOR

Stan Smith has lived most of his life in the Midwest United States and currently resides with his wife Trish in a house deep in an Ozark forest in Missouri. He writes adventure novels that have a generous sprinkling of science fiction. His novels and stories are about regular people who find themselves caught up in highly unusual situations. They are designed to stimulate your sense of wonder, get your heart pounding, and keep you reading late into the night, with minimal risk of exposure to spelling and punctuation errors. His books are for anyone who loves adventure, discovery, and mind-bending surprises.

Stan's Author Website
http://www.stancsmith.com

Feel free to email Stan at: stan@stancsmith.com
He loves hearing from readers and will answer every email.

ALSO BY STAN C. SMITH

The DIFFUSION series

Diffusion

Infusion

Profusion

Savage

Blue Arrow

Diffusion Box Set

The BRIDGERS series

Bridgers 1: The Lure of Infinity

Bridgers 2: The Cost of Survival

Bridgers 3: The Voice of Reason

Bridgers 4: The Mind of Many

Bridgers 5: The Trial of Extinction

Bridgers 6: The Bond of Absolution

INFINITY: A Bridger's Origin

Bridgers 1-3 Box Set

Bridgers 4-6 Box Set

The ACROSS HORIZONS series

1: Obsolete Theorem

2. Foregone Conflict

3. Hostile Emergence

4. Binary Existence

Prequel: Genesis Sequence

The FUSED series

Prequel: Training Day

1. Rampage Ridge

2. Primordial Pit

Stand-alone Stories

Parthenium's Year

Printed in Great Britain
by Amazon